Gray
Wolf
Mountain

GRAY WOLF MOUNTAIN

Jean Henry Mead

Medallion Books

Medallion Books

Printed in the United States of America

ISBN: 978-1-931415-37-8

Cover design by Bill Mead

First edition, August 2012

Other books in the Logan & Cafferty series:

A Village Shattered

Diary of Murder

Murder on the Interstate

Dedication:

For my friends and fellow mystery writers,
Jacqueline King and Alice Duncan

Chapter One

Dana unbuckled her seat belt and landed on the headliner. The side curtain airbag had ruptured, filling the Escalade's interior with gas and debris. Hand-masking her lower face, she felt as though she were choking.

Sarah! Her friend hung from her seat belt, apparently unconscious. Reaching to touch her hair, she called her name repeatedly, afraid the accident had broken her neck. Sarah groaned a moment later, much to her relief. When she was coherent, Dana told her between coughing spells that their SUV had rolled. She then cushioned her friend's head for the drop onto the headliner.

"Are you all right?"

Coughing, Sara pointed toward a side window.

Dana reached with the toe of her shoe, managing to open the driver's window. The passenger frame was bowed inward, preventing the door from opening, so Sarah would have to follow her through the driver's window. Once Dana had crawled onto the ground, she turned and stuck her head back inside. "Hurry, the Escalade might catch fire."

That got her moving. When they were both able to stand, Sarah groaned while rubbing the back of her neck. She then asked whether Dana had swerved to avoid hitting a deer.

Holding the sides of her throbbing head, Dana said, "No animals but I dodged a log before I heard a bang and the steering wheel jerked from my hands."

"I remember now. We were talking about the sale at Macy's and the next thing I knew I was hanging upside down."

"Are you sure you're not hurt?"

"We Caffertys have the skulls of mastodons—how about you?"

Nodding that she was okay, Dana peered at the Escalade, comparing it to a dead chicken with its feet in the air.

Sarah stood back to appraise the damage. "A shredded tire? I thought these new all terrains are guaranteed not to explode."

"Obviously not."

"Looks like it was hit by a cannon ball.

Dana noticed a hole in the fender near the driver's door. "What in the world—?"

"Somebody shot at us." Sarah turned to scan the terrain.

Crouching behind the Escalade, they searched the area for some sign of the shooter. When none was found, Dana crawled back inside to retrieve their cameras and purses. Moments later she handed them through the window to Sarah. Then, circling the vehicle at a distance, they took pictures of the disabled vehicle.

Sarah rummaged through her large leather bag. "Where's my cell phone? We need to call the sheriff."

"Calm down. It's in the side pocket." Shading her eyes against the afternoon sun, she noticed a dust cloud as a vehicle drove toward them. The older model, single-seated pickup truck was covered in rust and mud. When it stopped opposite them, a man much older than the truck leaned his head out the window to ask if they'd had an accident.

"Pretty obvious," Sarah muttered.

"I got a first aid kit in here somewheres."

When they said they didn't need the kit, he offered them a ride down the mountain. Glancing at her friend, Sarah said, "You have room for both of us?"

The old man opened the creaking driver's door. "Hold on a minute, ladies. I got some stuff to move around."

Stooped and slim as a broom handle, he shuffled around to the opposite side of the truck in his frayed plaid shirt and greasy, ragged overalls. Dana flipped her cell phone open and punched in 911. Wouldn't you know? No cell service. They would have to accept the ride. Offering to help their benefactor, they were waved off as he removed an aging yellow cat the size of a large Chihuahua. He then hauled out a battered plastic box with a cracked lid. Placing the box and cat in the bed of his truck, he retrieved several lengths of rope with hooks attached to both ends. That left something wrapped in a filthy blanket. When it slid to the ground they saw that it was a saber.

Sarah gasped and grabbed Dana's arm. "We don't want to put you to any trouble."

He cupped a hand to his left ear. "What's that you said?"

So he was hard of hearing. Sarah raised her voice.

"No trouble, young lady. I need to clean my truck out, anyhow."

"Young lady?" They looked at one another and grinned. "We haven't been called young in ages."

His returning grin had several teeth missing. "You two look mighty spry to me. Good lookin' too, if ya ask me."

That settled it. They would have to accept the ride, but neither of them wanted to sit next to him. The old man didn't appear to have taken a bath in months. Turning her back, Dana removed a coin from her wallet and flipped it on her wrist. Covering it with her palm she motioned for Sarah

3

to call it.

"Heads." Sarah whispered, crossing her fingers.

Sighing with relief, Dana showed her the coin.

"No problem. My sinuses are so clogged from all this mountain greenery that I can't smell a thing. But make sure you roll down the window."

The old man introduced himself as Gus Blake. Pulling a dusty rag from his back pocket, he flapped it in the breeze and proceeded to dust the seat. Finished, he bowed low and swept his arm in a welcoming gesture. Both women groaned as they climbed onto the lumpy seat. Something appeared to be growing out of the dashboard—what was left of it—but at that point, they couldn't gamble that something better would come along. There was a chance the shooter might drive down the rutted mountain road to finish them off.

Gus looked harmless enough. He was no taller than Sarah and weighed half as much. And there was no sign of a gun, unless it was hidden in the glove compartment. The cab smelled of grease and Gus, so Dana was quick to roll down the dusty window. Leaning her head far enough to whip her shoulder length auburn hair in the breeze, she inhaled deeply and glanced out of the corner of her eye at Sarah, who didn't seem to mind the scent of ode to a service station. Her short, curly blond hair never looked mussed and her presence made Gus look all the more grimy.

Gus cleared his throat. "You gals lookin' for a good time?"

Sarah laughed and asked what he had in mind.

"Barn dance tomorrah night down to the Grange Hall. I thought you two might like to go as my dates."

"When's the last time you had a date?" Sarah asked.

He shrugged and tapped the steering wheel with a crooked, arthritic finger. "It's been a while. There ain't a lotta single women here on the mountain."

Sarah turned in the seat to face him. "What makes you think we're single?"

"You ain't wearin' no weddin' rings."

"So you noticed that, did you?"

"Well, shore I did."

"You ever been married, Gus?" Sarah asked.

"My third wife died a coupla years ago."

"Three wives?"

"I've lived a long time and my wives just kinda wore out, if you know what I mean."

"No. We don't know what you mean."

"Ranchin' on the mountains takes a lot out of a woman. What with all the snow, high winds and rough country."

Worked them to death, Dana thought, shivering in the afternoon heat. Some men were heartless.

"So what do you do for fun? Cruise the mountain roads looking for damsels in distress?"

"Mostly I drive around lookin' for wounded gray wolves."

"I thought they were protected."

"They used to be but a law was passed that anybody with a gun can shoot 'em on sight."

Dana leaned around Sarah to ask, "But doesn't that upset the balance of nature?"

"Shore does, but the ranchers claim that wolves kill a lotta livestock."

Dana wondered what he did with the wolves when he found them.

"I nurse 'em back to health."

So Gus was a decent sort, after all. Poor old man had to do something with his time, and chances were slim he'd find another wife. Dana tuned them out as they progressed at a leisurely pace down the rutted mountain road toward the tiny town of Concord. Were the bullets that hit the Escalade from someone shooting at wolves? The shooter must have been awfully near-sighted or a terrible marksman to

5

mistake their SUV for a wolf.

Dana knew there wasn't a wrecker service or car rental agency in the town at the foot of the mountain, and she couldn't imagine Gus chauffeuring them all the way to the mansion. The neighbors would think they were slumming. She shrugged. Who cares what the snooty neighbors think? They'd never accepted her or Sarah since Dana's sister died, leaving her the mansion. Let them think whatever they pleased.

There was one small gas station in Concord and she insisted on buying Gus a tankful of gas. He didn't look like he had enough money to buy anything but the barest necessities, and his truck appeared to be held together with duct tape and baling wire. She wondered whether it would make it as far as Casper, where they could rent a car.

After Dana paid for the gas, she plucked her cell phone from her purse to dial 911. When a dispatcher answered, she reported the rollover as well as the gunshots. By the time she had finished, they were halfway to Casper.

"We need to call a wrecker for the Escalade," Dana said.

"Gonna cost ya a purty penny. Better call my cousin Bernie. Tell him Gus sent ya and he'd do it on the cheap."

Dana wondered if Bernie's wrecker resembled his cousin's pickup truck. She thanked Gus, telling him a sheriff's deputy would inspect the Escalade the following morning before it was towed away.

The old man nodded and said little more during the rest of the trip to Casper. It was nearing the dinner hour when they reached the edge of town. Dana had called ahead to reserve an SUV and hoped they would arrive before the agency closed. The aging truck might break down before they reached their rural subdivision.

The rent-a-car agency had already closed and Gus's truck was smoking as though the front tires had caught fire. What were they going to do now?

6

"Better head for the mansion," Sarah said.

"Good idee, I can hose the truck down in your driveway—if you got one."

Dana cringed, imagining Gus's truck leaking oil on her unblemished driveway. Nodding consent, they chugged off toward the old rural highway. She noticed that Sarah seemed to be holding her breath. An eternity later, the old truck died several feet from their circle drive and Sarah crossed herself, whispering, "Thank you."

Gus squinted at the setting sun when they left his truck. "Would you ladies mind helping me push the truck in the driveway?"

"Tomorrow morning." Dana said. "You can spend the night with us."

The old man turned to squint at the mansion. "Holy jeebers. That big house all yours? Looks like a fancy hotel to me."

"I inherited it from my sister, Georgi."

"She musta been as rich as Mister Romney."

"Not quite." Dana rubbed her throbbing head. "Tell you what, Gus. Leave the truck where it is and I'll buy you a better one tomorrow."

"Can't let you do that, ma'am. Gladys and me's been together nigh onto thirty years."

"Gladys?"

"My truck. I named her after my first wife and that didn't set too well with wives two and three."

Dana sighed. "Come in the house and we'll discuss the problem." *Maybe I can talk you into taking a bath.*

Gus grabbed his huge cat from the truck bed and reluctantly followed them around to the back entrance, which opened into a mud room. The moment Dana closed the door, Bert, their German Shepherd, bounded into the room to greet them. Skidding to a stop, he took one look at Gus and the cat and barked at full volume. Dana grabbed his collar, telling Sarah to retrieve some clothes from a nearby closet. Fortunately, she hadn't taken her former brother-in-law's clothing to the Salvation Army. He didn't need them in prison.

Sarah prepared dinner while Gus was cleaning up. They then ate in the kitchen so the formal dining room wouldn't intimidate their guest. Showered and freshly shaven with a razor he found in the bathroom cabinet, the old man didn't look quite so disreputable, although Rob's expensive clothing hung on him like a youngster playing dress-up. Dana noticed that his eyes were turquoise. No wonder he'd attracted so many wives.

Gus ate as though ending a hunger strike. During dinner, Dana asked about the wolf killings and why he thought she and Sarah had been the objects of someone's target practice. Shrugging, he asked if they'd noticed Gladys's puncture wounds.

Dana dropped her fork. "Someone shot at you?"

"More'n once. I reckon somebody don't like me savin' wolves."

"What happens to the wolves that recover?"

"I load 'em in the back of Gladys and take 'em further up the mountain to set 'em free."

The practice sounded dangerous and Dana couldn't imagine anyone nursing a wolf back to health.

Gus must have read her thoughts. "I have to muzzle 'em when they get better, but I think they know I'm tryin' to help. I only got bit once." Rolling up a too-long sleeve, he showed them the scars on his arm.

Sarah shook her head. "Why do you do it, Gus?"

"Somebody has to. There's already too many deer and elk around 'cause the wolves are dyin' off. Purty soon we'll be overrun with game animals that'll starve in the winter for lack of feed."

"Then why were wolves removed from the endangered

species list?"

"Politics, ma'am. Ranchers are tired of their livestock gettin' killed."

Dana stood to clear the table. "That's a real Catch 22."

"'S'cuse me?"

"We'll talk about it later over a glass of wine."

After the dishes had been done, they gathered in the richly furnished den. Sarah poured them each a goblet of red wine and they settled into soft, burgundy leather arm chairs. Gus reached down to pet their German Shepherd while his cat watched from a nearby chair.

"Better not take the dog to the mountain, ladies. He's the same color as the wolves. There's so many trigger happy hunters around that Bert needs a big orange collar—like the hunters' dogs wear—in case he gets loose."

Dana gasped. "You think someone would shoot him?"

"No doubt in my mind. He's a handsome feller and you can tell where he came from."

Sarah set her wine glass on an end table. "What do you mean?"

"He's from the Canidae species, like the wolves."

So Gus wasn't an illiterate, despite his obvious lack of education.

"You know a lot about wolves, don't you, Gus?"

"I been studying on 'em."

"What's to be done about the wolves?" Dana asked.

"Don't know, ma'am. Wish I did. All I can do is patch 'em up or bury 'em."

Dana showed Gus to the guest room and they turned in early, exhausted from the day's ordeal. She set her alarm for seven, planning to call a taxi to take them into town for the rental car. She would keep her promise to Gus to buy him a reliable truck after they met with the deputy on the mountain. Glancing out her bedroom window, she noticed that Gladys was missing. Who would have hauled the old truck away at this early hour? Grabbing her robe, she hurried downstairs where she found a note on the entry table. Gus had scrawled a brief message thanking her for her hospitality and telling her that he was able to start his truck and leave for home.

Disappointed, she knocked on Sarah's door before pushing it open. Sarah could sleep through a tornado and it required a bit of shoulder shaking to wake her. When she told her what had happened, Sarah's face fell.

"I like the old guy, don't you? I was hoping he'd stay around a while."

Dana nodded. "We need to get a move on if we're going to meet the deputy. Get dressed and we'll grab a bite. The rental agency opens at eight. No telling how long it will take for the taxi to get here."

Dana noticed a large bruise on Sarah's right leg when she swung them over the side of the bed. She had some bruises of her own and muscles that ached during the night. Yawning, she went back to her own room to dress. It would be a long day.

* * *

Later, as she drove the rental Buick up the mountain, Dana noticed a gray wolf racing across the gravel road. Braking, she sat clutching the wheel and inhaling deeply.

"Beautiful, aren't they?" Sarah said.

"Yes, but I don't want to provide Gus with another patient."

"Must be quite a few of them here in the mountains."

"And a lot of sheep and cattle ranches."

"I hope no one takes another shot at us, Dana."

"Amen to that."

The deputy was waiting for them. He had already inspected the Escalade and considered it totaled. He said they were lucky they hadn't been badly hurt in the rollover.

When asked if he'd noticed the bullet holes, he said he had and that it had happened before. But they had been unable to track down the shooter.

"Someone must know who's doing it," Dana said. "Doesn't everyone in a rural area know what everyone else's doing?"

The young deputy shifted his weight uneasily. "That's true, ma'am, but there're plenty of places to hide here in the mountains."

"Could it be one the ranchers?" Sarah asked.

"I doubt it. They're a friendly bunch, always looking out for each another."

"Maybe they don't like strangers."

The deputy laughed. "You're the only strangers I've seen up here in quite a while and I doubt anyone would shoot at a couple of older women."

Sarah frowned. "Older?"

The deputy ducked his head. "Sorry, ma'am. I-I didn't mean—"

"Don't worry about it," Dana said. "At least you didn't say old women."

She asked him about Gus Blake and wondered where he lived. Told his cabin was a mile off the main gravel road, she made a mental note to stop by his place to make sure Gladys had arrived home safely. She also wondered how many patients Gus had in his wolf clinic.

Chapter Two

Gus Blake's ranch house was even older than its owner. The patched, multi-colored shingled roof drooped above a small square of dried, splintered logs. Yellow wildflowers bloomed near the entry and Gladys was parked in a sagging shed adjacent to the cabin.

When Sarah knocked, Gus failed to answer his door. She said he might be around back caring for his wolves, so they trudged through ankle deep weeds to the rear of the cabin. They found him in another old shed the size of the one that housed Gladys. His back was turned as he bent over a makeshift bed placed on a battered table. The wolf appeared asleep but they stood back in case it wasn't. A dark cloth muzzle insured that Gus would not be bitten when the wolf regained consciousness. Dana also noticed straps which held the animal in place.

Gus turned to briefly eye them. "I knowed you'd show up sooner or later. How'd you find me?"

Dana smiled. "We never reveal our sources. Why'd you leave so early this morning?"

"Sylvia's not doin' so good." He pointed to a large wound

on the wolf's left shoulder. "Lost a lotta blood."

"Poor thing." Sarah reached to pet the wounded wolf.

"I wouldn't do that, ma'am. She's a wild critter that might come to and try to defend herself."

They stood watching Gus change a bloody bandage before Dana asked what they could do to help.

He stopped what he was doing to stare up at Dana, who towered over him. "If you really wanna help, instead of buyin' me a truck, build a new shed with bunks and cages for the wolves."

Dana didn't hesitate. "Consider it done. How about a metal building with a heavy lock so the shooter can't burn it down. Or get inside."

Gus's grin was wide and Dana thought he was going to hug her. "You're the angel I been prayin' for, ma'am."

"I think you're the angel, Gus. I don't know of anyone else who would risk his own life to save the wolves."

"They're just wild dogs that most people don't care about. But there is some that do. Like the Wild Life people."

"I don't understand why wolves were taken off the endangered species list. Weren't they nearly wiped off the planet in the nineteen thirties?"

Gus clenched his fists, his face turning an angry crimson. "It was Congress that done the deed in April, two thousand and eleven. They took protection for wolves in the Northern Rockies off the budget. A Montana senator and Idaho congressman made sure wolves was delisted even though some federal court declared it unconstitutional back in oh-nine."

If they can decimate the wolf population, Dana thought, they could do it to all wildlife, one animal at a time. They said goodbye to Gus and left him with his patient. On their way down the mountain, Sarah remarked that Georgi would be proud of the way Dana was spending her inheritance.

Dana's hands tightened on the wheel. "I'd rather have

my sister alive than all the money she left me."

"Of course you would, but at least you're putting it to good use."

"I hope you're right. Gus's wolves will probably be shot again after he patches them up. It seems so futile."

Sarah nodded. "Like sending an unarmed soldier into battle."

Dana made a mental list during the long drive home. Wondering whether the injured wolves would eat dog food, she decided to buy several cases of the soft meaty kind as well as the largest dog beds and cages she could find. A lumber yard would have the sheds and might know of someone who would assemble one for Gus. She'd ask Bert's veterinarian where to buy pet medicines and bandages. Gus must be paying for them with his social security checks. No wonder he looked homeless.

When they arrived home Sarah suggested they conduct online research before leaving on a shopping spree, so they trooped upstairs to Georgi's office. It was Dana's office now but she would always think of her sister sitting at the desk writing mystery novels.

Booting up the computer, Dana accessed the Wikipedia. "Look at this. Wolves only live six to eight years although some have been known to live as long as ten. That's shorter than most dogs' lives. And they weigh forty to a hundred and seventy-five pounds."

"That's more than Gus weighs. I wonder how he gets them in his truck."

"Gray wolves are about Bert's size and weigh up to a hundred and thirty pounds. Red wolves are the large ones that weigh so much more."

"I hope there aren't any red wolves on the mountain."

Dana shrugged and continued to read. "The wolves live and hunt in packs of six to ten and target large animals such as deer, moose and elk. Wolves eat as much as twenty pounds of meat at each kill, but when large animals aren't available, they eat smaller mammals, fish, lizards, birds, snakes, and fruit."

"Then I'm sure they'll eat dog food." Sarah leaned closer to the screen as Dana continued to read.

"Wolf packs have a strict hierarchy. There's a dominant male leader and his mate is usually second or third in command. This male and female are normally the only wolves in the pack to breed, but all the pack's adults take care of the pups by bringing them food and watching over them while the others hunt for food."

"How about that, Dana. Wolf baby sitters."

"Sounds very communal. Almost like a cult."

The desk telephone rang, startling them both. When Dana answered, a low, gruff voice warned, "Stay away from the wolves or you'll wind up in the same grave." Before she could reply, the call was disconnected.

The phone dropped with a clatter into the cradle.

"What's wrong, Dana?"

"I think *we're* on the endangered species list."

* * *

During the drive into Casper, Sarah tried repeatedly to dissuade Dana from continuing with her plan to help the wolves. "How in the world did the shooter know our phone number?"

"He could have traced the Escalade's license plate to us."

"But how could he have done it so fast?"

"He might be a public official. An officer of the law with access to transportation records."

"The deputy?"

"Maybe, but he didn't seem the kind to slaughter wild animals."

"He could have mentioned the accident to the shooter,

not knowing it was him."

"Or maybe someone who works in the records department who filed his report."

Sarah sighed. "Why us, Dana? We were minding our own business, just taking pictures of the mountain scenery."

"We might have taken pictures of something we shouldn't have."

"Like what?"

"A government installation or the shooter's hideout—"

"Let's check our cameras when we get home to see what we've got."

* * *

Their first stop was the pet store where they bought food, beds and cages, which filled the Buick's storage area. They then stopped at the clinic where the veterinarian told them where they could buy antibiotics online.

"At least the vet was sympathetic," Sarah said during the trip home.

"I realize there are ethics involved, but I had hoped to take everything to Gus tomorrow."

"He's done quite well by himself, Dana. Another day or two won't make that much difference."

They decided that the wolf needed antibiotics to cure the infection so Sarah suggested an overnight delivery. Dana agreed and ordered the medicines when they reached home. She had already bribed a building supply clerk to take a couple of days off to lay the foundation and assemble Gus's new wolf clinic.

But what if the shooter tried to prevent the shed from being built? Sarah must have read her thoughts. "What if the shooter carries out his threat? He might shoot that nice young man from building supply store. Or us as he threatened. I'm glad you reported him to the sheriff."

"I don't take kindly to threats. If he wanted to kill us,

he could have done so when he wrecked the Escalade. And if he were intent on killing someone, he would have killed Gus by now."

"But we weren't involved until the rollover, and *we* could have been killed." Sarah sat down heavily in a nearby chair. "You don't think Gus took a shot at us so we would help him—"

"And risk killing us? I think it was simply a warning to stay off the mountain. The shooter probably didn't intend for us to have an accident. He could have easily picked us off when we crawled out of the Escalade."

Sarah frowned and sank deeper in her chair. She said nothing for several moments as Dana scrolled through a list of online wolf sites. She then said, "I think we'd better leave for the mountain before daylight. Hopefully the shooter doesn't get out of bed until noon."

Dana stopped typing. "It's probably someone who doesn't have a nine to five job." She glanced at her watch. "It was about three in the afternoon when he shot at us on a Tuesday. What does that tell you?"

"He doesn't have a regular job, but he might have been on vacation."

"A vacation to kill wolves? Why on the mountain? He must live there."

Sarah sat bolt upright in her chair. "It could be a rancher with sheep or cattle that wolves attacked for food."

"Or someone else with a reason to hate wolves."

"It could even be a woman, Dana."

How many women would set out to eliminate wolves? Dana couldn't think of anyone that bloodthirsty. Was someone simply using the wolves for target practice? For what purpose? Was a paramilitary group training in the mountains for warfare, like the homegrown terrorists they'd encountered in Arizona? Or an army unit from a military base. She knew foreign troops were stationed at

Fort Guernsey, which wasn't far away. Was that why the government had delisted wolves from the endangered species program? She shivered, afraid she was becoming paranoid.

Dana's head throbbed and she closed her eyes to concentrate. They should have seen a doctor to check for head injuries. When she opened her eyes she saw that Sarah had fallen asleep, chin resting her chest. Maybe her friend was right. They should simply deliver the supplies to Gus and leave it at that.

They had a lot to discuss tomorrow when they returned to the mountain. And they had to find time to buy another car. What they needed was an armored vehicle.

Chapter Three

They left before dawn the following morning. Dressed in clothing resembling lumberjacks, they wore calf-length leather boots and wide-brimmed Aussie hats. Halfway up the narrow mountain road, Sarah remarked that they should have worn camouflaged uniforms.

Dana laughed. "Why? Are they in fashion?"

"No, but they'd make it easier to snoop around the mountain undetected."

"Put that on our to-buy list along with a camouflaged truck."

The road straightened when they reached the summit and started down another steep grade. Aspens lined both sides of the narrow road and a flock of wild turkeys paraded in the weeds as a young doe stood watching them, her ears standing at attention when the Buick passed by.

When they reached Gus's place, they assumed he was out back checking on his patient. He might even have another wolf by now. Dana wondered why the shooter hadn't buried his victims instead of leaving them lying in their own blood. He must know that wolves were cannibals who would feed on their own? She could understand a rancher defending his livestock, but why would he shoot at the Escalade? She and Sarah were minding their own business, not a threat to anyone, unless they saw something they shouldn't have. But what could that have been? Shooting their SUV and causing the rollover was a big mistake. Dana slammed her palm on the steering wheel. *The shooter doesn't know who he's messing with.*

"What's wrong, Dana?"

"This has gotten personal and I can't just drive away."

"I've been thinking similar thoughts. If we don't get ourselves shot in the process, I'd like to know who's demented enough to take his wolf vendetta out on us."

"Hopefully he hasn't shot any humans and I think we've covered every possible angle. Ranchers, lawmen, county employees, militia, terrorists, foreign troops—who else is there?"

When they reached Gus's ranch, his house appeared even more forlorn in early morning light. They sat a few minutes debating whether to knock or quietly trudge around back to the old wolf shed. A moment later Gus appeared at the front door, motioning them inside. The aroma of coffee permeated the small cabin and they followed him into the kitchen, just off the main room. The ancient stove stood on slender legs and appeared even older than its owner.

"Got some strong boiled java if you need an eye opener," he said. "I'm up a little late this mornin'. Didn't sleep all that good last night. Kept hearin' rocks hittin' the outside wall."

"Rocks?" Both women eyed one another as they repeated the word.

Sarah asked, "What did you do?"

"Nuthin'. I s'pose it was some kids up to a little mischief—Let 'em have their fun as long as they don't break the winders."

"It might have been the shooter sending you a warning.

He could have shot you when you opened the door to investigate."

Dana accepted a cup of coffee. "You need someone here to stand guard."

"Pshaw. I don't need no protectin'. It's the wolves that need it." A stricken expression crossed the old man's face and he set his cup down to limp to the door. The name "Sylvia!" sounded like a wail.

They followed him out the back door and across the field to the old wooden shed. The door was flung open and he grabbed a flashlight as he stepped inside. The beam found the bloodied body of the wolf outside her opened cage. Whoever had killed Sylvia must have used a hammer.

Gasping, both women fled outside, where Sarah lost her breakfast.

"Gus needs protection," Dana said when she was able to calm her friend. "That could have easily been him instead of the wolf."

Sarah wiped her mouth with the back of her hand and nodded.

A moment later the old man's stooped form emerged from the shed, his clothing stained with blood. "I couldn't save her," he sobbed. The lump in Dana's throat forced tears from somewhere deep inside, more for Gus than the wolf. The shooter was obviously a madman.

She should have delivered the supplies sooner. But what good was a locked metal shed when the lunatic had a hammer? Dana hugged Gus to her side. Poor little man had nothing more than saving wolves to live for.

Was the shooter hiding somewhere in the trees watching them? They needed to get inside. She handed the Buick's keys to Sarah to retrieve their purses. Dana remembered the .38 Smith and Wesson tucked in her purse and hoped she wouldn't have to use it. Gripping Gus's arm, she towed him into the house and seated him in a kitchen chair. She then rushed to a window to watch Sarah as she locked the passenger door. Holding the front door open, Dana took the handbags and ushered her inside. She was reassured by the weight of her purse that the gun was still there.

Now what? Should she call the building supply clerk and tell him not to come? She would never forgive herself if he were shot and killed. Dana plucked her cell phone from her purse and walked to the nearest window. No bars meant no cell service.

Gus was staring at her, the tracks of tears still visible on his ruddy cheeks. "Can't use them phones here, Miz Dana. My son brought me a store bought phone and couldn't get it to work. So he got me a laptop computer and taught me how to use it so's we could stay in touch. He gestured to the south wall where the satellite dish was located.

Dana's heart quickened. "Your son needs to stay with you, Gus. Or you move in with him."

"'Fraid not. He lives down in Colorado, and comes up ever' few months."

"But if he knows you're in danger—"

Gus's expression seemed to harden. "We ain't gonna tell 'im. He's got a passel of youngun's to worry about. Whatever happens to me don't matter none."

"We can't stand by and let some lunatic kill you and the wolves in your clinic."

Gus rose, nearly upending his chair. "It's time for you ladies to leave so's I can bury Sylvia." He headed for the back door.

Dana followed him into the yard where she told him about the supplies they'd brought for his wolf clinic. Gus's shoulders slumped when he turned back to face her.

"You two angels better stay away from now on. It ain't safe here on the mountain."

"We're worried about you, Gus."

"Ain't nuthin' you can do. Don't get me wrong. I appreciate what you done—"

A slamming sound startled them. A moment later, Sarah stuck her head out the back door to inform them the man from the building supply store had arrived. Dana groaned. Were any of them safe there now? What if the shooter decided to take them all out? She hurried around the small cabin to where a tall, dark-eyed young man stood beside his pickup truck. Hand on the bill of his baseball cap, he was squinting into the morning sun. He grinned when he noticed Dana jogging toward him.

"Tom Henderson," he said, extending his hand.

"I remember you from the store," she said, breathing heavily. "Come inside. There's something you should know."

Gus and Sarah were seated at the kitchen table when she led Tom into the room. Once introductions were made, Dana told him about the shootings and wolf killings, including the most recent one in Gus's clinic. Tom's face fell and his large fist pounded the table.

"I spent three tours in Iraq," he said, "so I know what a sniper can do. If I can survive enemy fire, I can get this job done too."

Dana touched his arm. "I have a thirty-eight revolver in my purse and I know how to use it. I'm willing to patrol the area while you two put the shed together." She turned to Sarah. "I noticed a rock pile on the ridge behind the house. Would you mind keeping watch from there?"

Her friend smiled. "You know I will."

Gus reached to pull a pair of binoculars from a kitchen drawer. "You can use these while I help Tom put the shed together." Shaking his head, he said, "Are you sure you wanna risk your lives to save the wolves?"

Dana sighed. "It's not just the wolves, Gus. The governor asked the Feds to delist grizzlies as well. They're already in danger of extinction because of beetles killing the white bark pine nut trees, the bears' main source of food, which they eat before hibernation here in Wyoming."

"Which animals are they gonna kill off next?" Gus said. "Mark my words. They'll be killin' all the big game animals by turnin' the state into a shootin' gallery?"

Tom agreed. "Grizzlies and wolves are keystone predators. They influence their habitat's entire ecosystem and keep the animals that eat plants in check. That in turn increases plant growth."

Gus agreed. "When there's wolves and grizzlies around we get bigger birds and more of 'em flying in from other places."

"Migratory birds?"

"Right, Miz Dana."

"So killing off both wolves and grizzlies really does upset mother nature."

Gus nodded as a cloud passed between the cabin and the sun, casting a dark shadow over those seated at the table. Dana shivered, envisioning an evil spirit glaring down on them. She glanced at Sarah, who slid lower in her rickety chair.

"That's not all," Tom said. "The petroleum industry has been drilling for some time in the Western part of the state, interrupting the longest wild game migration corridor in the country. That coupled with the wasting disease the big game animals are suffering from is going to eventually place them all on the endangered species list. It won't be long before my hunting license won't be worth the paper it's printed on."

So Tom was a hunter concerned with the dwindling supply of game animals. Dana asked where he had received his information and was told that he had studied forestry and animal husbandry in college before deciding to join the army.

Sarah had been quiet until now. "I read that all those wind turbines they're planting around the state are ruining the nesting habitants of quail and other birds and small animals."

"Yep," Gus said. "And there's a lotta mad homeowners whose houses wound up near them big windmills. All the red blinkin' lights and loud hummin' noises are enough to drive you bonkers, I'd say."

Tom said that Wyoming had been a nice, quiet place to live while he was growing up until the energy development companies discovered it. The power companies had continually raised residents' rates to pay for supplying electricity to other states.

Gus rose from the table. "I reckon we'd better git started before the shooter comes back." He paused to look each one of them in the eyes. "I hope you know what you're gitting yourselves into."

Dana checked her revolver to make sure it was fully loaded. Accompanying Sarah to a pile of boulders on the rise, she helped her make a comfortable perch of grass, which was already turning yellow from lack of moisture. Satisfied that Sarah could successfully sweep the entire area with Gus's field glasses, she adjusted the brim of her hat and began her walk around the small ranch's perimeter. The men were already nailing boards together to contain a concrete pour for the foundation.

Dana hadn't walked more than a few hundred yards when she recognized Sarah's shrill whistle. Turning, she saw her friend frantically waving her hand holding the binoculars, the other pointing off to the West.

Chapter Four

Dana was out of breath when she reached Sarah's perch. "What's wrong?"

"Smoke. It's coming from that grove of trees on the next rise."

Dana shaded her eyes against the sun's glare, wishing she had worn sunglasses. Sarah was right. A column of smoke rose from the trees and was blowing in their direction. She yelled at once to Tom and Gus, who were finishing the concrete forms.

"Git in your car and leave," Gus yelled back. "The fire's headin' this way."

Sarah climbed down from her perch. "Better listen to him or we'll all be crispy critters."

Dana gripped her arm and urged her toward the cabin. "We'll drive to the ranger station," she yelled to the men, "and send some firefighters up here."

When they reached the SUV, Dana noticed Tom running toward the fire with a shovel. Gus limped after him, a hoe in hand. She hoped they weren't going to try to fight the fire on their own. Backing onto the narrow dirt road, she created a cloud of dust when she stepped down hard on the accelerator.

"Keep an eye on your cell phone, Sarah. Dial 911 as soon as you see a bar."

"If you don't slow down, we'll be seeing the Pearly Gates." Sarah slapped herself on the forehead. "How do we get ourselves into these messes?"

Dana glanced at her friend. "Trouble's imprinted in our DNA. Keep your eyes on your cell and I'll keep mine on the road."

A moment later Sarah shrieked, "I have a bar," and began punching in numbers. Dana listened as she described the area where the fire was located. Sarah groaned when she clicked off. "It'll take at least forty-five minutes for the volunteers to reach the cabin."

"What about the forestry service?"

"There's another fire on the other side of the mountain."

"You don't suppose the shooter set them both?"

Sarah cringed. "A sniper, wolf killer, and arsonist all rolled into one? Now I'm getting nervous."

The narrow road, lined with thick stands of evergreens, curved sharply and plunged down another steep slope. Dana applied the brakes and hit a patch of sand that sent them sliding off the road. Leaning against the headrest, Dana agreed there was nothing more they could do. Turning the Buick around, she headed back up the slope.

"What are you doing?"

"We'll help fight the fire until the volunteers arrive. At least we can hose down the cabin before it burns."

Smoke was visible as soon as they topped the rise. The fire seemed much worse and had nearly reached the road. If they continued, they would be trapped on the other side. Dana stomped on the gas and raced past columns of billowing smoke. When they arrived at the cabin, she jumped from the Buick and ran toward the men hacking at the ground several hundred yards from the cabin. Two men had joined Gus and Tom on the fire line but their efforts seemed fruitless. There were too many trees surrounding the cabin that would catch fire from blowing sparks.

Dana jogged up to them asking for another hoe to help fight the blaze. Gus stopped chopping long enough to point at a shed near the one which housed his pickup, and she raced off in that direction. Sarah joined her there, asking if she had lost her mind.

Telling Sarah to spray the cabin, Dana selected a long handled hoe from the tools in the shed and hurried back to join the men. The heat from the fire was nearly unbearable but she continued to chop at the hard ground, knowing they weren't making enough progress. Bending so that her hat partially shielded her face from direct heat, she realized that her cheeks were wet with tears. The trench they were digging was less than a foot wide and a hundred feet long. She knew their efforts were futile and it wasn't long before her companions came to the same conclusion.

"Fall back to the cabin," Tom yelled and they took off running. Everyone except Gus, who limped as fast as his legs allowed. Dana turned back to help him but he shrugged her off.

"Drive outa here," he insisted. "Before it's too late."

Sarah was alternating the flow of water on the roof with the ground surrounding the cabin. One of the strangers took the hose and pointed toward the Buick. The fire's roar was so loud that Dana couldn't hear what anyone was saying but she obeyed when Tom repeatedly waved her off in the direction Sarah had taken.

When she reached their SUV, Sarah insisted, "It's too late. We need to get out of here."

Dana hesitated. What about the men? Were they going to stage a last ditch effort to save the cabin? What if they left too late? The four of them could escape together in Tom's truck, but would Gus try to save Gladys? What if the pickup didn't start? Biting her lip, she decided to wait a few minutes to determine what they would do. The lanky man with the hose still aimed the stream of water at the cabin's roof. She then noticed Gus limp toward the old shed that housed Gladys. Less than a minute later, a spurt of smoke shot from the shed and the old truck backed into the yard.

Tom motioned for the neighbors—if that's who they were—to follow him to his truck and they took off running. Dana surmised that the men had arrived on foot. Mesmerized by the erratic scene, she sat transfixed at the wheel of the SUV as everyone else was in motion. A chunk of burning limp grazed the windshield as she watched Gus's old truck continue to back toward the Buick.

"Let's go," Sarah said, "before he runs into us."

Dana spun the tires as she backed onto the narrow road. From the corner of her eye, she watched Gus stop his truck in the yard and limp toward the front of the cabin. She stomped on the brakes, nearly throwing Sarah against the dashboard.

"Seat belt," she yelled as she threw open the driver's door and ran toward the cabin. Dana grabbed Gus's arm when she reached him, preventing him from going inside. Angry, he managed to twist free.

"I gotta save my pictures. The cabin's gonna burn."

Dana glanced back at the fire, which had already leaped the firebreak. Sparks and debris flew past and she feared their clothes would catch fire. Pushing open the door, she urged him inside. A small bookcase stood adjacent to his ancient recliner and he handed her several photo albums, which she carried to the door. Turning, she made sure he was following as she ran to the SUV.

Was he going to make it? Gladys belched smoke as she backed onto the road. Dana sighed as she pulled forward, keeping an eye on the rearview mirror. Sparks bounced off both vehicles as they headed east.

"You risked your life to save these old albums?" Sarah carefully turned a page.

"Gus. Not the albums. I was afraid he'd try to save the cabin. And die trying." She glanced into the mirror to make certain Gus was still following.

"I can understand. There're a lot of memories on these pages. Look at these women. They must have been his wives."

Dana glanced briefly at a tattered page. The oblong photographs were attached to black pages with small triangular corners. She hadn't seen albums like those since her grandfather died and left family pictures to her in his will.

Sarah laughed as she held a page for Dana to see. "This must be Gus when he was young. Not bad looking. No wonder he's had so many wives, one right after another."

"It's his eyes, Sarah. I've never seen anyone with eyes that color."

"Yes, beautiful eyes that are awfully sad right now. How would you feel driving off, knowing your house was burning?"

Dana caught movement from the corner of her eye and immediately applied the brakes.

"What are you doing? We're not far enough from the fire."

"Someone dressed in black with long hair was sitting on a boulder off the left side of the road, watching the fire. When we stopped, he or she dropped off the other side and disappeared."

"The shooter!"

They couldn't stay there a moment longer. If the stranger had a rifle, they would be his next targets. Or Gus. The Buick started forward and picked up speed. She prayed that Gus hadn't noticed the man and would continue following them. She held her breath as she watched Gladys in the rearview mirror. The old pickup didn't stop and she released a stream of breath. They weren't out of the woods yet. She prayed the maniac would be satisfied with burning Gus's cabin and leave his vendetta at that. A few minutes later she was convinced that her hunch was right.

Tom's big Chevy pickup stopped along the road and he walked with the two other men back to talk to Gus. Dana left the Buick and followed him to make sure that Gus was all right. Smiling sadly the old man said, "Now I know what's it like to be homeless."

Dana patted him on the shoulder. "You have a home with us until your son—"

Gus stared at the tops of his well-worn boots. "Don't think so, ma'am. The only home I ever knowed was here on the mountain. And the wolves need me."

"I think you need to come home with us for a few days until you sort things out."

Tom agreed but Gus's neighbors offered to let him bunk with them. Before Dana could protest, they shook hands and the agreement was made. Sighing, she knew Gus would have been uncomfortable at the mansion, but worried that he was still in the shooter's sites. There was no way to protect him.

"I'll buy you a shotgun," she said.

"Thanks all the same. I got me one behind the pickup seat."

"Then keep it with you at all times. You know we'll worry about you."

The two neighbors wore worried expressions, a middle aged man and a young man who, although he didn't resemble him, must have been his son. It had probably just occurred to them that they were placing targets on their own backs by offering Gus refuge. But they were all targets standing there in the middle of the dirt road. Dana suggested they leave the area. Gus, however, insisted that he drive his neighbors back to save their own cabin.

"Volunteer firemen should be workin' the fire by now," he said as he opened his driver's door. His neighbors climbed in and Gladys managed to negotiate a U-turn. Hands waved from both windows as the ancient truck jerked forward, sputtering and belching more smoke.

Sarah patted her arm. "He's a grown man, Dana. We can't protect him from himself."

"He risked his life to save his albums, yet he left without them. That must mean he plans to get in touch. *If* he survives."

"Maybe that's his way of insuring the pictures survive."

Tom stood watching the old truck navigate the narrow rutted road, seemingly unsure whether he should follow. Dana started the Buick and sat watching the young man in her rearview mirror, hoping he wouldn't follow Gus, although she knew the old man needed someone with Tom's firearm's expertise. Tom was a good man and she didn't want either one of them in the shooter's crosshairs.

"Let's go, Dana. It's a long drive down this road."

Dana bit her lip, undecided what to do. When Tom came alongside the Buick, she lowered her window to thank him for his help. The expression she had seen earlier lingered on his handsome face. He was obviously still wondering whether he should return to the fire.

"Tom, would you mind leading the way? I have a talent for getting lost and we've never been down this road past Gus's ranch."

"Okay, Miz Logan. You hired me so you're the boss, but I just might come back—"

"The volunteers have probably contained the fire by now. There's no reason for you to stay."

"Even so—"

"Don't jeopardize your job, Tom." *Or your life.* "It's not worth it."

Head down, he kicked at small rocks in the road as he made his way back to his truck. If I had a son, Dana thought, he'd be a lot like Tom. Or a son-in-law. She thought of her daughter, Kerrie, and wondered whether she had decided to marry the FBI agent who had nearly gotten her killed. Mothers never stopped worrying about their offspring, no matter how old they were.

Sarah must have read her thoughts. "Have you heard from Kerrie lately?"

Dana eased her foot onto the accelerator before she answered. "Not since last week. She's still working for the Denver news magazine, waiting to see if Roger's supervisor is going to transfer him to Cheyenne."

"How do you feel about their relationship, Dana?"

"I have mixed feelings. I haven't quite forgiven Roger for using us as decoys to catch those Arizona terrorists."

"I know, but he was just doing his job and almost died himself."

"I'm aware of that and I'm not going to try to sway Kerrie in her decision whether to marry him."

Sarah asked if she would tell her daughter about Gus and the wolf killer. Dana had considered telling Kerrie but knew she'd be on the first plane to Casper. She loved a good feature story.

"I think not. The shooter has enough people to shoot at without risking Kerrie's life."

When Tom's pickup disappeared around a sharp bend, two short masked men dressed in dusty black clothing appeared on either side of the road, guns aimed at their windshield.

Chapter Five

Sarah's scream unnerved her. The Buick fishtailed to the side of the road and a moment later both men pointed guns at the side windows. Dana heard one of them yell for her to open the driver's door. She rolled her window down an inch from the top and tried to calmly ask what he wanted. Her heart threatened to pound from her chest. Apparently frustrated, the gunman rested his gun against the glass at face level and demanded she leave the Buick. Sarah was experiencing a similar scene on the passenger side but the man had a high pitched voice, more like a young woman.

Her hand covering the lower part of her face, Dana whispered to her friend. "They're young and would have shot us by now if that's what they intended. Don't get out, whatever you do." She knew Sarah was on the verge of hysteria.

Dana leaned closer to the window. "Young man, you've had your fun, now step aside so that we can go home."

"Get out," he yelled or I'll shoot your door lock."

"Our friend in the pickup ahead of us is an Iraqi War veteran. He's well-armed and will turn around as soon as he notices us missing." Dana prayed Tom had a gun with him. "You don't want to get in a firefight with him, do you?"

Although the black mask covered most his face, Dana could sense his frustration. His companion on the other side of the Buick turned to listen and yelled that they should leave.

A moment later, Tom's Chevy came barreling around the curve, effectively ending the planned kidnapping. He was out of the truck, revolver in hand in a matter of seconds. Both black-suited kidnappers disappeared into the trees and thick undergrowth on either side of the road.

"The cavalry's here!" Sarah's lips quivered as her smile broadened.

Not a second too soon.

Tom came running toward them. Telling them to leave, he returned to his truck to negotiate a U-Turn as Gladys had done earlier. Dana floorboarded the SUV, leaving Tom in a thick cloud of dust. Was he planning to go after the thugs? She should have stayed and used her own gun as backup. When she glanced at Sarah from the corner of her eye, she realized her friend was hyperventilating. Now was not the time to play Annie Oakley. The sheriff and his deputies could go after the masked men. She wondered if they had a hideout in the mountains.

An hour and a half later they pulled into the mansion's circle drive. Dana could hear the phone ringing but it stopped as she fumbled with her key in the lock. She nearly tripped over Bert, who was waiting for her, his tail wagging wildly. The call back number was from the sheriff's office. Tom must have reported the fire and the masked men who tried to kidnap them. Why hadn't she thought to call during the drive home? She attributed her lack of forethought to exhaustion and her attempt to calm Sarah, who had fallen asleep not long before they reached the mansion.

When she returned the call, she was routed to the deputy

who had investigated the Escalade's rollover. He had spoken to Tom and wanted Dana's version of the *story*.

"Story? You must have heard about the fires on the mountain."

"Yes, ma'am. But I want your version of what happened."

Dana told him everything she could remember, but something was troubling her. Details buried in the deep recesses of her mind refused to come forward. She'd probably wake in the middle of the night with the answers.

Checking her watch, she realized it was time to start dinner. While she was chopping vegetables for a salad, the phone rang a second time and Sarah took the call in the next room. Curious, Dana walked into the dining room where she overheard her friend talking about the fire and attempted kidnapping. When Sarah noticed her, she handed her the phone.

"It's Kerrie. She's going to catch an early flight in the morning from Denver."

"You told her?"

"I'll see you before noon," Kerrie said in her ear. "I haven't had a good feature story in quite some time. This one sounds better than the Arizona terrorists."

Dana glared at Sarah, who turned and left the room.

"I don't think you should come, dear. Men with guns are running around the mountain setting fires and killing wolves."

"Sounds like a great story."

Kerrie clicked off before Dana could protest further. So much for leaving the wolf killings to the sheriff. They'd have to accompany her daughter to the mountain to watch her back.

The phone rang again as she made her way to the kitchen to give Sarah a thorough scolding. Bert trailed after her, his tail still wagging. The caller was Tom with a report on the fire and his conversation with the sheriff's deputy.

"Fire's contained near the old man's cabin. Some of the logs are scorched but he can move back in as soon as the embers die out. Trouble is, another fire started near the summit where Gus takes his wolves when they recuperate."

Dana's sigh of relief became a gasp. "That means the wolves will be moving to lower ground where the shooters can pick them off."

"I'm afraid so."

She asked if he knew how many people were involved in the wolf killings. He said he would discretely ask around and let her know. She knew Kerrie would be investigating and that she and Tom would eventually team up to discover who the culprits were. Thank heavens Tom was a recent war veteran who could protect Kerrie. But what about *his* job?

* * *

Kerrie's flight arrived at the airport at 10:20 the following morning. Dressed in designer jeans and a peasant blouse, she resembled a runway model. Dana's chest swelled with pride when she noticed her approach, her long auburn hair swinging as she walked.

After crushing hugs all around, the three women picked up Kerrie's luggage at the carousel and trooped out to the rented SUV. Maybe Kerrie would help her choose the right car when they arrived in Casper. She was seriously considering a camouflaged Jeep.

"Can we do it later, Mom? I'm anxious to get started on this wolf investigation. Are you sure no humans have been killed?"

"Not to my knowledge, but we're worried about Gus. I don't know how many animals he's rescued but it made him unpopular with the wolf killers. I wish I knew how many people are involved."

"I'll change clothes when we get to the mansion. Then

we can drive up there."

"You need someone to protect you—someone handy with a gun."

"How about you, Mom? You're a crack shot. I've seen you in action."

"I was thinking of someone with more experience."

"You have someone in mind?"

"Yes, but he works at a building supply company during the day."

Sarah laughed. "And you call *me* a matchmaker."

"I'm not matchmaking, Sarah. I can't think of anyone better suited to protect us—there's also a young deputy working the case. I think you should talk to him before we drive to the mountains."

Dana called Tom's cell phone when they reached home. She asked whether he was interested in pursuing the matter further. When he said he was, she thought he must miss the action he experienced in the army. She offered to hire him as Kerrie's bodyguard if he were willing to take a leave of absence from his job. He said he'd been looking for another position and agreed to start the following morning.

Kerrie descended the stairs from her room as Dana replaced the receiver. Dressed in a jade green shift and strap sandals, her hair pulled into a chignon, Kerrie would have no problem impressing the sheriff's deputy, or the sheriff himself.

"First stop the sheriff's office, then we'll go from there." Kerrie slung a camera case over her shoulder and placed a recorder in her travel bag.

Dana told both women about hiring Tom during the drive south. Kerrie didn't seem happy about confining her investigation to the sheriff's office, but agreed. The following morning was soon enough to drive to the mountain. She also agreed that buying a camouflaged Jeep was a good idea, if they could find one that afternoon. Sarah then told her of their own online research, which Kerrie jotted down on a pad from her purse.

After dropping Kerrie off at the sheriff's office, Logan and Cafferty cruised the car dealerships, where they finally spotted the Jeep. While Dana was negotiating with a salesman, Kerrie called, saying she was finished interviewing the deputy. Sarah drove back to pick her up while Dana signed the paperwork and wrote a check for the Jeep. The salesman was attaching a temporary sticker on the license holder when Sarah drove back onto the lot.

Kerrie volunteered to drive the Jeep while they followed her to the mansion. During the drive, Sarah remarked that hiring Tom was a stroke of genius. She wondered whether Dana had an ulterior motive.

"I think Kerrie's unofficially engaged to Roger Brandt."

"I always thought he was too handsome and full of himself to make a good husband. Maybe Kerrie will change her mind after she meets Tom."

"Now who's matchmaking, Sarah?"

"Guilty as charged. I enjoy bringing people together."

Dana pulled into the passing lane to close the gap with the Jeep, which Kerrie seemed to enjoy driving. "Why don't you concentrate on Gus? He's obviously unhappy without a wife or live-in companion."

"If he wasn't so busy saving wolves, he probably would have found one by now. Besides, Gus has more important things to worry about. Saving his own life as well as the wolves."

"I wonder if we can talk him into staying with us for a while."

Sarah slowly shook her head. "He was adamant that he wouldn't leave the mountain."

"Maybe I should hire an older housekeeper—a widow—and invite Gus to dinner."

"Good thinking, Dana. That just might work."

At least it would take our minds off the madmen on the mountain for a while.

Chapter Six

Tom arrived at seven the following morning. Dana was impressed that his outfit matched their camouflaged Jeep. Inviting him in, she led the way to the kitchen for a cup of coffee. Kerrie sat on a tall stool at the island, sipping chai tea topped with whipped cream. A thin white line rimmed her upper lip, which she hastily wiped off when introduced to Tom. Both smiled shyly and lowered their gazes to their respective mugs.

Sarah was busy packing a picnic lunch for their trip to the mountain. When the basket had been filled to the brim with sandwiches, chips and a potato salad she'd made the night before, she pronounced them ready for the trip.

"Are you sure there's enough room in the Jeep for all four of us, Mom?"

Tom set his cup down. "Might be a good idea if I follow in my pickup." He then asked Kerrie if she'd like to ride along.

She hesitated.

Her mother said, "With your long legs, it might be more comfortable not sharing the backseat with the picnic basket." From the corner of her eye Dana noticed Sarah use her hand to cover an encroaching grin.

An hour later the two vehicles pulled into Gus's yard, which still harbored patches of smoldering grass. The west side of the cabin was scorched but the asbestos shingles had probably saved the cabin from burning. The yard surrounding three sides of the cabin was the color of charcoal briquettes.

Tom was already out of his truck and motioning them to remain seated. Stomping the ground with his combat boots, he made his way to the cabin. When no one answered, he tried the knob and pushed the door open. A moment later the door opened again and Tom was alone. Shaking his head, he walked to the Jeep.

"Cabin's been trashed, Miz Logan, and there's no sign of Gus Blake."

Both women gasped. "Was there any...blood?"

"Hard to tell. The place is a mess."

"We'd better call the sheriff."

"No cell phone service here," Sarah reminded her.

Dana opened her door and left the Jeep. Kerrie was already standing nearby, adjusting her sunglasses. Reaching into her purse she extracted a digital camera. For the next few minutes, she snapped pictures of the blackened land as well as the cabin. Kerrie then followed Tom to photograph the cabin's interior, carefully avoiding any remaining hot spots. Dana and Sarah stepped single file in her hiking boot prints.

Tom was right. Whoever trashed the cabin did a good job. The old furniture was in pieces, the cushions ripped to shreds and strewn about the room. Dana was surprised the culprits had not set fire to the cabin's interior. Maybe they wanted Gus to discover what they had done to his possessions. Poor Gus. He didn't have much to start with. Now what was he going to do? If he were still alive.

Dana retrieved a picture with broken glass from the floor. A middle-aged woman with a lovely face smiled back at her. Another one of Gus's wives?

When Kerrie finished snapping pictures, she asked if there were other buildings to investigate. Dana opened the back door and was shocked to find all that remained of the outbuildings were smoldering piles of wood. Someone had wreaked havoc on Gus's small ranch.

Dana insisted they find an area with cell service to report the vandalism and Gus's disappearance. He might be staying with the neighbors and they should investigate before calling the sheriff's office. Tom suggested they first locate a cell service area. They should call in a report before they searched the surrounding area for a neighbor who might know Gus's whereabouts. They needed additional manpower to locate the old man.

How had Gus's simple acts of kindness spiraled into such devastation? It didn't make sense. There had to be a hidden agenda, but how were they going to discover what it was? If Kerrie hadn't arrived to investigate, they could have left the case up to the sheriff's office. Or could they? Both she and Sarah were deeply concerned about Gus and couldn't bring themselves to sit on the sidelines, without trying to help.

A mile or so later Tom pulled off the side of the road and Sarah noticed two bars on her cell phone. Dana picked up her own phone and punched in the number on her speed dial. She'd had plenty of reasons to call the sheriff's department before. She then noticed that Kerrie had left Tom's truck and was smiling at him. So they were getting along.

When she clicked off, she told Sarah that a deputy was on his way to Gus's cabin and should arrive within the hour. That would give them time to explore the woods adjacent to Gus's ranch for neighbors. Dana prayed they'd find him there.

They drove slowly back along the dusty, washboard road toward Gus's place, watching for small side roads or lanes leading to other ranches. When they neared the burned area, Tom's brake lights appeared along with a right turn signal. They followed him down a narrow lane through heavy brush. No wonder they hadn't spotted a neighbor sooner.

The lane curved off to the left toward Gus's small ranch where they saw a barbless wire fence running between the two properties. This had to be the neighbors who helped fight the fire. A curve to the right brought them within sight of a cabin apparently as old as Gus's, with an equally sagging roof. A large dog bounded toward them when the cabin door opened and a lanky, overall clad man stepped into the yard. Dana recognized him as one of the neighbors who came to Gus's rescue.

Tom left his pickup but must have warned Kerrie to stay inside. The dog looked friendly when Tom offered the back of his hand to sniff. He seemed satisfied and signaled them to join him. They were all soon questioning Frank Toliver about his neighbor.

The lanky older man pulled the brim of his battered western hat lower on his shaggy head. "Haven't seen him since yesterday when we put out the fire. I told him he was welcome to stay with me and my son, but he insisted on going home."

Dana's heart sank as she gripped Sarah's arm. She knew her friend was on the verge of tears. "Do you have any idea where he might have gone?"

"No, ma'am. He keeps pretty much to himself. Doesn't visit much."

Kerrie asked how he felt about Gus rescuing wolves.

Reaching down to pet his dog, he said, "Gus told me this one was the gentlest wolf pup he ever rescued. He couldn't save the mother and rest of the litter, but he brought Jenny home to me."

"Jenny?"

"I named her after my wife 'cause her fur's the same color as Jenny's hair before she died."

Frank shook his head when Dana asked if he'd seen strangers in the area during or after the fire. "With all the smoke and volunteer firefighters in their uniforms and helmets, it was hard to tell who was here and who wasn't. My son Pete and I came on home while the volunteers were still hosing down the hot spots."

"Where's Pete now?"

"He works during the week at one of the cafes in town. Yesterday was his day off."

Kerrie moved closer with her camera.

"Don't like to have my picture taken," he said. "Might break your fancy camera."

"When we find Gus, I'm sure he'd like a copy." Kerrie snapped two additional frames.

Tom scrutinized Frank as though he were a bug under a microscope. "Aren't you afraid the shooters will kill your wolf dog?"

"I keep her close. She doesn't run loose like other dogs and doesn't seem to mind. She's got a crippled leg from when she was shot as a pup, but it doesn't slow her down much." He reached again to ruffle her fur. "Jenny's my buddy."

Dana hoped the shooters didn't know about Frank's wolf. She didn't bark at their approach and the cabin was well off the dirt road hidden in trees and thick foliage. Thank heavens the fire hadn't reached that far.

Kerrie asked if there were other neighbors in the area who might know Gus's whereabouts. She wrote down the names as he remembered them and gave directions. From his expression, he didn't hold out much hope for Gus's survival.

They thanked him and drove back to the dirt road. Tom turned left to find the first neighbor on Frank's list. Dana checked her watch, remembering the deputy who should arrive within half an hour. She wondered if he were the same one who investigated their rollover.

They couldn't tell whether the next neighbor was male or female when the shack door opened. Frank had said Bobby Gear but had he meant Bobbie? The person who answered the door was rotund and dressed in a loose fitting long sleeved denim shirt and baggy jeans, which Dana thought were a bit heavy for late June weather. Frizzy red hair flared like a huge Afro, uncombed and partially tangled. Thick brows lifted above large dark eyes, which stared at them as though they had dropped in from another planet.

Kerrie asked if Gus Blake had been in the area that day.

"What's he done this time?" a husky voice asked.

"Nothing illegal but we're afraid he's gone missing."

"Look for the damned wolves and you'll find him." With that the neighbor turned and disappeared back inside.

"Not very neighborly." Sarah did an about face and walked back to the Jeep.

"Was that a man or woman?" Dana wondered when she sat behind the wheel.

"Definitely a man. No woman would let herself go that badly."

"We'd better return to Gus's cabin before the deputy gets there." Dana signaled to Tom and backed onto the dirt road. It wasn't much more than a quarter of a mile when they reached the burned area. The deputy's patrol car was already there. When he saw them approach, a scrubbed face young man, who seemed as young as a high school student, left his car scowling.

"You have a key to the place?" he asked when Dana left

the Jeep.

"The door's unlocked and the cabin's been trashed."

"How do I know you didn't trash it?"

"You're joking, aren't you?" Dana felt heat rise to her cheeks.

"No, ma'am. I'm quite serious. Where's the owner of the cabin?"

Dana stamped her boot, raising a small cloud of ashes. "That's why we called you up here. Gus Blake's missing and someone tossed his cabin."

By then Tom, Kerrie and Sarah had joined them. The deputy ordered them to stay put while he checked out the cabin. Long moments passed before he returned holding Gus's saber covered in dried blood. Dana forced back the lump in her throat as Sarah began to wail.

"You're all coming back to the station for questioning."

"But aren't you going to find out what happened to Gus?" *Or his body?*

"He's apparently been run through with this sword. I doubt it's necessary to call for a manhunt."

"But he might be still alive."

The deputy stared at Dana as though she were insane. It was no use trying to reason with him. He'd already solved the case. She thought of her friend Sheriff Grayson in California, and remembered his ineptness when he first took office. This young man could have been his clone.

* * *

They followed Tom's truck down the mountain to the county seat, the young deputy bringing up the rear. They were wasting precious time instead of combing the brush for some sign of Gus, or questioning more neighbors. Someone must know what had happened to him. He might even be hiding out somewhere on the mountain.

An hour and a half hour later, the four of them left the sheriff's station angry and frustrated at how slowly the wheels of justice seemed to turn. They had been warned not to return to Gus's cabin but no one had told them to stay off the mountain. So they continued their search for witnesses. Someone had to know Gus's whereabouts.

The next neighbor on Frank Toliver's list lived in a spacious ranch house surrounded by mature pine trees. Neatly dressed and wearing a Stetson, he admitted to knowing Gus although he hadn't seen him in months. Dana reasoned that he wouldn't be saddened if something had happened to the old man. He had his livestock to protect.

The rancher stopped them when they turned to leave. "I hear he has a lady friend—a widow who lives a mile or so past the grange hall. You might check with her."

So Gus had been holding out on them. Despite his age, he was quite a flirt, making them believe he was lonely and in need of companionship. He probably had a harem hidden away on the mountain. One of them may have become jealous and decided to do him in. Dana shook her head. She'd been watching too many late night TV movies and reading too many novels. The wolf killers had either kidnapped Gus, killed him or both. They needed to find him or his body.

Chapter Seven

Marietta McIntyre's house sat sheltered from the wind between granite boulders, which seemed to dwarf her home. A neat flower garden was the only real color in the vicinity. The wood frame house was earth colored with a dark green tin roof. Everything else, including the vegetation, had faded to tan and pale yellow in the hot June sun.

A petite woman answered her door dressed in calico, which covered all but the toes of her western boots. Her snowy white hair, piled high into a bun, only reached to Dana's shoulder. When she learned the reason for their visit, she invited them into her home. Plush burgundy Victorian furniture reminded Dana of her grandmother's home with its velvet drapes and patterned art glass chamber lamps.

Once seated, Kerrie pulled a notepad from her purse and began asking questions.

"I haven't seen Gus in several days although he left an email message yesterday morning."

They all leaned forward, anxious for an explanation.

"He said he would come for dinner last night but he

didn't show up, so I thought his truck might have broken down. He doesn't have a phone, you know."

"Does he always keep his dates?"

Marietta laughed. "Yes, but I wouldn't call it dating. We're just good friends. Companions."

"Do you know where Gus would go if he were in danger?"

"In danger?"

"Hasn't he told you about people shooting wolves?"

Marietta bit her lip. "I know that he takes in injured animals but he didn't tell me someone's shooting them. I guess he didn't want to worry me."

"What about other ranches where he might take refuge?"

"Gus has a friend he calls his brother, although I don't think they're related. His name's Albert Gorring and his ranch is over near Granite Creek.

Kerrie asked if strangers had been asking questions about Gus. Marietta frowned and shook her head. "You're the first people I've seen all week. We don't get many visitors here."

Dana was concerned. "Do you have a weapon of any kind to protect yourself?"

My late husband left me a sawed-off shotgun but the kick nearly knocks me down. I also have a thirty-thirty Winchester rifle, a Smith and Wesson revolver, and an old derringer. After all these years, I'm still a damned good shot."

Dana warned her of allowing strangers into her home and suggested visiting family members for a while. She was surprised when Marietta admitted she had no family and that her home was the only one she'd ever known.

"She'll be fine," Tom said when they left. "I'll bet she can hit a rattlesnake at forty paces, if she's lived here all her life."

Dana was still worried and even more convinced that something terrible had happened to Gus. It could take years to search the mountains and they'd probably never find him. She asked Kerrie who was next on the list.

"Two names left besides Albert Gorring. According to Frank's directions, the closest one lives about a mile down this road."

Henry Thompson wasn't home but his wife answered their knock. The mobile home had been modified with a wooden porch that stretched the length of the trailer. Frances Thompson invited them in and offered them cans of Coke. Hot and thirsty, they accepted before Kerrie began her interview.

"Gus is a friendly old duffer," Frances said. Pulling her long, gray streaked hair behind her ears, her brown eyes sparkled when she laughed. "I remember the time his old truck broke down in front of our place and he needed a lift to get some tools."

"Have you seen him in the last couple of days?"

"No, but I seen his truck go by with somebody else driving it."

"When?"

"Yesterday morning after Henry went to the field."

"Did you recognize the driver?"

"It was somebody wearing a black hat pulled down low over his forehead. He had his elbow on the window with his hand on the side of his face, so I couldn't tell who it was."

"Are you sure it wasn't Gus?"

"I never seen the old man dressed in black and the arm wasn't wrinkled like Gus's."

"Did you see it come back this way?"

"No, ma'am, but I was busy finishing a quilt." She indicated a comforter neatly folded on the dining table.

"What about the wolf killings? How do people around here feel about Gus saving the wolves."

Frances hesitated. "Most folks just think he's a crazy old man who has nothing better to do. They know that the wolves he saves are just gonna get shot again and die."

"How do you feel about the wolves?"

The woman shrugged. "As long as they don't bother us, we don't mess with 'em. We don't believe in killing for no reason."

When she couldn't offer additional information, they thanked her and left. The sun was nearly tree top level and it was a long drive home. Should they chance another visit? Dana thought it was best if they return to the mansion to regroup. She didn't relish driving down the narrow, curving mountain road after dark.

* * *

Tom made sure they were safely inside when they reached the mansion. Dana thought she noticed him wink at Kerrie when he said he'd see them the following morning at seven. Kerrie smiled and waved goodbye.

"I think I'll ride with Tom tomorrow." Sarah's grin was wicked.

"Oh, no you won't," Kerrie said. "We've got an interesting discussion going on that's not quite finished."

"What's that?" her mother asked.

Smiling, Kerrie unlocked the front door and took the picnic basket from Sarah. "I might just tell you about it. Someday."

Both sets of brows raised as they followed her inside. Bert was waiting for them, barking as though he needed out.

"Poor boy left alone all day." Kerrie knelt to pet him.

"That's because Gus advised us not to take him along. He looks too much like a wolf," Dana said.

Sarah retrieved Bert's leash and stooped to attach it to his collar. "I'd feel much safer with him along. His police dog training will come in handy for sniffing things out. He might even be able to find Gus."

The implication was the old man's body, but neither woman would say the word. Bert had been a drug sniffing dog and Dana didn't think he had been trained to find cadavers.

"Bert can ride along in the backseat of the Jeep. The tinted back windows make it hard to see inside. Besides, who has a wolf riding around in a Jeep?"

Bert yipped and danced in place. While Sarah led the dog outside for a walk, Dana and her daughter went to the kitchen to find something for dinner. They settled on frozen pizza because everyone was tired.

"We should have invited Tom to dinner."

"Not quite yet, Mom. We're just getting acquainted."

"Okay. What do you have planned for the rest of the week?" *Besides riding around with Tom.*

"I don't think a week's long enough to wrap this thing up." Kerrie opened the oven door and shoved the pizza inside.

"I had hoped you could stay longer."

"The only reason my boss allowed me to stay this long is because we haven't had a good feature story all month. I'm lucky she's interested in saving wolves and other wildlife."

"I hope we haven't taken on more than we can handle, dear."

"We've always managed in the past, although we've never had a case quite so mysterious."

"Gus must have known the shooters would come after him. I wonder why he didn't set up some kind of defense system."

Kerrie took a seat at the kitchen island. "Maybe he's a fatalist. Like a captain who goes down with his ship. If he can no longer save wolves he might feel that he has nothing left to live for."

"Gus's too spunky for that. I know he'd find a way to

discover who's responsible for shooting the wolves."

"He's had plenty of time to do that, Mom. And what about the dried blood on his saber?

Dana shrugged. "What if someone broke into the cabin and attacked Gus. What if he ran *them* through with his sword?"

"What if *he* were run through and they buried him on his ranch?"

Remember what the Thompson woman said about seeing his truck go by with someone else at the wheel? There's no mistaking that truck of his."

"We should have looked closer for blood stains. We can do that tomorrow if the sheriff's department hasn't locked the cabin."

Kerrie smiled. "Good thinking. Let's do it early. I'll call Tom and ask him to come at six instead of seven."

Dana reached into her purse. "I have his number in my wallet."

"That's okay, Mom. I have it on my contact list."

Chapter Eight

They were ready when Tom arrived, Sarah yawning and Bert running about the house excited because he's been told he was going along. Another picnic lunch had been packed along with a plastic container of dog food and gallon of ice tea. The .38 Smith and Wesson was still tucked in Dana's purse but she had the feeling she was forgetting something.

The sun had risen above the mountain peaks by the time they pulled into Gus's yard. Dana expected yellow crime tape surrounding the house but none was visible. She was even more surprised to find the door unlocked. Sun streamed through the living room windows and the mess looked even worse than the day before. Had the culprits returned looking for something they may have missed? Experiencing a cold chill, Dana rubbed her arms. What if Gus were buried beneath all this rubble?

Tom's baritone voice startled her. "I brought a shovel along just in case. It looks like we should start in here but we could be arrested for disturbing the crime scene."

"You're right." Dana pulled on a pair of rubber gloves.

"Let's sort through this stuff to look for blood stains. Try not to make it obvious we've been here."

"Looks like somebody already has."

"I'm aware of that. They must have returned to look for something."

"By the looks of this place they found it."

Sarah entered the cabin with Bert. Unclipping his leash, she told him to sniff. The dog hesitantly rooted under the edges of the nearest pile of debris and jerked his head up to sneeze. Ashes had drifted into the cabin and who knew what was hiding under the debris. Dana stooped to lift a few newspapers, magazines and single sheets of paper drilled with holes down the side that must have come from a notebook. Nothing suspicious that she could find. Thank goodness Gus had rescued his photo albums the day before. But would he ever see them again?

By that time Bert had plowed his way through to the middle of the room and was sniffing the remains of torn cushions. Something hung from his mouth, which he shook back and forth as though to dislodge it. He obeyed Sarah's command to bring it to her and obediently dropped it at her feet.

"Let's see that," a husky voice said.

When they looked up, a large woman dressed in a deputy's uniform stood on the threshold with her gun aimed at them. "What are you people doing besides disturbing a crime scene?"

Dana tried to remove her gloves behind her back. "Looking for our friend Gus Blake, who lives here. We helped him put out the fire yesterday that nearly destroyed this cabin."

"So you returned to finish the job, I see." She waved them against the far wall with her gun. Pulling the radio from her belt, she used her thumb to turn it on. It didn't take long to realize that radio reception was unavailable.

"Whoever set the fire came back to trash the cabin," Dana said.

"So what are you doing poking around in the mess?"

"Looking for blood stains or anything else that will help us find our friend, Gus Blake."

The deputy holstered her gun. "This is a police matter. Not a case for amateur sleuths."

Sarah brightened and stepped away from the wall. "As a matter of fact we are amateur sleuths."

"Don't tell me you've been watching 'Murder She Wrote' reruns?"

"No, ma'am. We've solved a number of murder cases. You can call our friend, Sheriff Walter Grayson, in California. He'll vouch for us."

Kerrie handed her mother a notepad and Dana jotted down Walter's number, which she handed to the deputy.

Frowning, she pocketed the number without looking at it. "All right, sleuths, what makes you think somebody came here to kill a harmless old man?"

Dana sighed. "He was saving wounded wolves."

"So I've heard."

Bert had returned to sniffing through the trash and they were told to restrain him and take him out of doors. Sarah protested that the German Shepherd was a former drug sniffing police dog and could help solve the case.

"Let me get this straight. You think Gus Blake has hidden drugs in his cabin?"

"No!" they said in unison. "But someone else might have."

Dana filled the deputy in on all that had happened since the rollover. She was then introduced to Kerrie.

"Isn't there enough crime in the big city to keep you busy without snooping around here?" The deputy's sarcasm was lost on no one.

"Nothing to compare with what's happening in the

mountains." Kerrie removed her media I.D. from her wallet to show to the suspicious deputy. "I only have a week to wrap up the story. That's why Mom and Sarah came to help."

"What's *your* connection?" she asked Tom.

"Miz Logan hired me as a bodyguard to protect her daughter while she investigates."

The deputy shook her head in apparent disbelief. "That's pushing the envelope, people. You don't really expect me to believe all that? I think we'd best take a trip to the sheriff's office."

"But we were there for over an hour yesterday," Dana protested.

"That was before you were caught disturbing evidence."

The deputy followed them down the mountain to the sheriff's office where they each signed a statement and were released on their own recognizance. They were also warned not to interfere in the investigation.

It was past noon when they left the sheriff's office so they stopped at a park to eat their lunch, wondering what to do next. Kerrie reminded them that she still had two more interviews, people who knew Gus and might have some idea where he was. But was that considered interfering in the investigation? Kerrie suggested that Dana and Sarah take Bert home while she and Tom drove back to the mountain.

The two women reluctantly agreed. While driving back on the Interstate Dana asked what Bert had unearthed from the floor.

"I didn't get a good look at it because the deputy scared the willies out of me, but I think it was a bloody piece of clothing. Probably one of Gus's shirts."

"He had blood all over his clothes when he tried to save the wolf. Remember how he looked when he left the shed?"

"So any bloody clothes we find can be wolf blood, not Gus's."

"Let's hope so, Sarah. Knowing Gus, he had an escape plan worked out well in advance. I can't believe he would have allowed anyone to take him prisoner."

"He did say he owns a shotgun and I'll bet he knows how to use it."

"Gus might have tracked the shooters to their home base and—"

"And what, Dana? The poor man was limping the last time we saw him. I don't think he could have tracked anyone very far, especially in that old truck that smokes so badly that you can spot it a mile away."

Dana applied the brakes and drove across a shallow gully between the north and southbound lanes.

"What in heaven's name are you doing?"

"Going back to the mountain to see if Gladys burned in her shed."

"But Frances Thompson said—"

"What if she was lying?"

"Why would she, Dana?"

"She and her husband could be the shooters."

"They're not young enough."

Maybe their children are. I saw sheep grazing behind the trailer."

"But why would anyone steal that rusty bucket of tin and bolts? Everyone knows it belongs to Gus."

Twenty minutes later the Jeep was again climbing the narrow mountain road. Once they left the patched and pot-holed pavement and turned back toward Gus's ranch, they noticed a dark gray van parked along the edge of the property about a quarter of a mile ahead. Sarah warned that it could be the shooters, so Dana backed to where they could watch the cabin through unburned trees on the opposite side of the road.

Dana left the Jeep without completely closing the door. There was enough brush to hide her as she climbed a slope across from the cabin and crouched to watch for anyone leaving. She could see the collapsed shed and didn't think the old pickup was beneath the charred boards. Afraid the men would notice the Jeep when they left, she hurried back to drive it out of sight. A little used trail presented itself several hundred feet away and she eased the Jeep around a bend and parked along the dirt road. She and Sarah then climbed higher up the slope until they could see Gus's front door through the trees. They then sat down to wait.

Several minutes later two people dressed in black clothing left the cabin and looked about before climbing in the van. Their faces were hidden in the shadow of black baseball caps. Without the masks they appeared quite young. One of them carried a bundle under his right arm and a handgun in the other. His partner opened the van's driver's door and within a matter of seconds the van raised a trail of dust as they sped to the east out of sight.

"We should have brought binoculars," Dana said. "That's what's been in the back of my mind all day."

"Dare we search the cabin now that they're gone?"

"If we get caught, we'll be spending time in jail."

"You're right. And it looked like they found what they were looking for."

Dana rose from her flat rock perch. "We'll drive by the cabin to make sure Gladys isn't buried under the shed. Then we'll know that Gus's probably in hiding."

"I hope so, Dana, but how far could he have driven in that old truck?"

"Not far, but there are plenty of hiding places here on the mountain that we're not aware of. I think we need to talk to Frank Toliver again."

They stopped by Gus's cabin for a quick peek inside. The vandalism seemed even worse than the day before, if that was possible. What did the two people find in the rubble? Whatever it was, she hoped they were satisfied and wouldn't return.

Gladys wasn't in her shed so they drove to the Toliver ranch. Frank wasn't home but his son Pete was. He took his time answering the door. When he did, he said his dad had driven to town for a month's supply of groceries. He didn't expect him home for several hours. Sarah questioned how they could keep that much food from spoiling.

"Mostly can goods and Dad has an old freezer out back. He usually doesn't buy that much food but he must have a good reason. He left me a note on the table."

Short and slender, he had a buzz cut that looked as though he were in military boot camp. He stepped inside to retrieve a sheet of paper, which he handed to Dana.

"Have you seen Gus since the fire?"

"No, ma'am. I hope he's all right."

"You haven't been to the cabin?"

Pete shook his head. "Dad went over this morning before I left for work and I haven't seen him since."

Dana handed the note back, asking, "Are you sure that's your father's handwriting?"

He studied the note carefully. "It does look a bit different."

Dana told him about Gus's disappearance and said that Frank may be missing as well. The young man steadied himself against the door frame before inviting them inside. His tan seemed to have disappeared as he sat in the nearest chair. He was asked if he knew of a hiding place where both men may have gone. He said he didn't know. Dana handed him a card with her phone number and email address so he could contact her if either man returned. She also warned about the men dressed in black driving a dark gray van. He could be their next victim.

"By the way," Sarah said. "Where's Frank's wolf dog?"

"Dad must have taken her with him. I haven't seen her around."

Dana asked that he search the area and report anything suspicious or out of place. When he agreed, they left for home. The sun was setting and Dana wanted to leave the mountain before dark. She wondered how Kerrie's interviews had gone and hoped they were on their way home.

* * *

The Jeep pulled in behind Tom's truck in the circle drive. They found him and Kerrie seated at the kitchen table drinking ice tea and laughing about something they didn't care to discuss. When asked how the interviews went, Kerrie shrugged.

"Neither man was home."

Disappointed, Dana sat across the table from them and reported the news about Frank and Gus.

"That does seem strange, Mom. We'd better go back first thing in the morning. I've only got four days left to investigate."

"I know, dear, and we're very worried about Gus, not to mention Frank and his wolf dog. The shooters may have found out about Frank and kidnapped both men after doing away with the dog."

"Or killed them all," Sarah said.

"Ma'am," Tom said. "Is it possible that Gus rode to town with Frank to get his own supplies?"

"It's possible, but what happened to the old pickup truck?"

"That's a mystery, all right."

"Maybe they hid the truck so the shooters would think Gus died in the fire."

Dana sighed. "I think they were watching from the slope across the road after they set the fire. That's how Sarah and I were able to spot them when they left the cabin."

Sarah drew a circle with her fingertip on the table. "I'd sure like to know what they were looking for and what they carried from the cabin."

"And I'd like to know what it has to do with the wolf killings." Dana rose from her chair to refill the ice tea glasses.

"It could be a subterfuge to disguise what they're really after," Kerrie said. "They could be dealing drugs or contraband weapons or—"

"But how was Gus mixed up in it?"

Sarah said, "He probably didn't know what was hidden in his cabin. I doubt he ever locked his doors."

How were they going to determine the real reason for Gus and Frank's disappearances? Dana hoped they hadn't been followed. The gunmen already knew her phone number, so they must know where she lived. She hated the thought of another trip to the mountain, but it seemed the only way they were going to find the answers. Tom agreed to meet them at six the following morning and left before they could ask him to stay for dinner.

Chapter Nine

Dana wondered whether her German Shepherd was psychic when Bert barked five minutes before the alarm went off. He must enjoy the trips to the mountain. Faint light filtered through her bedroom window and she groaned and turned over for a few minutes' sleep. But sleep eluded her. She wasn't sure why the dog had barked. Had someone followed them home from the mountain? Dana mentally cleared away the cobwebs. If the wolf killers had followed them home, they would have struck during the night, not at daybreak.

Dragging herself to the window, she peered through the curtains, noticing Tom's truck parked out front. How long had he been out there? Dana threw on her robe and descended the stairs to open the front door. Bert was waiting for her, his tail beating a steady rhythm on the hardwood floor. Motioning for Tom to come inside, she shuffled to the kitchen to plug in the coffee pot. The early morning hours were about to do her in.

Tom entered the kitchen with Bert at his heels. "Morning, Miz Logan. I'm a little early."

Dana sighed. "I was afraid you'd spent the entire night

out there."

"I thought about it, but I needed a shave and shower."

She smiled. *Got to look your best for my daughter.* "Sit down and have a cup of coffee as soon as it's ready. We need to discuss today's schedule."

"Kerrie said she wants to return to Granite Creek to interview Albert Gorring."

"I think Sarah and I will stay here to scan all the pictures we've taken on the mountain. That may be why someone shot at us."

"Good idea. I'm sure the men in black will be watching for your Jeep."

Kerrie entered the kitchen, surprised to find Tom there. Immediately turning around, she rushed back upstairs. Dana noticed that she had failed to put on her makeup.

"She forgot something, Tom. By the way, how are you two getting along?"

She could have sworn that he blushed. "Just fine, ma'am. I was about to ask your permission to take your daughter to the Saturday night dance. Since I'm in your employ, I didn't know how you'd feel about it."

"You have my permission as long as you don't let her out of your sight." *Kerrie would be furious if she overheard me saying that.*

Dana dropped the subject when she noticed Sarah standing in the kitchen entry rubbing her eyes. Opening a cupboard, she removed a waffle iron and plugged it in. "Breakfast will be ready in a few minutes."

Half an hour later, Dana watched Tom's truck leave with Kerrie in the passenger seat. She prayed the black-clothed thugs didn't remember Tom's truck but she didn't think they would be looking for him at Granite Creek. As soon as the plates had been loaded into the dishwasher, she and Sarah trooped back upstairs to plug their memory cards into the computer. Scrolling through each frame, they enlarged them to scrutinize carefully.

Dana leaned close to the screen. "Looks like something black stuck in that pile of boulders."

"Too thin to be a man."

"It's shaped like a rifle."

"Looks like a limb to me, Dana. But what's that dark thing back in the bushes?"

"Utilities probably."

Dana scrolled through several dozen photographs before returning to the box. "We need to check that out."

"Let Tom do it tomorrow. I'm scared witless to go back to the mountain. You know they're looking for us."

"We need to find out whether Frank Toliver returned home."

"If his son doesn't call by noon, we can call him at work."

Which café did Pete Toliver work in and how many cafes can there be in a town the size of Concord? She shared Sarah's reluctance to return to the mountain but needed to know what had happened to Frank as well as Gus. Marietta McIntyre might know. They should have asked Gus's lady friend for her phone number or email address. Dana decided to check her own email.

"Sarah, look at this." The subject line said "We're safe!" She quickly opened the message and was shocked to find a brief note from Gus. How did he get her email address? She then remembered the card she had given Pete Toliver with her cell number and screen name.

The message said, "Don't come back to the mountain. It's too dangerous. Frank and I are hiding out near Granite Creek with my cat and Frank's dog. The bad guys don't know we're here so don't tell anybody. We'll be in touch." The note wasn't signed.

Both women sighed with relief that both men were alive. Dana then wondered how Gus had been able to get

71

in touch with Pete. Probably on Frank's cell phone while his son was at work. But why hadn't they called instead of emailing her? And why did Frank have cell service and Gus didn't?

"Dana, what if the bad guys captured Pete and found the card you gave him. They could have sent that email message to keep us off the mountain."

Sarah was a worrywart but she could be right. What should they do? Dana picked up the phone to call Kerrie. When told what had happened, her daughter said they would ask Albert Gorring whether the two men were hiding on his ranch when she interviewed him. They were on their way there now. Gorring's ranch was the logical place for them to hide. But what about Frank's son?

Dana pulled a phone book from a desk drawer to call the cafes in Concord. When the first one didn't answer, she checked her watch. Too early to call? One of them had to be serving breakfast. Her third call produced results.

"Pete didn't show up for work this morning," the manager told her.

When she explained that his dad was missing, the woman's voice lost its hostile tone. "Then why didn't he call and let us know?"

"He might be missing too."

Dana hung up the phone and told Sarah to get ready to leave for the mountain. Despite her friend's sputterings, she managed to pack a lunch and store water bottles and dog food in the Jeep. By nine o'clock they were on their way. The sky was gloomy with low hanging clouds as they started up the mountain toward Frank Toliver's ranch. The weatherman confirmed her suspicion that it was going to rain and it wasn't long before they were in the midst of a downpour. Dana pulled off the road in the foothills to wait out the storm. She'd lived in Wyoming long enough to know that most storms passed through within an hour or two, often less. This downpour slackened in less than ten minutes so Dana decided to proceed.

The pavement ended at the summit and they began a long downhill run on a muddy dirt road. Sarah shrieked when the Jeep slid sideways almost off the road, which prompted Bert to bark from the backseat. *Why didn't I just turn around and go home? Dana* shifted into four wheel low and crept to the bottom of the grade where the road crossed a narrow bridge. As soon as the shoulder widened, she drove onto the grassy shoulder and continued up another grade. She knew it was at least another two miles to the Toliver ranch and getting stuck would make them sitting ducks. She could feel Sarah glaring at her from the passenger seat although she didn't say a word.

The Jeep slowly made its way along the shoulder, leaving tracks in the weeds. It was raining again, more a heavy sprinkle than steady rain, but was it enough to keep the shooters off the road? Low clouds swept in creating fog so dense that it was nearly opaque. What kind of weather was this for late June? Wyoming weather at seven thousand feet.

They were in open range country and she didn't want to risk running into a stray cow or rancher on his way to town. No one in his right mind would drive in this weather, including the shooters, unless it was a dire emergency. It was too late to decide whether finding Gus and the Tolivers *was* an emergency. Driving back into the mud, she told Sarah to watch for animals and the edge of the road. There were sheer drop-offs in some areas and she cringed, imagining the Jeep tumbling into space and landing on the rocks below.

Crawling forward at five miles an hour they managed to reach the burned area and Gus's ranch without passing another vehicle or knocking down a rural mailbox. The wind had picked up and fog was less dense at the lower elevation, making it easier to locate the lane bordering Gus's ranch.

When they reached Frank's cabin, Dana rapped at the door and waited. When no one answered, she tried the knob. The door swung open to reveal another vandalized cabin. Motioning Sarah to join her, she shouted for her to bring Bert along.

The dog immediately went to work sniffing the mess. A moment later he turned toward them with a bloody hiking boot hanging from his mouth. Dana's heart leaped into her throat. Whose boot was it? Gus's, Frank's or Pete's? The boot was small, which eliminated Frank. Could it have been Frank's wife's boot? He might have kept Jenny Toliver's boots as remembrances, but a bloody one? She might have been wearing them when she died, but was she involved in an accident or did she die of natural causes? She would ask Marietta McIntyre.

Sarah leaned to take the boot from Bert. "Well, at least the deputy isn't here to arrest us for tampering with evidence. And I doubt she'll be willing to drive up the mountain in this weather."

"I wouldn't be too sure." Dana pulled on rubber gloves from her shoulder bag and handed a pair to Sarah. "Don't touch anything else until you put these on."

"What about the boot?"

"What size is it?"

Sarah walked to the window and looked inside. "It's an old boot and hard to tell the size. Looks like a six and a half."

"I wonder if Pete's feet are that small."

"It's possible. He's not very big and may have inherited his stature from his mother."

Dana glanced into the yard to determine whether they'd been followed. "Let's look through this mess before we have company."

Where was Pete? Had he gone to Granite Creek to join his father? As soon as they had cell service she would check for messages and call Kerrie. Hopefully, she and Tom had reached Albert Gorring's ranch by now.

They found nothing unusual in the debris to suggest that violence had taken place in the cabin, other than the bloody boot. The furniture appeared to have been demolished with a sledgehammer, the couch cushions ripped to shreds as though someone had searched for something hidden inside. A few paperback books had been pulled apart, the pages scattered about the room. That made no sense unless it was done simply for affect.

When they looked in the bedrooms and kitchen, they found the drawers had been upended to scatter the contents on the floors. Except for one bedroom. They wondered who slept there. The bedding had been shredded as though an animal had attacked them. Were the shooters trying to place the blame on the wolves?

Half an hour later they were ready to leave, with no clue as to what had happened. Sarah carefully wiped her fingerprints from the boot and left it where the dog had found it. How long had the boot been bloody? It appeared to have been for some time. Dana thought again of Marietta McIntyre and wondered whether they dare pay her another visit without placing her life in danger.

A light wet fog still veiled the entire area but she decided to drive over there. The shooters wouldn't expect them to be on the mountain in this weather.

Marietta wasn't home or she was afraid to answer her door. Had she also disappeared and had her home been trashed as well? Dana pressed her nose against the window and cupped her hands around her eyes to peer inside. The drapes had been drawn and she couldn't see a thing. When they tried the single garage door it was locked.

Sarah whispered, "Let's go. This place is giving me the

creeps. It feels like someone's watching our every move."

Dana's heart sank. They should have looked for Gus's computer. Was that what one of the shooters carried under his arm when the two men left the cabin? While she was trying to decide what to do, Sarah noticed a car driving toward them. When it stopped, they noticed the county emblem on the door.

"Out sleuthing again, I see." The voice was all too familiar.

"We came up to visit Pete Toliver,"Dana told the deputy. "When he wasn't home we decided to talk to his friend, Marietta, but she's not home either. We didn't even stop at Gus Blake's cabin." She then told her about her early morning email.

"You came up in this weather? Why didn't you call the sheriff's office?"

"Because Pete Toliver didn't show up for work and he seems to be missing."

"An even better reason to call the office."

"I didn't want to call in a false report, so we decided to check it out ourselves. I just pulled over to call." Dana crossed fingers in her lap to nullify the lie.

The deputy left her patrol car and walked over. "Then why didn't you?"

Dana told her about Kerrie's call and that all three men were missing. She also filled the deputy in on her suspicion that the shooters had stolen Gus's laptop and emailed her that morning. She suspected that Pete Toliver had been kidnapped and her card found in his wallet.

The deputy mulled that over for a moment before she told them to drive home and stay there. Someone would stop by to take their statements. No more sleuthing, the deputy warned, or they would be considered *persons of interest*.

Before she turned to leave, the deputy told them she had contacted Sheriff Walter Grayson and he had vouched for them. But that didn't give them the right to interfere with the investigation. "By the way, he asked that you pick him up at Natrona County Airport tomorrow. He said he'd call later to let you know the flight number and time of arrival."

Dana groaned. She didn't want Walter flying back to Wyoming when he was so close to retirement. Maybe he could help but she doubted it. By the time he had a handle on the case there would be dead bodies littering the mountain.

The rain had moved on, leaving behind an anemic sun to burn off remaining fog. They needed to leave before the shooters discovered them there. What about the deputy? She didn't seem concerned about her own safety. She probably felt secure that the shooters wouldn't harm her for fear the mountains would be crawling with deputies.

Dana drove the downhill mountain curves slower than usual as she considered all the implications. Was the bloody boot Pete's and had they killed him and searched his pockets? Where were Gus and Frank? She remembered the man's voice who warned her of an early grave. Had he carried out his threat with Gus and the Tolivers? There had to be something else going on besides the wolf killings.

They needed to get in touch with Marietta McIntyre to warn her again that she was in danger. Did she know more than she had told them and had the gunmen gotten to her as well?

Chapter Ten

Kerrie discovered early on that Tom was a country music fan. An old cowboy song played loud enough to be heard above the air conditioning unit which rattled in time to the music. Tom was not only handsome, he was well versed in current events as well as history and anthropology. So he was easy to talk to when he wasn't singing along with Hank Williams or Lefty Frizzell.

When the song ended she reached to turn down the volume. Tom glanced over at her and raised a brow as though to say, "This had better be important."

"I need some background for my feature story."

"Such as?"

"I know you keep up on the news and I wondered if crime is a problem in this state."

"We have an occasional murder, wife beatings, drunken brawls, drug busts—but nothing like you have in Denver."

"That I'm aware of. What I'd also like to know is how environmentally aware are people here and how do they feel about wolves and game animals killed needlessly."

"I can only speak for myself, Kerrie, but everyone I've

talked to is against slaughtering animals, unless of course it's wolves, bears or other wildlife killing their livestock."

"I'll have to research Wyoming's demographics."

"We have slightly less than half a million people although it's the tenth largest state. And some twenty-five percent of our residents are from other places, so they carry their own opinions about the wolves. Why do you ask?"

"I just wonder if most people here really care about the wolf killings."

"I'm sure they do. There are several organizations devoted to fighting the current laws that allow shooting them on sight."

"Less than half a million people, huh?"

"I'd like to increase the population by two or three. How about you?"

Surprised, Kerrie ducked her head to scribble notes, ignoring his blatant attempt to take their budding friendship to the next level. She knew he expected an answer and mumbled, "Someday, maybe, after I'm tired of working."

"I thought you wanted to write mystery novels like your aunt."

"I do, but I can't see myself changing diapers and writing novels at the same time."

"All in good time," he said smiling.

"Back to work. What do we know about Gus's friend, Albert Gorring?"

"Not much. I remember meeting him as a kid before he moved away. I find it impossible to believe that he'd slaughter animals. Or kidnap Gus and the Tolivers."

"What about the other neighbors?"

"There's one left on the list—someone I haven't met, so he must have moved to the mountain within the last five years. We need to talk to him after you interview Albert Gorring."

An hour later, they found the Gorring ranch. Albert was a pleasant man about Gus's age and size. Dressed in denims and a western hat and boots, he looked like a successful rancher. When told of his friend's disappearance, he paced his living room trying to think of somewhere Gus might have gone.

"If his old truck broke down, he could be anywhere."

Kerrie said, "I think he left with Frank in his newer model pickup, but we can't be sure."

"Did you talk to his friend Marietta?"

"We did. She told us to get in touch with you."

Two grooves deepened between Albert's eyes. "Frank Toliver's a good man. I hope the two of them left together, but if they're not headed this way, I have no idea where they may have gone."

Tom asked if he knew of a hiding place where Gus may have played as a boy. A cave or hideout that might have survived the years.

Albert shook his head. "Wait a minute. Gus's dad had an old fishing lodge on a stream that he inherited from his own dad. He used to fish from his back porch. I'm not sure I remember exactly where it was but I'm willing to have a look."

"What about Frank's son Pete? Have you heard from him and what do you know about him?"

The old man seated himself in an arm chair. "Frank adopted Pete when he married Jenny. He loved that boy as though he were his own. It was about the time I bought this ranch and moved away, but we never really lost touch. And, no, I haven't heard from the young man."

Kerrie looked up from taking notes. "So the three of you were boyhood friends?"

"Yes, good friends and I often regret moving away."

"Do you know of anyone who would want to harm Gus?"

Albert paused. "I don't imagine he's too popular with the local ranchers. Saving wolves who might attack their livestock doesn't earn him many friends in the ranching community."

Kerrie asked why he and Frank had better educations, and was told that Gus's mother died when he was eight and his father didn't insist that he attend school. "Maybe because his old man quit school in fifth grade to help on his family's ranch and didn't think that schooling was that important."

"So how did the three of you remain friends?"

Albert chuckled. "We'd meet up after school down by the creek where we'd toss in a line wrapped around a branch to fish."

Kerrie asked how he felt about killing wolves, knowing that he owned livestock.

"I have mixed feelings on the subject, as I'm sure my fellow ranchers do. I don't cotton much to slaughtering animals, but if I catch one killing my sheep, I'll shoot 'em."

They left after Albert promised to drive to the mountain to locate Gus's old fishing lodge. Kerrie had given him two of her business cards, one for home and the other for his wallet. She also warned him to be careful. He said he would call if he found the lodge or located his friends.

"What did you think of him?" Kerrie asked when they left the ranch.

"A nice old guy who cares about his boyhood friends. I think he'd do just about anything for them."

"I hope he goes armed and with someone else when he explores his old mountain haunts."

"He will. I'm sure of it."

* * *

Dana's cell phone rang as they reached the summit

where the muddy road merged with the pavement. Cell service at last. When she pulled off the side of the road, a quick glance at the screen told her it was Kerrie.

"Mom, Gus and Frank aren't here. Gus's friend Albert Gorring says he hasn't heard from him."

"What about Frank's son Pete? Have you heard from him?"

"No, Albert hasn't heard from him either."

"Do you think Albert might be hiding them and afraid to tell anyone where they are?"

"No, I think he's telling the truth, but I'm worried that something might happen to him on the mountain, along with Mrs. McIntyre. I don't think either one of them realizes the danger they're in."

* * *

The phone rang minutes after they reached home. Walter was calling to announce his arrival time. When Dana tried to talk him out of flying to Wyoming, he insisted that she and Sarah were in danger and that he couldn't allow anything to happen to them.

Dana hung up frustrated.

"When's he coming?" Sarah asked.

"His flight arrives tomorrow afternoon at two-twenty-five."

"You don't seem happy about it."

"We agreed that he would stay in Modesto until he officially retires."

"If you love him it shouldn't matter."

"That's the problem. I just don't know. I'm grateful that he tried to help us solve the terrorist murders, but since he's been gone I've wondered how I really feel about him."

"You'll know when you see him, Dana. I wish someone was willing to fly back and forth across country to see me."

Dana didn't want to discuss her relationship with Walter, or even think about it. "We need to get hold of Marietta and warn her again about the wolf killers. I hope she's in the phone book." Thumbing through, she found an M.A. McIntryre listed with a Concord address. Did the town limits extend that far? She dialed the number and heard an automated man's voice ask that she leave a message. What should she say?

After a moment's hesitation she decided. "Marietta, this is Dana Logan calling. It's urgent that you return my call. It concerns Gus Blake and Frank and Pete Toliver." Leaving her number she replaced the receiver.

"Now what, Dana?"

"I thought I'd search the data bases for Gus and the Tolivers to see if there's anything in their backgrounds that could explain their disappearances."

The desk phone rang at her elbow, startling Dana. Marietta was returning her call. Dana detected a note of fear in her voice and asked if she had been home earlier when they knocked at her door.

"I'm sorry. I didn't want anyone to know I'm home. Two men wearing black outfits knocked at my door early this morning before the foggy rain storm. When I didn't answer, they tried to break in. I guess something scared them away. I would have shot them, you know."

Dana sighed with relief, thinking it was too bad she hadn't shot them. It would have solved at least one problem, although dead men couldn't be forced to tell where their victims were. She then told her that Frank's cabin had also been vandalized and that the three men were missing.

"Please come and stay with us Marietta. You're not safe there."

"I can take care of myself."

"I know you can but you have to leave the house sometime

to buy supplies. Why don't I have someone pick you up and bring you here?"

"Because Gus might try to get in touch."

"He hasn't emailed you?"

"Not since I invited him to dinner."

That settled it. If Gus had actually emailed Dana, he would have also sent a message to Marietta. The shooters had his computer but did they also have Gus? And why trash Frank's cabin as well. Nothing made sense.

"Do you know where Gus and Frank might be hiding?"

"If they're not with Albert, I have no idea."

Chapter Eleven

Brent Green's small ranch was located several miles from the Tolivers and they stopped in unannounced to see him. The wiry little man was friendly enough and didn't seem surprised that Gus and the Tolivers were missing.

"I knew something like this would happen," he said. You can't go around saving wolves in cattle and sheep country. I don't know how many times I told Gus that."

Kerrie wished she had brought along her tape recorder, although she doubted Brent Green would have been as candid. "What about Frank and Pete Toliver? Were they also saving wolves?"

"Not to my knowledge although Frank had a wolf pup the last time I saw him."

"How well do you know Pete?"

"Haven't seen him in a while, but he was a wild youngun' after his ma died."

"How wild?"

"Oh, nothing real bad. He just didn't want to take his dad's advice. But I suppose that's true of all kids nowadays."

Kerrie asked if he knew of any place where Gus would

have gone to hide on the mountain. Shaking his head, he said, "Not unless they went to the old fishing lodge on the stream in the woods. Us kids used to camp out there sometimes."

When asked to give them directions, he said his memory was failing him. Was he telling the truth or trying to protect his old friends?

Further questions received similar statements of failed memory, so they thanked him and left, exacting a promise that he would get in touch if he remembered anything else.

* * *

Tom and Kerrie arrived at the mansion around three that afternoon, smiling and seemingly happy. Dana remarked that the interviews must have gone well and they both nodded. Kerrie briefly told her about them before the phone rang. She then excused herself to talk to Roger Brandt in another room. Dana decided not to ask about her relationship with Roger until her daughter brought it up.

A frown had replaced her smile when she returned to the kitchen and Tom asked if anything was wrong. Kerrie shrugged off whatever was bothering her and reminded him that there was still another friend of Gus's to be interviewed. Dana tried to dissuade her from returning to the mountain but Tom agreed that the neighbor might know where Gus and Frank were hiding, if they were still alive.

"Someone from the sheriff's office will be here to take a statement sometime this afternoon," Dana said. "Maybe you should wait for an escort."

Kerrie protested that she only had a few days left to wrap up her research. She didn't want to waste a minute of the time she had remaining.

Dana's frown matched Kerrie's earlier one. "If the

gunmen got a good look at Tom's truck they might recognize it and shoot at you."

"We'll be careful, Miz Logan. I doubt those guys are watching the road twenty-four/seven. They must be hiding out with sheriff deputies investigating."

"Please make this your last trip to the mountain, Kerrie. The story's not worth risking your life."

"We've been in riskier situations before, Mom. Remember the serial killer in the San Joaquin Valley, our local drug gang, and the terrorists in Arizona?"

"How could I forget?"

Tom reassured her that he was well armed and that the shooters had only killed wolves. "Warning shots fired into my truck can be repaired."

Before Dana could protest, Tom took Kerrie's arm and they left without a backward glance. Sarah appeared as concerned as she was. "Something's going on between those two."

"Don't I know it? I'll have a serious talk with Kerrie when they get back. *If* they come back."

Sarah reached across the table to pat her arm. "They will. I have every confidence in Tom. He's lived through three war zones, Dana."

"That doesn't mean he'll survive an attack on the mountain." Dana rose from the table to grab the phone. "I'm going to call Marietta again and tell her that she can come here with Tom and Kerrie."

Dana gave up after ten rings. Marietta had said she wouldn't leave the house, so something must have happened to her? Had she also disappeared? Dana dialed Kerrie's cell phone and asked that she stop by Marietta's house to persuade her to come to the mansion. Kerrie said they would try and promptly clicked off. What was going on with those two?

"Do you think she's going to dump Roger for Tom?"

"Who knows, Sarah? We have more pressing problems to worry about, such as keeping Kerrie and Marietta alive. I wonder why Marietta's answering machine didn't click in. You don't suppose the shooters set fire to her place?"

"You're not thinking of driving up there again, are you?"

"Grab Bert's leash. Let's go."

* * *

The road was muddy when the pavement ended. Tom noticed deep ruts made by several vehicles that had traveled the road since the rain. Two of them must have been made by the Jeep. There was also a single set of wider treads that had gone up the mountain and not returned. That made Tom even more watchful. He glanced briefly at Kerrie, noticing her profile framed with an abundance of auburn hair. Why hadn't he met her sooner before she became engaged to the FBI agent? Tom hoped Roger Brandt realized what a lucky guy he was. Maybe that's who she had been talking to on the phone when she came back looking like a thunder cloud. And maybe he had a chance with her after all.

"Look out!" Kerrie screamed.

A short, black-clothed shooter stood in the middle of the road with an AK-47 pointed at the windshield.

"Duck," Tom commanded as he stepped down hard on the accelerator. He could feel Kerrie's head touch his thigh as he threw his own head against the side window. The bullet made a hole in the windshield as well as the back window but he kept the pickup floorboarded. He wasn't sure whether the bump he felt was a rut in the road or the truck had mowed down the shooter. Wrestling the wheel to regain control of the truck, he managed to round a curve without leaving the road on a downhill grade lined with aspens.

He warned Kerrie to remain out of sight. "Another shooter might be stationed further down the road."

"Oh, my Lord. Did you run over him?" She raised her

head high enough to stare at Tom. "You're not hurt, are you?"

"I'm fine. Keep your head down until we're out of firing range."

"Shouldn't we go back to see—?"

"If someone's with him, he'll open fire. I can't risk getting you killed." He looked in the rearview mirror but his back road was obscured by trees.

"They're no longer just shooting wolves, Tom. Shooting at us means they probably killed Gus and the Tolivers."

"I'm afraid you're right. We need to find another way out of here."

"I'd better not try interviewing the last neighbor. It would put him in danger."

"What about the old lady?"

"Mom wants us to rescue her, if she's still alive. Do you remember where she lives?"

Tom glanced again in his mirror. It was impossible to determine whether they were being followed. He told Kerrie to sit up and watch her side of the dirt road for any kind of movement. What the hell was going on? This wasn't ranchers protesting wolves. It was more like open warfare, although no soldier in his right mind would stand in the middle of the road and aim at a speeding truck. They had to be civilians, possibly high on drugs or alcohol. That made them even more dangerous.

"How far to Marietta's ranch?" Kerrie still held a hand to her chest and appeared to be hyperventilating.

"Couple of miles. Did your mother tell her we're on our way?"

Kerrie nodded, apparently still out of breath.

"There's another curve coming up. Look back to see if anyone's following."

Kerrie rolled down her window and looked back, her long hair whipping about her face. She said all she could see were thick stands of aspens growing on both sides of the narrow road. Tom told her to call 911 as soon as she had cell service. She discovered two bars and punched in the numbers, but before she could tell the sheriff's department their location, she lost the signal.

"Keep trying. We may need reinforcements."

* * *

"Shouldn't you call Kerrie and tell her we're on our way?"

"You can try but there are only certain areas on the mountain where cell service is available, Sarah."

They were approaching the foothills and Dana was relieved that the dark clouds and fog had departed for Nebraska. The late afternoon sun shone brightly, which Dana hoped had dried the mud. Kerrie must be interviewing Gus's neighbor by now. Hopefully she and Tom hadn't seen another fire on the mountain. Sarah shook her head when Dana asked if she had been able to reach Kerrie. She and Tom must be traveling in a dead spot.

The pavement was dry when they left the foothills but the deeply rutted road past the summit slowed them down. Halfway down the grade, they noticed a black bundle off the side of the road and Dana stopped the Jeep to investigate. Protruding from the mound of clothing was a mean looking rifle.

Dana stepped from the Jeep and cautiously moved forward. Kicking the gun aside, she looked down on a black-masked face. Pulling the mask free, she saw that the shooter was young and had traces of mascara smudged beneath her eyes. She couldn't tell if the victim was still alive and knelt to take a pulse when a car came to a halt behind the Jeep.

"You just couldn't stay out of it, could you?" The deputy stood with hands on her ample hips.

"We stopped when we saw her lying in the road." Dana raised the young woman's arm and noticed black nail polish. "There's a faint pulse. You need to call an ambulance."

The deputy waved her off and took her place. "You're right. I'll call in a helicopter to take her to the hospital. Get in the Jeep and stay there."

"I'm surprised she didn't notice that nasty looking rifle," Sarah said, once Dana was back behind the wheel.

"I don't think she noticed the walkie-talkie in the shooter's jeans pocket either. That means there was a spotter nearby. I wonder why he or she didn't come to the shooter's rescue."

The deputy walked over a few minutes later. "Unless you want me to haul you two back to the station, you'd better turn that Jeep around and head for home. Deputy Arnold's on his way to interrogate you."

"Interrogate?" Sarah said. "We're not criminals."

The deputy's expression said otherwise.

Dana made a U turn and drove back up the grade. The mud had hardened into small ridges, making for rough travel. The Jeep jerked sideways and she fought the wheel until they reached the pavement.

Sarah leaned to look back in her side mirror. "We should have told her about Marietta."

"The deputy has her hands full with the injured girl. She's also a target if there's another gunman in the area. I asked Kerrie to persuade Marietta to leave the mountain with her and Tom."

"I hope they can, Dana."

"We'll call the sheriff's office as soon as we have cell service to let them know Marietta's in danger."

"After all the warnings we've received to stay off the case?"

"You're right. We'll tell Deputy Arnold when he arrives at the mansion."

Dana picked up her cell phone to call Kerrie, but there

was no answer. They must still be in a no service area.

* * *

The deputy was parked in the circle drive when they reached the mansion. Tall, middle aged and grim-faced, he followed them into the house. Refusing a glass of ice tea, he began his questioning as soon as they were seated in the living room.

After Dana had described their rollover, he wanted to know why they continued to travel to the mountain, knowing they were in danger.

"We thrive on adrenalin rushes," Sarah said, smiling.

"Meaning you two have death wishes?"

Dana frowned. "My friend's being facetious. Actually, we've solved three other murder cases, including my sister's death."

"Licensed private detectives?"

Sarah cleared her throat. "My late husband was a licensed PI."

The deputy glanced at Dana for confirmation. When she nodded, he asked why they had gotten involved.

"Wouldn't you if someone shot up your SUV and caused a rollover?"

"I'd report it to the sheriff."

"And if you received threatening phone calls?"

Deputy Arnold began taking notes. When he finished, he advised them to find another hobby and to stay off the mountain. Dana then told him about Marietta. He said he'd check into it. She wondered when he would.

* * *

Tom's pickup pulled onto Marietta McIntyre's property and Kerrie was relieved that the house had not been burned. Leaving the truck before Tom could stop her, she ran to the front porch and knocked.

"Mrs. McIntyre, it's Kerrie Compton. My mother, Dana Logan, sent me to talk to you. Please let me in."

When no one answered the door, she repeated her earlier plea. At last a woman's voice said, "Go away before I have to shoot you."

"Shoot me? We came to save you from the killers. Please open up."

Several moments later, the old woman opened the door a crack.

"You need to pack a bag and come with us. It's not safe here." Kerrie then told her what had happened and asked that she take a look at the bullet hole in Tom's windshield.

Marietta hesitantly stepped onto her porch to peer at Tom's truck, a rifle clutched in her hands. "When did that happen?"

"A few minutes ago, on our way here."

Marietta retreated back across the threshold. "If they're shooting at you, why should I come along?"

"We're not going back the same way and we need to get you out of here before you disappear like Gus and the Tolivers."

"They won't get *me*," she said, closing the door in Kerrie's face.

Kerrie's voice rose in volume. "They'll burn you out of your house, like they tried to do to Gus's cabin."

The door opened and Marietta reached for her arm. Pulling her inside, she said, "I'm bringing all my guns along and my family pictures and—"

"Bring whatever you like, but hurry."

A knock at the door startled them. "It's me, Tom. Open the door."

"He's my friend. He'll help us carry out your things. Please hurry."

Marietta laughed. "When you get to be my age, there's

no such thing as hurry."

Kerrie estimated her age as mid-eighties but she seemed to get around quite well. She had no doubt that Marietta could take care of herself unless she was caught in a fire.

Within half an hour Marietta's possessions had been loaded into the bed of Tom's truck. The old woman made herself comfortable in the backseat where the windows were tinted. She was so small that she sank into the cushions like a young child. Once on their way, she gave them directions to a little known trail that would lead them down the south side of the mountain to a gravel road that would take them into Concord.

Kerrie worried the killers would burn Marietta's house for spite. Then her mother would have a permanent house guest at the mansion, unless Dana decided to build Marietta a new home. Her mother's generosity was going to eventually bankrupt her.

Kerrie turned in the seat to tell Marietta that Albert Gorring was on his way to the mountain to search for Gus's old fishing lodge. Did she know where it was? Marietta thought for a moment before she remembered.

"Take the next lane on the right for about two miles, then make a left at the castle rock."

Kerrie asked if Gus had taken her there to fish.

Marietta ducked her head. "That and a little hanky panky, but that was years ago between his first and second marriages."

"Why didn't you marry him, Marietta?"

"I was still married to my third husband who'd left for parts unknown. I had to wait till I could afford to divorce him. The last two wanted me to sign my ranch over to them."

What a mountain Peyton Place.

Chapter Twelve

"Watch for the old lodge in those trees to your right. I haven't been here for a while but my memory's still pretty sharp."

Tom followed Marietta's directions while Kerrie scanned the area for any movement along the trail. She shivered when she noticed the bullet hole in the windshield. How many shooters were out there with guns pointed at the truck? And what would they do if the first shooter had been killed?

Marietta pounded the seat back with her small fist. "Stop the truck. That's the lodge over there. I'll go call for Gus so he won't be afraid to come out—if he's in there."

Tom advised her to take a gun along. He'd serve as backup with his hunting rifle. Kerrie accompanied him to a copse of trees where they watched as the old woman climbed a slope to the lodge porch. Standing back, she called Gus's name. When no one answered, she called for Frank and Pete. Raising her shoulders, she turned back in their direction. Tom motioned her to stay where she stood. He then moved forward with Kerrie following. When he reached the door, he knocked, turned the knob and pushed the door open with his rifle barrel.

The lodge appeared to be unoccupied but Tom wasn't taking any chances. Telling the women to stay outside, he searched each room but found nothing that would indicate that Gus or anyone else had been there recently. The dusty, rotting wooden furniture reeked of mold and he knew the roof must leak.

"Let's get off the mountain," he said as he left the lodge.

"What about Albert?" The old woman plucked a cell phone from her purse. "We need to tell him to stay away."

Kerrie said, "I'm afraid it's too late. He left well ahead of us this morning. I wonder where he is."

Marietta punched in the numbers and waited. A few moments later she reported that he wasn't answering his phone. She then left a message that Gus and Frank weren't at the fishing lodge and that he should leave the mountain at once.

Their backseat navigator then repeated directions to the little known trail that would take them into Concord. The rough path proved more suited to mountain goats than a four wheel drive pickup. Bouncing their way down the mountain they finally arrived at a paved road. Nearly an hour later they reached the mansion and helped Marietta unload her possessions. Staring at the impressive house, she said, "I would have dressed better if I'd known you were bringing me to a fancy hotel."

Kerrie laughed as she used her key to open the door to the foyer. The aroma of broiled steak greeted them, making Kerrie's stomach growl. Following the scent they found her mother and Sarah busy in the kitchen. Both women smiled and Sarah leaned to hug their tiny guest.

During dinner Marietta told them that Gus had received several death threats but had shrugged them off as pranks.

"He wouldn't listen to reason and I've been worried about him ever since."

How long had Gus been saving wolves? Dana asked, and the old woman said as long as she had known him.

"Not just wolves but stray dogs and cats, even injured birds. I remember a newborn antelope he named Andy, whose mother had abandoned 'cause he was sick and couldn't stand. Gus fed him calf's formula from the feed store with a baby bottle until he died. He buried him behind his house and carved a small plaque with his name on it for the grave." A small tear hesitated on Marietta's cheek. "He's such a good man."

"Then why didn't you marry him?" Sarah asked.

"Because all his wives have died on the mountain and I was afraid..." her voice ended in a sigh.

The phone rang and Dana left the table to answer the call. When she returned she said, "That was Albert Gorring. He said a masked man threatened him on the mountain and demanded that he leave. He reported it to the sheriff's department as soon as he reached home."

"How did he know our number?"

Kerrie said she had given him her cards before they left his ranch. "Thank heavens the shooters didn't kidnap Albert. They must not have known his connection with Gus and Frank."

Dana shook her head. "If there are only two shooters, that could explain not kidnapping or shooting Albert. But I wonder if the second one knows the young woman was hit by Tom's truck."

Tom said, "It doesn't make sense that the other shooter didn't know. If the woman we hit had a walkie-talkie in her pocket, someone further up the mountain must have told her we were coming. Why else would she have been standing in the middle of the road pointing the gun at us?"

"There's very little traffic on the road so someone must have recognized your truck, Tom."

"Then why leave the woman lying there? If she were dead, someone should have dragged her body off the road."

"Unless they didn't have time."

Tom screwed his face into a scowl. "If that's true, someone else came along between the time Kerrie and I drove through and when you and Miz Cafferty discovered the body."

"I wonder if it was Albert Gorring." Dana glanced at Marietta. "How well do you know Albert?"

"Well enough to know that he would never get mixed up in some crazy wolf killing gang."

* * *

Dana awoke after one o'clock, so restless that she couldn't go back to sleep. She went downstairs to heat a cup of chai tea and trooped back up to her computer. Scrolling through a series of people finder websites, she selected one and typed in Albert Gorring's name. His age was listed as 85 along with his address and family members. When she paid the fee to check on his background she found that he had no criminal record. He was simply listed as a Wyoming rancher.

Now what?

She decided to check up on Frank Toliver but had similar results. So she typed in Gus Blake's name. To her surprise Gus had been arrested twice for civil disobedience. She wondered whether it had something to do with the wolf killings. The sheriff's department could tell her, but would they? She was afraid that she had already become a persona non grata.

Jeff Mailer's name popped into her mind and she decided to call him later that morning. Her former bodyguard had helped to solve former cases by providing invaluable information.

Walter was arriving that afternoon and had seemed jealous of Jeff. How was he going to react when he learned Jeff was on the payroll. Should she wait to hire Jeff until Walter flew back to California? No, time was precious. Gus and Frank could be badly injured and in need of rescue. And what of Frank's son Pete? How did he figure into the scenario? As far as she knew, he'd had nothing to do with the wolves. But she typed in his name.

Nothing came up and she looked again at Frank's brief biography. Pete's name was listed as his family, as was his mother Jenny. She must have died recently or the webmaster had been lax in removing her name.

Dana crossed the hall to her bedroom and promptly fell asleep. The alarm woke her at seven and she went back to sleep. At eight, Sarah woke and reminded her that they needed to pick up Walter at the airport. Sarah had a crush on Walter although she now denied it. Dana often wished that he were in love with Sarah instead of her. It would make life so much easier.

Kerrie was using her laptop at the kitchen table when Dana dragged herself into the room. She headed for the coffee pot and was grateful that Sarah had brewed a fresh carafe. Caffeine was exactly what she needed to jump-start her entire body, not to mention her brain.

When asked, Kerrie said she was researching wolf killings and found that wolves were shot from the air in Idaho, Montana and Canada. "They've killed over six hundred wolves in the Keystone pipeline area alone."

"Why around the pipeline?"

They claim the wolves are killing the caribou but there's evidence that pipeline construction has destroyed the caribou's natural habitat, causing them to die off."

"So they're blaming caribou deaths on the wolves?"

"Right. And in the Upper Yukon region, the biggest

aerial wolf kills are taking place to boost caribou and moose numbers for big game hunters. Biologists have been strapping radio collars on the wolves to keep track of their numbers and locations. And the park service is concerned that there will only be about a hundred wolves left in the entire territory while boosting the caribou herd to a hundred thousand."

"Just so the hunters can go in and kill the caribou?"

"Yes. But the worst thing they're doing in the lower forty-eight states is gassing wolf pups in their dens and burying them alive. They're also sterilizing adult wolves when there's a state quota for live animals."

Dana shuddered. "That's like throwing bagged kittens into the river to drown. I can understand sterilizing wolves to keep the population down but killing puppies in such a barbaric way—"

"I know, Mom. I've got a good feature story now but some of the puzzle pieces are still missing."

"That reminds me. I'm going to call Jeff Mailer to help with the investigation. He has some good sources within law enforcement."

"Great. I only have three days left."

Dana reminded her daughter that Sheriff Walter Grayson would arrive that afternoon from California. Maybe he could learn something from the local sheriff's department.

"Stanton County officials are pretty tight lipped about their cases, but Walter can be persuasive."

"The sheriff also helped to save my life in that decrepit house in the San Joaquin Valley. I'll always be grateful to him for that, as well as you, Mom."

Dana patted her daughter's shoulder and began preparing breakfast. She wasn't looking forward to Walter's arrival and hoped that he didn't plan to stay more than a few days. His standing marriage proposal weighed heavily on her mind. She wasn't sure how she felt about him. He was more than a friend but she wasn't ready to make a firm commitment. He planned to retire soon and move to Wyoming. He expected her to marry him and she would have to decide soon.

* * *

Walter's plane arrived half an hour late, increasing Dana's anxiety. She had decided not to marry him but wouldn't tell him until he was ready to leave Wyoming. He was the first passenger off the plane and jogged toward her with wide spread arms. She went into them and accepted his enveloping hug. Closing her eyes, she breathed in his scent and felt comforted in his embrace. She knew she loved him but was it enough? She would worry about his proposal later. They needed to concentrate on solving the wolf killings and the disappearance of Gus and the Tolivers.

During the drive back to the mansion, Dana filled him in on everything that had transpired, from the rollover until the recent hiring of Jeff Mailer. She knew he wouldn't be happy about Jeff's involvement but the former police officer's law enforcement contacts would help with the investigation. Walter, on the other hand, was an out of state sheriff who had no connections in Wyoming. He surprised her by simply nodding and saying nothing. He must have finally realized that Dana had no romantic interest in her former bodyguard.

Jeff's nondescript car was parked in the driveway when they reached home. Walter smiled when he shook Jeff's hand, surprising Dana even more. Sighing with relief, she led them into the living room where Tom and the three women were seated. Once the introductions were made, they began a brain storming session starting with the disappearances.

Marietta was asked whether she knew of any other

place the three men could be hiding. Shaking her head, she said she had racked her brain but could not come up with anywhere other than the lodge. She concluded that the three men must have been killed and buried on the mountain.

"But the injured woman was left on the side of the road to die," Tom said. "That makes no sense."

Kerrie said she had called the hospital to ask whether the young woman had survived. Listed as Jane Doe, the only information available about her condition was that she was still alive. Jeff rose saying he would check with his sources at the police department. He then left the room.

Dana noticed Tom hanging his head and guessed that he was feeling guilty about the woman's condition. She dismissed the urge to hug him and remind him that Jane Doe could have killed both him and Kerrie.

Turning to Walter she said, "Would you mind visiting the local sheriff to find out what you can about their investigation?"

He smiled with that lovesick expression she hated. "Glad to, dear."

Biting her lip, she offered to drive him to the sheriff's department. The others declined to ride along and she knew they thought that she and Walter wanted time alone.

Jeff returned with good news. "She's still alive and they think she's going to make it. But she's not talking to anyone. She won't even tell them her first name."

"No I.D. on her at all?" Walter asked.

"None. She must have expected capture."

"You mean like one of those suicide bombers?" Sarah said.

Jeff smiled. "Something like that."

This mystery is getting curiouser by the minute. "Why would a pretty young woman risk her life to keep people off the mountain?" Dana said. "And was she waiting for anyone who happened along or just those of us who know Gus?"

Tom said, "Her walkie-talkie convinces me that she was in contact with someone within a short distance. A spotter. I don't think she would stand there all day holding that heavy gun until someone came along."

Jeff agreed. "From what you've said, they must have recognized your truck from the time you scared off the two shooters who threatened Dana and Sarah."

Tom stood, apparently restless. "I wonder what would happen if you and I drove back up there in another vehicle, Jeff."

"Depending on how many's left, we're liable to get shot."

Dana asked them to wait until Walter learned how the sheriff's investigation was going. Maybe the other suspect had been taken into custody. They agreed and Dana asked that Tom remain at the mansion to protect those who stayed behind. She then asked Jeff to contact as many sources as possible to find out all he could.

* * *

"I'm beginning to feel like a drill sergeant," Dana said as she drove toward the Stanton County Sheriff's Department.

"You'd make a good sheriff, Dana." Walter reached across the seat back to massage her neck.

Dana sighed. Her big teddy bear of a man didn't give up. "What are you going to ask the Stanton County sheriff?" She was glad Walter had worn his uniform.

"I'll ask how the investigation's going and if he knows of Gus Blake's whereabouts."

"Please find out as much as you can about Jane Doe. She seems to be our only link to solving this mystery."

"Will do, love. Are you going to sit out here and wait?"

"Call me on my cell when you're ready to leave. I have some investigating of my own to do while we're in town."

Dana left for the local newspaper office the moment Walter entered the building. It was still early and she knew the weekly newspaper had appeared on the stands the day before, so the editor might have some time on his hands. Jackson Winters was a tall man in his mid-sixties with a wide middle and thinning white hair. He smiled when he greeted her at the front counter and invited her back to his office.

She asked him when the all-out war on wolves had begun and if he knew of anyone with a grudge against Gus Blake. Leaning back in his swivel chair, he bit his lip as though in deep thought.

"It's been a coupla years and I heard that old Gus was trying to save the wolves."

"How old is he? Do you know?"

"Oh, he's in his mid-80s. He and my dad were friends. Gus's a good man but I'm afraid he stepped on the wrong toes."

"Do you have any idea who it might be?"

"I have my suspicions but Sheriff Ed asked me to keep a lid on the story for a while. That's why it hasn't appeared in the paper."

"But what about the people who might drive up the mountain—"

"The word's out. Something like that spreads around town like a flash flood. Everybody knows to stay away from the mountain."

Dana breathed a sigh of relief although disappointed the editor wouldn't offer an opinion. Handing him her card, she explained why she was involved in the case and asked that he contact her if he had a solid lead. He nodded agreement but Dana wondered whether he actually would. She was well aware of small town politics, especially when it involved strangers. She and Sarah hadn't lived in the area long and were considered outsiders.

She decided to talk to the librarians, who usually knew what was going on. She'd cross her fingers and say she was a writer—like her sister Georgi—who was researching a book about the wolves. The small library was located off the main street and she hoped that Walter wouldn't call before she had a chance to question the librarians.

* * *

Maude Anderson was an angular woman with gray hair pulled into a bun behind her neck. Peering questioningly at Dana over half glasses balanced on her long nose, she seemed too busy to cooperate. Dana recited her rehearsed speech about wolves and asked if the librarian could direct her to local news reports about previous incidents on the mountain.

"Are you one of those wildlife defender people?"

Dana cringed at her sarcasm. She must be a rancher's wife.

"No, I'm just writing a novel about the wolf killings. Maybe you've heard of my sister, who was also a writer?"

The woman raised a brow.

"The mystery novelist, Georgiana Turnsby."

A smile cracked the stony face. "She was one of my favorite authors." Motioning Dana to follow, she led her to a small library table, saying she would search for the files on her computer. In the meantime, Dana could read the latest issue of the *Stanton County Gazette*.

Knowing how Walter loved to talk to other lawmen, she hoped the local sheriff did as well. Thumbing through the newspaper, she noticed a photo of someone in a hospital bed, with the caption, "Do you know this woman?" So the sheriff *was* trying to learn her identity, but why hadn't he given the photo to Jackson Winters for his small weekly newspaper? Surely Winters had seen *the Gazette* by now. On second thought, maybe the photo would appear in next week's newspaper.

The librarian returned with several issues of both newspapers, warning Dana to read them carefully. They were the library's only copies. Dana agreed and zeroed in on the editorial page of the *Weekly Observer*, Winter's newspaper. The editorial was in favor of delisting northern Rocky Mountain wolves, citing recent livestock kills. The newspaper was also in favor of drilling in wilderness areas and planting more wind turbines No mention was made of wolf kills but cattle and sheep deaths figured prominently in the editorial.

The sheriff must not like the *Observer's* policies, which may be why he hadn't kept Winters informed of the recent wolf killings and the unidentified young woman in the hospital. *The Gazette* seemed more concerned with environmental issues and wildlife management. One article in particular caught Dana's attention. The headline read: *Suspicious Activity on the Mountain has County Officials Concerned.* The article went on to say that reports of guns fired in the Bear Creek area had been received from area ranchers during the non-hunting season. The remains of wolves, coyotes and smaller fur bearing animals were found skinned and heaped in piles along the creek banks.

Selling the skins of animals couldn't be the reason for the animal slaughter. The wounded wolves Gus found hadn't been skinned. What was going on?

Dana's cell phone rang and Walter said he was ready for pickup. There was a laugh in his voice so she assumed that he'd gained some valuable information. He was waiting for her at the curb and began filling her in on everything he'd learned before he fastened his seat belt.

"Someone identified the girl. Her name's Rhonda Bailey and she's a nineteen-year-old college student."

"Are you sure, Walter?"

"Yep. They got a positive I.D."

"Any prior arrests?"

"Just one. She was a member of a protest group in Laramie last year."

"Protesting what?"

"The delisting of wolves."

"You're kidding."

"'Fraid not. A group of six college kids threw pop bottles at a pickup truck that kept circling the block to harass them."

Why would someone who protested the delisting of wolves fire at people who were trying to help? Dana felt a headache coming on. The entire scenario was overwhelming. She needed to return home to meditate.

Chapter Thirteen

When they returned to the mansion Jeff Mailer said he had news for them. His source within the police department reported that a group of students had staged a rally the previous weekend at a Casper mall. They carried placards with pictures of wolves and were handing out leaflets to passersby.

"Was Rhonda Bailey among them?"

"She was."

Exhausted, Dana dropped into the nearest chair. "Then why was she standing in the middle of the road shooting at people?"

"Maybe she thought Tom was one of the wolf killers."

"That makes sense. But it doesn't explain why the shooters left her lying in the road."

Jeff rubbed his chin which already sported a shadow. "I'm wondering where she got her hands on an AK-47 and whether she was alone."

"She's still not talking?"

Jeff shook his head. He said the Casper police were checking into it because the rally had taken place within their jurisdiction. They reported that no incidents of violence or disturbances had happened at the mall, but that a number of shoppers had joined the students in the rally, which had spilled out into the parking lot.

Dana knew there was growing public awareness of the senseless aerial wolf killings to further the sport of big game hunting. Why didn't they just confine their wolf killings to hunting seasons with hunters on the ground? At least give the animals a fighting chance.

She noticed everyone else's absences and asked where they had disappeared. Jeff said that Sarah had borrowed his car to drive Marietta to town to buy more clothing and that Tom and Kerrie left for Laramie.

"Did you tell them what you just told me, Jeff?"

"Yes, ma'am. They decided to do some investigating on their own when I gave them the names of the students who took part in the rally."

* * *

"How long will it take to drive to Laramie, Tom?"

"A couple of hours."

They talked about the case during the drive to Albany County and the university. Tom had called ahead to ask his friend who worked in the registrar's office to contact the students who took part in the rally. He hoped some of them would show up for an interview.

Four of them were waiting in the cafeteria, where Kerrie questioned them not only about the rally but Rhonda Bailey. Three of the students were young men, the other an attractive young woman named Annie Woods. She said her friend Rhonda had gone alone to the mountain, taking her brother's gun with her.

"But why would she shoot at a pickup truck? She might have killed the driver."

"I talked to her on the phone this afternoon. She said

the gun had been modified and had a hair trigger. She only meant to scare away the people in the truck."

Kerrie was taking notes. "Was she shooting at everyone or just that particular truck?"

"Her boyfriend told her to shoot at the truck."

"On a walkie-talkie?"

Annie shrugged. "She didn't tell me that."

"Who's the boyfriend?"

"Some guy who lives on the mountain. She didn't mention his name."

"Why'd she go alone?"

"No one wanted to go with her. Carrying placards is one thing. Shooting at people is another."

The young men agreed they wanted no part of Rhonda's crazy plans.

Kerrie looked to Tom who leaned forward in his chair to ask, "Do you know the boyfriend's name or why Rhonda was taking orders from him?"

They all shook their heads.

"Rhonda's a very secretive person," Annie said. "I think her boyfriend told her not to say anything because it could get him in trouble."

We need to talk to Rhonda right away to make her understand that three men's lives are at stake. Kerrie thanked the students and took the arm Tom offered when the questioning session was over. Checking her watch, Kerrie decided they should visit Rhonda Bailey that evening after dinner. She knew the girl was tight-lipped, but there must be some way to pry the information out of her. Kerrie would consult with Jeff and Walter about the girl at dinner.

* * *

The others were seated at the dinner table when they arrived back at the mansion. Marietta was helping in the kitchen and appeared with a large platter of roast beef when Kerrie and Tom sat down. Kerrie repeated her earlier request that her mother hire a housekeeper-cook to help with the chores. Strands of Dana's hair had fallen across her forehead and she appeared to have had little sleep.

Sarah said, "I've been telling her that since we moved in here."

Dana explained it away with, "No housekeeper in her right mind would have stayed with drug addicts trashing the house and a terrorist making himself at home while we were in Arizona. I don't want to place anyone else in danger."

Her mother's reasoning made sense but Kerrie hated to see her working so hard when she didn't have to. Turning to Walter, she asked what he'd learned at the sheriff's office.

"They're not saying much and they don't seem happy that we're sticking our noses into the case."

"I think that woman deputy would like to lock us up," Dana said. She then asked Kerrie what they had learned from the students.

"Rhonda Bailey is very secretive, according to her friend Annie Woods, and she's definitely involved in the wolf killings. We're going to pay her a visit tonight at the hospital."

Jeff said that Rhonda would be under guard because she was probably going to be charged with attempted murder. He still had his police badge and might be able to get them into her room for a few minutes.

He suggested they take flowers and a box of candy with them, but advised them not to tell her they were the couple she shot at. "Tell her you attended the rally in Casper and that you sympathize with the students' cause. She might let something slip about her boyfriend."

"But what if she recognizes us?" Kerrie said.

"I doubt she will. I'm sure all she saw was the pickup

truck while she fumbled with the gun. I also doubt that she's proficient in handling an AK-47."

Sarah wondered whether Rhonda had been one of the two masked people who had stopped her and Dana along the dirt road. "The one on my side wasn't very big and had a voice pitched higher than most men."

"If you're right," Dana said, "there might only be two of them instead of an organized gang."

"Then why would they set fire to Gus's ranch? That makes no sense if they're in favor of saving wolves? Then, again, it may have been someone else."

Walter suggested they might have an ulterior motive and that saving the wolves could just be a cover. Jeff agreed. But a cover for what?

Jeff said, "I've been trained in reading body language and would like to observe the young woman's reactions while you talk to her."

Kerrie thought Jeff's suggestion was a good one. Time was running out and the case was getting more complicated by the minute. After dinner she helped to clear the table before she and the two men left for the hospital in Jeff's car. During the thirty-five minute drive, they discussed various possibilities concerning motives for the fire, but came up with nothing concrete. Hopefully, Rhonda Bailey would provide the answers.

Jeff warned them when they reached the hospital that, depending on the deputy standing guard, his badge might not get them into Rhonda's room.

Kerry felt deflated but hoped for the best. When they approached the room, Jeff said he couldn't believe his luck. Grasping the deputy's hand, he slapped him on the back.

"Jeff, old buddy. I haven't seen you since the funeral. How've you been?"

"Great. It's good to see you again, Hal. We missed you at the station when you signed on with Sheriff Johnston."

Jeff briefly told his old friend about his involvement in the wolf killing case and asked if he would allow them a few minutes with Rhonda Bailey.

The deputy chewed his lip. "Make it quick and don't mention this to anyone."

"That's a promise. I owe you one." Jeff motioned Kerrie and Tom to follow him into Rhonda's room. They found her asleep with no other visitors. Setting the vase of roses from Dana's entry table on Rhonda's bedside stand, Tom cleared his throat while holding the box of candy he bought at the local grocery. Her head wrapped in a helmet bandage, the young woman opened her wide blue eyes and gasped when she saw them. Kerrie held her breath, afraid they'd been recognized.

"We heard about your terrible accident on the mountain and wanted to bring something to cheer you up."

Rhonda smiled when she noticed the flowers and Tom's offering.

Kerrie moved closer and took Rhonda's hand. Stroking it, she asked how the accident had happened.

Rhonda hesitated. "A pickup truck was speeding and hit me on the road."

"How awful, dear. I read in the newspaper that they found an assault rifle lying in the road beside you."

"I was hunting wild turkeys with my friend."

With an AK-47? "Your friend wasn't with you when it happened?"

Rhonda's eyebrows pulled together. "No, he was further up the mountain and didn't see what happened."

"I'm surprised he's not with you now."

Pulling her hand away, her voice took on a defensive tone. "He was here earlier but had to leave."

"What about your parents? Do they know you're here?"

Rhonda's eyes narrowed. "They live back east and can't afford the plane fare."

Kerrie knew she wanted the conversation to end and would soon claim fatigue. "We were at the rally last week and regret that we didn't have time to join you and the other students in your protest of the wolf killings."

Rhonda shrugged. "That's okay. I'm not really into protests."

"Then why—?"

"My boyfriend's idea. I just went along for the ride."

Kerrie's heart quickened. "Was he at the rally?"

"Yeah, but he didn't stay long."

Kerrie decided the truth was the only way to learn the young man's identity. Telling her that she was writing a feature story about the wolf killings, she said she wanted to contact the other students for interviews about the rally. Would Rhonda give her their names?

Rhonda's face took on an angry expression. "Are you the ones who talked to my friends in Laramie today?"

Kerrie nodded. She then told her about the three missing men and that they might have been murdered. A slight smile played across the young woman's lips and she turned over in bed, her back to them. She said nothing more. Glancing at Jeff, Kerrie noticed him tapping his watch. Leaning to pat Rhonda's back, she wished her well and they said their goodbyes.

When they were seated in Jeff's car, she asked what he'd learned from their visit. He said the girl was scared and that she wouldn't tell anyone her boyfriend's name. They would have to talk to the male students again to get a complete list. But Rhonda would probably call her friends to warn them not to tell.

If Walter goes with us to Laramie wearing his uniform, it might scare the truth out of them.

117

Chapter Fourteen

They drove to Laramie in Jeff's car early the next day. Jeff's body language skills were invaluable, especially when talking to the students. But if Rhonda had called her friends, the trip could be a waste of time. Kerrie was desperate. She only had two days left before she had to return to Denver.

Two students showed up for questioning, Annie Woods and a lanky young man named Cameron Frazier. Annie's attitude was belligerent until Kerrie explained that three men's lives depended on the information she provided.

Annie removed her glasses to rub them on her blouse. "Does Rhonda know about this?"

"Probably. Her boyfriend's tied into the disappearances but we're not sure how." Kerrie asked if they remembered a man who accompanied Rhonda to the rally but didn't stay long.

Both students shook their heads. "There were so many people milling around that it could have been anybody," Cameron said.

Walter pulled a notepad from his shirt pocket to take notes. He asked for the names of the students who took part in the rally. "All of them," he said in an authoritarian voice. "Withholding evidence is punishable by law."

Kerrie thought he was a bit over the top but it seemed to have the desired effect on Annie and Cameron. They didn't hesitate to give up the names of the original students who took part in the rally: Four males and three females. They had already talked to two of the girls and Cameron, so that left four students to contact before they left town.

"Are you sure you don't know Rhonda's boyfriend's name?" the sheriff asked. They both said no. He then asked Annie to call her friend and ask who he was.

"I can't do that, Sheriff. Rhonda would never speak to me again."

Walter heaved a heavy sigh and rolled his eyes toward the ceiling.

"Let me explain this to you again, young lady. Three men are missing. If we don't find them soon, we'll be burying them."

Annie chewed her lip before taking out her cell phone. Turning her back, she walked to the other side of the room. A few moments later she reported that Rhonda had gone missing from the hospital.

The sheriff slapped his hat against his thigh and motioned for the others to follow. "Is she telling the truth?" he asked Jeff when they left the room.

"Apparently so. I didn't see any eye movements that would indicate she was lying."

"Then we need to contact the hospital."

"There was a guard on duty last night. How could she have escaped?"

"Even guards have to take bathroom breaks," Walter said.

Kerrie hurried back into the room to learn where

the other students lived while Walter called the Stanton County sheriff's office. A deputy confirmed that Rhonda Bailey was missing and that an APB had been issued. Kerrie remembered the smirk on the young woman's face before she turned her back on them at the hospital. She must have known she was going to be rescued. Obviously by her boyfriend. Kerrie hoped none of the other students were missing.

A few minutes after they left the university, they pulled in front of a modest single story house on the edge of town, where two of the students were living. The grass needed mowing and the car parked at the curb could use a wash job. Kerrie was afraid they weren't home until she heard music blaring when she opened the car door. Annie and Cameron had been warned not to call and tell them they were coming.

Jesse Colter slouched to the screen door when the sheriff knocked on the frame. Tall with a thatch of multi-colored hair and a multitude of tattoos and body piercings, he invited them into the living room littered with textbooks and clothing. Pushing various items to the floor, he motioned for them to be seated. A few minutes later his roommate Jennifer Carpenter appeared dressed in cropped denim shorts and a mini top. Dark-haired and dark-eyed, she didn't quite reach Jesse's shoulder.

They had agreed beforehand that Walter would conduct the questioning and Jeff perched on the lumpy couch to watch them closely. When asked who had organized the rally, they both said that it had been Rhonda Bailey. Surprised, their visitors exchanged glances.

"Was her boyfriend involved in planning the rally?" Walter asked.

They both shrugged. "If he was, we weren't aware of it."

"What's his name and where's he live?"

Jesse cocked an eyebrow as though questioning the reason for the visit. "Rhonda plays around so who knows who she's sleeping with on any given day."

"Are you sure she didn't mention his name?"

"Positive, sheriff."

"Did you ever see them together?"

They both shook their heads.

Walter told them about the missing men but didn't mention Rhonda's disappearance. He glanced at Jeff, who didn't indicate they were lying. Checking his watch, Walter rose from his rickety chair and handed them each a card. "Call the minute you remember who this guy is or have any information about the case." He then told them that Rhonda was missing. Jennifer gasped and slid to the floor to hide her head on her knees. Jesse seemed to pale when he heard the news, but neither said another word.

"They know something," Jeff said when he was once again behind the wheel. "Whether they'll call with information is in question."

The sheriff checked his list. "Two more to go before we'll head back north."

After a quick burger for lunch, they stopped at a mid-town apartment building. Bryan Johnson lived on the third floor and took his time answering the door. Dressed in jeans and a tee shirt, his blond mop was uncombed and he appeared to have recently gotten out of bed. Yawning, he held the door open for them.

The apartment was neat for a college student and nicely furnished. His must have an affluent family. Bryan didn't seem the least bit nervous but was obviously struggling to stay awake.

"Late night?" the sheriff asked.

Bryan nodded and told them to have a seat. The couch looked comfortable so everyone but the sheriff sat down. After Walter explained the reason for their visit, Bryan said that he vaguely remembered a guy who talked with Rhonda but left a few minutes later. He couldn't remember anything about him except that he had short brown hair. He didn't know his name. After Walter told him about the three men's disappearances, he handed Bryan a card and asked that he call if he heard anything about the missing men or Rhonda's boyfriend's identity.

Back in Jeff's car, he confirmed what they had all decided, that Bryan Johnson was telling the truth. Their next stop was Alan Riley's apartment.

Alan lived in a newer apartment building two blocks to the west. Average height with a sprinkling of freckles across his nose, he looked like an older model Opie. His grin was disarming and he flashed perfect white teeth at Kerrie throughout the sheriff's interview.

He didn't know Rhonda's latest boyfriend and wondered why she had organized the rally when she didn't seem all that interested in saving wolves. The seven students had ridden to Casper in someone's van. He didn't know who owned it.

"Was the boyfriend in the van?" Walter asked.

"Not unless Rhonda's going with Bryan. That girl gets around."

Back in Jeff's car, Tom remarked that he was surprised none of the students lived on campus. He deduced that they must all be on full scholarships or have student loans. Kerrie dropped her notepad into her purse. "That makes sense. Those who have to work to pay for tuition and books probably don't have the time to get involved in social issues."

"So who do you think the illusive boyfriend is?" Walter asked. "One of the boys I just questioned?"

Jeff started the engine. "I didn't detect anyone lying. I think it must be someone else. Maybe not a student at all."

* * *

The drive back to the mansion seemed to take forever, with everyone immersed in their thoughts. There was a lot to consider. Kerrie went over her notes, trying to find a discrepancy in the students' stories. Maybe Jeff was right. Rhonda's latest boyfriend must be an older man who was using her for some illegal purpose. But what? And why stage a wolf rally when Rhonda didn't care about the wolves.

Walter turned in the front seat to ask if either she or Tom had noticed anything suspicious at the scene where Rhonda had fired at them.

Tom grinned halfheartedly. "All I saw was an assault rifle aimed at the windshield and the bullet hole after I ducked. A few inches to the right and she would have nailed me."

Kerrie wondered aloud if Rhonda had been charged with attempted murder. Walter shook his head. "Last I heard no charges had been filed, but you can be sure Rhonda's cute little butt will be tossed in jail as soon as they find her. An APB went out as soon as they heard she was missing."

"I think the students know more than they're willing to tell," Jeff said, "but no one seemed to out and out lie."

"Kids tend to alibi each other, whether they're guilty or—" The sheriff's cell phone rang and he groaned when he noticed the caller. Cupping his hand around the phone, he talked in low tones, which Kerrie was unable to understand.

Clicking off, he said, "Looks like the three of you are on your own. I've got an urgent case to handle back home." Turning to Jeff, he asked to be dropped off at the airport as soon as they reached Casper. He then called to arrange a flight. His next call was to Dana to apologize for his departure.

Kerrie knew her mother would be relieved. Walter was a nice guy but Dana wasn't ready to marry anyone. The sheriff's persistence was wearing her down and Kerrie knew that she was vacillating. As soon as they dropped Walter off at the airport, Jeff called his friend at the police station for an update on Rhonda Bailey. When he hung up, he reported no word yet on an arrest or information about Rhonda's whereabouts.

Tom said he'd call his friend at the college to get the girl's home address and any other information available. Kerrie listened to his uh-huhs for some time before he ended the call.

"Rhonda's records have been sealed by local police at the request of the Stanton County Sheriff's Department, but my friend Bob made a copy before they were turned over."

"Yes! When can we see them?"

"He's fedexing them this afternoon. But if word gets out, he'll lose his job."

"Hallelujah for friends." *Maybe, just maybe we can crack this case before I have to leave.*

Tom took an off ramp onto the rural highway. "Don't worry, Tom. We won't say a word."

Twenty minutes later they pulled into the mansion's circle drive. Dana was waiting for them in the foyer, a worried expression on her face.

"What's wrong, Mom?"

"I just received a call from someone who said that Rhonda Bailey's body was found on the mountain. It sounded like a warning for us to stay away."

"Who made the call?"

"I don't know, but it sounded like the same voice that warned us we would wind up in a grave with the wolves."

"That's strange," Kerrie said. "Whoever's shooting wolves isn't bothering to bury them. Maybe it was a crank call."

"How many other people know about Rhonda's disappearance?"

"Hospital employees and the police. And don't forget the boyfriend."

That poor girl," Sarah said.

"Not as innocent as you may think. She was about to be charged with attempted murder."

Jeff said he'd call the police department for an update on the crime. If they were unaware of Rhonda's death, he'd report the anonymous call.

"But it's in another county," Kerrie protested.

"They'll pass along the information to the Stanton County sheriff."

"Too bad Walter had to leave," Kerrie said. "He could have called them."

Dana nodded, her relief evident. "He can still call from California."

Tom reminded them that his friend was sending Rhonda Bailey's records, which should arrive the following morning. They could then contact her family. Maybe they knew who Rhonda was dating.

Sarah said. "You don't think her boyfriend killed her, do you?"

"A good possibility," Jeff replied. "She was probably taken from the hospital to keep her quiet."

"Then Gus and his neighbors must be dead."

A gloomy silence fell over the group as Dana led them into the living room. When they were seated, she served them each a glass of wine. Marietta then bustled into the room wearing an apron that almost reached her shoes. She announced that dinner was ready.

No one seemed in the mood to eat but they followed her into the dining room, where the table was loaded with food. Marietta would have made a great short order cook, Kerrie thought as she scooped mashed potatoes onto her plate.

Dana said she had an idea. "If we take a caravan of

vehicles up the mountain, the shooter won't dare try to take us out."

Tom nodded agreement. "We'd better wait for the Fedex delivery and make a few phone calls first."

"I was thinking of going tonight at dusk so we'll be hard to see."

"What's the point of going," Jeff said, "if the shooter doesn't see us?"

"He'll be able to hear all three vehicles, which should scare him off."

He frowned. "How will we be able to find anything in the dark?"

"We can park at Gus's ranch and spread out to locate a building with its lights on."

"That's a lot of territory to cover."

"But lights are visible for miles."

Sarah's eyes brightened. "She's right. That's how we tracked down drug dealers in the mountains.

Jeff said it was risky. But he'd accompanied them on the trip to South Dakota in search of the murdering drug dealers, so he knew what they were capable of.

"Then it's settled," Dana said. "It won't be dark until nine o'clock so we have some time to prepare."

Kerrie thought about the dance she'd planned to attend with Tom that evening, but solving the case was more important. She hadn't heard from Roger for several days and wondered if the engagement was in danger of extinction. She would try calling him tomorrow, if he could be reached. The F.B.I. agent was often incognito.

* * *

The six of them drove up the mountain in Jeff's car, the Jeep and Tom's truck. They left the mansion at eight and it was twilight when they reached Gus's place, without incident. There didn't appear to be any burning embers, but they had all worn boots just in case. Each carried a gun, except for Sarah, who held her baseball bat.

"Spread out," Dana whispered. She and Sarah walked down the dirt road toward Frank Toliver's small ranch, their flashlights held low and shining through their fingers. Tom and Kerrie left in the opposite direction and Jeff and Marietta trudged around back.

When they were halfway down the narrow lane, Dana noticed a muted light in Frank Toliver's window. She then heard a door slam and an engine start. She and Sarah crouched in the tall buck brush with their heads down. When the pickup drove past, Dana noticed the license plate holder had no light, but the last number was visible from the taillight's glow. A seven.

"Who was that?" Sarah whispered.

"I wish I knew. Let's have a look inside the cabin."

"What if the pickup driver notices the cars at Gus's place?"

"I'm more worried that he'll spot Kerrie and Tom walking along the road." Dana decided to first return to Gus's ranch to let the others know what they'd seen.

Jeff and Marietta were seated in his car when they jogged back to Gus's ranch. Jeff was trying to get a signal on his cell phone although Marietta told him it wasn't available. Kerrie and Tom hadn't returned. When Dana told Jeff what they had just seen, he agreed they should return to the Toliver cabin, but would wait for the missing duo.

It wasn't long before Kerrie and Tom showed up, breathing heavily. They had dived into the brush the moment they saw headlights, but had been unable to get a license number. Piling into their vehicles, they drove single file to the Toliver Ranch.

Once back on foot, Dana asked if they were trespassing.

"I'm afraid so," Jeff said, "but with the Tolivers missing,

who's going to report us?"

Jeff tried the cabin door and found it locked.

No crime tape graced the property, which made Dana wonder if the sheriff's deputy had investigated the vandalism or even reported it? And who just left? If the vandals had returned, what had they taken?

Marietta said that mountain people rarely locked their doors. If someone wasn't home they were welcome to make themselves comfortable until the owner returned. It was a long held practice since territorial Wyoming, because severe winter weather forced travelers to take shelter wherever they could to insure survival. The practice had continued on the mountain.

"Too bad we couldn't have followed the guy who left," Tom said.

Kerrie's sigh was heavy. "And where is Rhonda's body? That could have been her in the pickup truck."

Jeff said he would call his friend at the P.D. first thing in the morning. In the meantime, Dana could call Walter to ask if he'd get in touch with his counterpart in Stanton County. She hesitated, saying the sheriff had probably just reached home from his flight and was tired.

"I'll call him, Mom, if you'd rather not talk to him."

Dana reached to pat her daughter's arm. "No, I'll call as soon as we reach home." *But I won't tell him anything else or he'll be on the next flight back.*

Chapter Fifteen

Marietta wanted to check her house before they left the mountain. It was several miles from the Toliver ranch and in almost total darkness. A near eclipse of the moon and thick stands of trees on either side of the road blocked out most of the starlight.

Tom led the way because he was well acquainted with the mountain road and knew that animals were often out feeding at night. When they reached Marietta's house, she was the first to notice a broken window. When she shrieked, Dana knew the house had been vandalized. Fumbling with her key, the old woman managed to open her door and flip on an overhead light.

"Oh, my Lord," she cried. "I knew I should have stayed here to protect my property."

The devastation was complete. Someone had taken an axe to the furniture and heaped the contents of drawers on the living room floor along with ripped cushions from Marietta's overstuffed furniture. Her landscape prints had been slashed and ripped from their frames. The walls had also been hacked in a number of places and broken dishes littered the kitchen floor. Contents of the cupboards and refrigerator had also been strewn about the room.

Dana tried to comfort her but Marietta was inconsolable. *This is my fault. I shouldn't have insisted she come to stay with us. But what if the shooter had kidnapped or killed her?*

"We'll help you clean this up," Sarah said when Marietta stopped wailing.

"There's nothing left to save. We'll have to shovel it all out and haul it to the dump." Marietta stooped to dig through the mess on the living room rug. When she straightened, she said, "They've taken my pictures. What would they want with them?"

Dana patted her shoulder. "You're alive. That's all that matters."

Marietta turned to wade through the mess. They heard her cry out when she reached her bedroom. "They've slashed my clothes."

Why would someone do that to a poor old woman? And who was next on the maniac's list? Dana remembered that the Toliver cabin intruder was headed down the mountain to town.

"We need to leave now," she said. "I'm afraid the same thing's going to happen to the mansion."

They left as soon as they could persuade Marietta to accompany them. It was slow going down the narrow, curving mountain road and required a lot of concentration. Dana glimpsed the lights of Concord at the foot of the mountain as well as the red flashing lights of dozens of wind turbines in the distance. She wondered how the town's residents blocked the lights from their homes.

After they passed through Concord, Tom picked up the pace until they were speeding down the interstate. If a patrolman happened to be on the road, he'd have to follow them home to write a batch of tickets. It was a quarter past eleven when they pulled into the circle drive and Dana breathed a sigh of relief when she noticed all the yard lights were on. She could also hear Bert barking. Rushing to the front door, she was stopped from going inside by Jeff, who had drawn his gun. When he eased the door open Bert nearly knocked him down. Grabbing his collar, Dana restrained him while Jeff reconnoitered the house.

He returned several minutes later to report that a back window had been broken but that Bert must have scared the intruder away. Dana crouched to hug the German Shepherd and kiss the top of his head. He had earned a steak for breakfast the following morning.

Jeff said that he had seen a piece of plywood in the garage the previous day and asked if he could use it to board up the window. Tom offered to help and they left for the garage together.

Sarah retrieved a broom and dust pan from the closet. "The neighbors are going to love us."

"I'm sure they'll be getting up a petition soon to have us evicted from the neighborhood," Dana said. "First drug dealers breaking in and trashing the house and now this."

Dana noticed that Marietta was sitting with her head in her hands. She suggested that the old woman go to bed. When led upstairs, Marietta asked why all this was happening. Was it because of the wolves?

"It's gone far beyond the wolves and we're going to find out why."

Downstairs Kerrie was helping Sarah clean up the broken glass while Tom prepared to leave. Dana apologized for the broken dance date and reminded Tom of Kerrie's engagement to Roger Brandt.

"Your daughter's a great gal, Miz Logan. Please let me know if it doesn't work out between them."

Dana smiled. "I'm sure *she'll* let you know herself, Tom."

"I hate to see her leave."

"I'll miss her too."

Kerrie stood in the doorway, a dust pan full of glass in hand. "What's all this about missing me?"

Tom took the dustpan and emptied the glass in the trash. "Mind if we have a little talk before I leave?"

Kerrie glanced at her mother, who shrugged and turned away. "Sure. Come on upstairs for a few minutes."

Dana listened to Kerrie's door close and wondered about their relationship. She didn't think it had developed beyond friendship, but Kerrie hadn't heard from Roger in almost a week. She must be having doubts about their engagement. He could be on a government assignment but surely there was a way for him to get in touch. Maybe her estimate of the FBI agent had been right. Dana liked Tom and if Kerrie fell in love with him, she would be living nearby. Smiling, she made her way to the back of the house where Sarah and Jeff were still cleaning up. A piece of plywood had been wedged in the frame and affixed with duct tape. Sarah had that look in her eyes and Dana wondered whether Jeff was aware of Sarah's infatuation.

"It's almost midnight," Jeff said. "I didn't think you'd want me hammering at this time of night. If someone tries to break in now, the plywood will make such a racket when it hits the floor that Bert will wake up the neighborhood."

Jeff was staying in her former brother-in-law's room overlooking the rear yard. She knew he'd be listening for a possible break-in. Dana hoped Sarah wouldn't distract him from his job.

Tom left smiling several minutes later and Dana secured the dead bolt behind him. Brewing herself a cup of tea, she followed the others upstairs to bed. Sarah had moved her things into Dana's room and was sharing her king-sized bed while Marietta was occupying her room. Dana knew she wouldn't get much sleep that night. There were too many things to consider and Sarah was already snoring.

Next morning they gathered around the breakfast table to discuss the day's plans. Kerrie said she was going to call her editor to ask for an extension but wasn't optimistic about her chances. The doorbell rang and Tom was waiting on the doorstep. He had come early in case they decided to leave for the mountain. Kerrie's smile was radiant, which her mother didn't fail to notice. Or Sarah, who winked at her from across the table. Dana then remembered her planned call to Walter and left the room. He wasn't available but his secretary promised to relay the message.

Dana tried to remember if the deep-voiced caller had hinted at the location where Rhonda Bailey's body had been found. Maybe she had repeated the information to Sarah, but her friend was talking to Jeff in low tones when she returned to the kitchen and she didn't want to disturb them. Kerrie and Tom were also huddled together deep in conversation. When she looked for Marietta, she found her watching Bert eat the steak she had prepared for his breakfast. The dog was happily consuming his reward.

Leaning against the fridge, Dana sighed and crossed arms. She'd done a lot of sighing lately. Silently counting to ten, she said, "Well? What are we going to do today? Any ideas?"

Tom and Kerrie reluctantly ended their conversation but Jeff and Sarah continued talking. Kerrie wanted to know whether Dana had called Walter and whether the girl's body had been found. When Dana said no, Jeff checked his watch and decided to call his friend at the police department. When he returned to the kitchen he said searchers were on the mountain but Rhonda's body had not been found.

Kerrie disconnected her cell phone from the charger. "I'll call Annie to find out whether Rhonda called her after she left the hospital. I'll put her on speaker phone."

They gathered around Kerrie as she made the call. Annie was at first hesitant to talk but opened up when told that Rhonda might have been killed.

"She said she was going to the mountain with a guy who her boyfriend sent to get her."

"Did she give you his name?"

"No, she was very secretive about it."

Kerrie glanced at a note Jeff had handed her. "Did she say where they were going?"

Annie sounded as though she were crying. "She told me not to tell anyone."

"Listen to me, Annie. We may still be able to save Rhonda *if* we can find her. You've got to help us. The man who took her from the hospital may be the one who kidnapped the three men we told you about."

Annie was quiet for several moments before she said, "Rhonda mentioned something about a cabin on the backside of the mountain where her boyfriend's staying, but she didn't tell me his name."

"Did she say why? Or how long she planned to stay there?"

"No, it sounded like whoever she was with took the phone away from her. I tried to call her back but she didn't answer."

Kerrie gave her a cell phone number to call if she heard from Rhonda, and thanked her for the information. She then disconnected the call.

Tom said there were quite a few cabins on the eastern slope of the mountain. They should get started if they were going to check them out. Marietta would be a good source of information about who lived where. And with searchers on the mountain, the shooter must be hiding out.

The doorbell rang and a Fedex delivery man handed Dana a large white envelope. When she checked the return address she saw that it was from the university. Pulling the tab on the back, she withdrew a sheaf of papers from the envelope and walked back into the kitchen while reading them.

"It's not good news, folks. Rhonda didn't list any relatives on her university application. She claimed orphaned status. Looks like we've hit the proverbial brick wall."

"I don't believe it," Kerrie said. "Rhonda told us in the hospital that her parents live back east and can't afford the plane fare to come out here."

Dana tossed the envelope on the kitchen island and reached for her purse. "I guess we can check it out later. Our chariots await. Let's go check out the cabins."

* * *

They arrived at the Toliver ranch by nine o'clock in Jeff's car and Tom's pickup. No one was in the area and the cabin was still locked, so they continued on toward Marietta's ranch. The old woman made a verbal list of cabin residents as Dana wrote them down.

"Last I heard, the Brady's sold their cabin to some guy from Denver, but I've never seen him around."

"That's strange," Dana said. "Why would someone from Colorado—with all those mountains nearby—buy a cabin in Wyoming?"

"Less expensive," Jeff suggested. "And more remote."

That made sense. Dana had heard of well-known gangsters hiding out in the Wyoming mountains as well as Butch Cassidy's wild bunch and the James gang. They'd had their own experience with a vicious drug gang months earlier. She asked Marietta if she knew the cabin's location and the look she gave Dana said she'd asked a stupid question. She knew every inch of the mountain.

The cabin in question was perched on a ridge overlooking a vast expanse of the valley. The perfect place for a hideout. Jeff and Tom parked several hundred feet from the lane leading to the large log cabin with a glass A-frame façade. Dana calculated its worth at half a million dollars, even in a depressed market. Whoever lived there was definitely not on welfare.

Their two bodyguards inched their way up the long driveway and took up positions on either side of the impressive double entry doors. Dana feared that if anyone were home, they would have seen them approach unless they were occupied elsewhere on the property. She watched as they waited on the front steps, then circled the house to the back of the lot. Glancing at Tom's truck, she noticed Kerrie taking pictures through the windshield.

It seemed an eternity before the two men returned, shoulders slumped as though disappointed. When Jeff opened the driver's door he confirmed that no one was home and no vehicles were garaged.

Marietta told them of other cabin owners who vacationed there from the East during the summer. She didn't suspect any of them of illicit activities and maybe the new owner of the Brady cabin was as clean as a bar of soap.

Where were the searchers? They hadn't seen another soul since arriving on the mountain. Jeff signaled Tom and Kerrie for a conference and they stood around the nondescript car, trying to decide their next move. Marietta suggested calling Walter again for news about Rhonda Bailey. Maybe he had tried returning Dana's call while they were in a no service area. Dana could call from Marietta's ranch while she sifted through the rubble.

When Dana called, Walter answered after the first ring, nearly shouting, "Where've you been?" He'd been in touch with the Stanton County Sheriff's Department and was told that they'd received a similar call about Rhonda Bailey, but *deep throat* had only given them a general location.

Dana tapped the speaker icon on her smart phone. "Where in general, Walter?"

"I was told at the bend of a stream near an area called Elk Creek. That's all they could tell me."

Marietta must know where Elk Creek was located. Dana knocked and entered the vandalized ranch house where she found her sitting on the floor crying over her ruined possessions. Dana knelt to take her in her arms, reassuring her that she would replace her furniture.

The old woman raised her tear stained face and said the furniture was irreplaceable. It had belonged to her grandmother. When asked about the Elk Creek area, she allowed Dana to help her to her feet and lead her back to Jeff's car. She then gave directions to the creek, where they found a group of people spread out along the bank.

Jeff approached a man who seemed to be in charge. They spoke for some time before he returned to his car to report that a pair of women's shoes had been found in the bushes along the bank.

"They haven't been there long and appear to belong to a young woman."

"Why?" Dana asked.

"A pair of high heel platform sandals. Not something you'd wear to walk along a creek bank."

Sarah gasped. "They must belong to Rhonda Bailey."

"My thoughts exactly."

"Can we join the search party?"

"I asked and Hanson wanted to know why, so I told him Kerrie's an investigative reporter and that Gus Blake is a friend of yours. So he agreed as long as you turn over anything you find."

Dana opened the passenger's door as well as one for the backseat. She wasn't sure whether Marietta was up for the search but was told in no uncertain terms to try and stop her.

139

Jeff suggested they drive further downstream away from the other searchers. The creek was filled with rocks that could snag pieces of clothing and provide other evidence. So they climbed back into his car. Jeff stopped again a quarter of a mile from the other searchers and he and Tom removed their boots to cross the stream. Thick brush lined both sides of the bank and the women moved carefully, searching for anything unusual.

Sarah shrieked when a tan snake with diagonal markings slithered onto the bank. Dana rushed over to make sure it didn't have a rattle. Marietta laughed. "Don't know your snakes, do you? That one's harmless enough."

Jeff whistled and held up an article of wet clothing. He and Tom then examined it closely before tossing it to the ground. "Man's shirt, size extra large," he yelled across the creek.

Dana sighed with relief. At least it wasn't Gus's or the Tolivers. None of them were heavy enough to wear a shirt that large.

Swirling water lapping the rocks was mesmerizing. Dana felt the urge to sit on the bank and close her eyes to meditate, but forced herself to part the undergrowth to search for clues. She noticed Marietta further downstream crouching to peer at something in the water. When she straightened she yelled and waved her arms.

"Over here. Everybody, quick, come here." She removed a hand from her mouth and retched into the stream.

The two men made their way downstream in the water, carefully balancing themselves on flat rocks as Dana, Sarah and Kerrie hurried down the bank toward Marietta. Dana instinctively knew what she had found and didn't want to look. The three women slowed their pace until Jeff and Tom reached the scene. They knew when they saw the expressions on the men's faces.

"Stay back," Jeff warned. "You don't want to see this."

Taking Marietta's arm, he gently led her back to Dana.

"Is it Rhonda?"

"I'm afraid so. She's face up in the water and she's been brutally beaten." Jeff suggested they return to the car while he and Tom dragged the body from the creek.

Concerned that Marietta was in shock, Dana held onto her as they made their way back upstream. The old woman said nothing during the trek and remained silent in the car until Dana asked how she was.

"There's not much hope now for Gus," she said. "I know I'll never see him again."

"There's always hope," Dana said. "Are you sure he didn't tell you something before he disappeared that might help us find him?"

Marietta wiped her mouth with a tissue Sarah had handed her. "I've replayed every word he said to me the last time I saw him, and the only thing I recall is that he said something about searching the Internet for somebody. But he didn't say who."

Dana asked if Gus had said why.

"Just that he had suspicions that the man wasn't who he thought he was."

Tom and Jeff returned, wiping hands on their jeans. "We'd better get on back upstream to report this to the search party," Jeff said. "This makes it murder one, not just kidnapping. I'm not too optimistic about our chances of finding the three men alive."

Sarah placed a hand on Jeff's arm. "Shouldn't we search further downstream for other possible murder victims."

Jeff looked to Dana for approval but she was undecided. She didn't know whether any of her companions were ready to discover more bodies. Kerrie then reminded them of her pressing deadline.

"All right, Jeff, we'll search further after we notify Mr. Hanson of Rhonda's body." She looked to Marietta, who nodded her consent.

The rest of the afternoon provided a futile search and they left the stream just before dusk, tired and happy to have found no additional bodies. Where were Gus and the Tolivers? Marietta couldn't think of another place to search unless the killer was hiding them in one of the vacation cabins.

Chapter Sixteen

The quiet was deafening that evening at dinner. Exhausted from the day's travails, they all seemed to sink permanently into their dining room chairs. Before the meal ended, Kerrie broke the silence with her conclusion that if the killer was hiding in a vacation cabin, the lights would be on at night.

Everyone groaned but Tom volunteered to drive Kerrie there. Dana protested that it was too dangerous. The shooter had been upgraded to a killer. But Kerrie was insistent. Her job was on the line.

Marietta wrote a list of cabin owners and starred the ones who weren't at home. There were only four at the present time and she told them the best way to sneak up on each cabin.

"They pay me to keep a watch on their places while they're gone," she said. "I use my old Ford." Reaching into her purse she withdrew a set of keys, telling them to take the pickup parked in her garage, *if* it were still there. Everyone knew what she drove and would think it was her.

Kerrie smiled and reached to hug her. "You're a lifesaver,

Marietta."

"I hope so. Gus's life may depend on us."

Kerrie and Tom left immediately in his pickup. It was nearing eight o'clock so the killer should still be up by the time they reached the eastern slope of the mountain. Kerrie's heart thumped in her chest. They probably should have asked for backup, but the woman deputy they'd encountered earlier would probably prevent them from investigating further. Why were officials moving so slowly? Didn't they have a clue?

Tom warned Kerrie to remain in the truck while he unlocked Marietta's garage and flashed his light inside. The old pickup was still there and undamaged. Backing it into the yard, he ran over to open Kerrie's door and help her into the ford. With the lights on low beam they chugged up the nearest grade and headed toward the cabins. Kerrie had memorized Marietta's directions so they wouldn't draw attention to themselves by reading the list by flashlight.

The first cabin was an A-frame with a front redwood deck. No light was visible from the gravel road but Tom cut his own lights and stealthily climbed from the Ford. Kerrie did the same on the passenger side, not quite closing the door. They stood and listened to the night sounds, hearing nothing more than crickets and night birds calling. Tom whispered that he was going to tiptoe onto the porch and peer through the edges of the front windows in case the killer had hung blankets to darken the rooms.

A few moments later he returned. "Let's go," he whispered. "I don't think anyone's here."

Climbing back into the old truck, Tom started the engine and they crept down a steep grade until they found the lane Marietta had described, which led to the second cabin. Setting on a ledge, the small log house faced outward into what they had been warned was a deep canyon. Unless they wore parachutes, they shouldn't step off the path. No lights were visible so Tom repeated his tiptoe approach with a carefully muted flashlight. Kerrie held her breath until he returned.

"Nothing I can detect. Let's find door number three."

Kerrie prayed they weren't being watched as they drove quite a distance to the third cabin. Tom had to unlatch a ranch-type wire gate to gain access to the property and Kerrie waited until he returned after some twenty minutes of investigation. Frightened when she heard a cracking sound, she squeezed her eyes tight to listen but heard nothing more.

When Tom finally returned, he said, "I thought I saw a flash of light at the rear of the cabin but it was probably just a lightning bug."

"Are you sure?"

"Yeah, I hung around to make sure nobody was back there. Or inside."

She told him about the cracking sound she'd heard and was told it was probably an animal stepping on a limb. One more cabin to go. This one had to be the killer's hideout or they were back to square one.

They saw headlights before they reached the cabin. Tom shut off the Ford's lights and pulled off the road into some undergrowth. Thank heavens the old truck was a faded green. When the pickup truck drove by, Tom waited several minutes before he pulled back onto the road. The cabin was somewhere ahead off a narrow dirt road leading to a precipice. The climb was steep and required a few minute's driving time. Kerrie wasn't about to stay in the truck, so she followed Tom up the narrow path. Tom stopped and she ran into him. Pulling her close, he whispered, "Do you see that faint glow in the window?"

She admitted she had. "Looks like a night light."

"That pickup must have left this cabin."

"What'll we do?"

Tom pulled a gun from his belt. "Knock and ask for directions, *if* someone's in there."

Kerrie fumbled in her fanny pack for her mother's borrowed gun.

"Stand to the right of the door when I knock and take your cue from me." The tone of his voice precluded an argument. He sounded like a drill sergeant.

"Yes, sir, I'm right behind you."

Tom knocked and stepped aside, as Kerrie did beside him. When no one answered, he knocked again.

"Listen," Kerrie whispered. "I thought I heard someone groaning." There it was again.

Tom handed his revolver to Kerrie and threw his shoulder against the door. Kerrie heard a cracking sound but the door remained in place. Her bodyguard then kicked the knob with his boot heel and the door sprang open. The only light in the room was a child's night light placed low near the floor by the couch. Kerrie's flashlight discovered a coffee mug filled with cigarette butts on the lamp table. No wonder the room had an offensive odor.

Someone groaned and they flashed their lights along the baseboards as they entered each room. In the second bedroom they found a small man tied like a rodeo calf with a blindfold and wad of cloth stuffed in his mouth. Tom quickly removed the mask and gag and began to untie him.

"It's Gus Blake," Tom said. "Thank God he's still alive."

When the little man tried to stand he fell sideways. Tom caught him before he hit the floor.

"Who did this to you?" Kerrie ask.

"Water," Gus croaked.

Kerrie rushed to the kitchen to get a glass. When she returned with the water, she found Gus lying on the bed gasping for breath.

"What's wrong with him, Tom?"

"I'm not sure but we need to get him to a hospital. He's either hyperventilating or having a heart attack."

Kerrie pulled Gus into a sitting position. "Find a couple of aspirin in the medicine cabinet. Hurry!"

Tom returned with an aspirin bottle and Kerrie insisted that Gus place them under his tongue before swallowing them. Tom then checked the other rooms before picking up Gus and carrying him to the truck. Kerrie climbed in beside him and strapped him in as Gus's head lolled to one side.

Kerrie prayed during the entire trip down the mountain to the nearest hospital. Gus was still alive but, because of his age, the emergency room doctor didn't give them much hope that he'd survive.

"What if he dies before he can tell us who kidnapped him, Tom? And what could have happened to Frank and Pete Toliver?"

"The crime lab will go over every inch of the cabin and dust for prints."

Kerrie plucked her cell phone from her pocket. "We need to let Mom know."

Her mother sounded worried when she answered the phone. Before Kerrie could tell her what had happened, Dana said she'd received another warning phone call. "Jeff says we need to have a tracer placed on our line."

"Mom, we found Gus Blake."

"What?"

"He's alive, but barely. We brought him to the hospital."

"We'll be right there." Dana hung up before Kerrie could tell her that the Tolivers were still missing.

Half an hour later, everyone was present in the waiting room. Kerrie and Tom took turns telling the others what had happened on the mountain. Dana then told them about the phone call. "He said he was going to burn down the mansion and kill all of us if we don't stop investigating the wolf shootings."

Kerrie pulled her mother to her feet to hug her. "Why are you and Sarah such magnets for murder?"

"Just lucky, I guess."

A pudgy doctor with ink black hair streaked with white approached them with a scowl. "Mr. Blake has been transferred to ICU. He seems to be responding to treatment but we won't know his true condition until sometime tomorrow. No sense you all staying here tonight."

Jeff briefly filled the doctor in on the kidnapping-murder case and said that the patient required protection. He asked Dana first, then volunteered to stay until the police provided a guard. The doctor nodded, then motioned for Jeff to follow.

Tom would fill in for Jeff until he returned to the mansion. That meant sleeping across the hall from Kerrie in Jeff's room. Dana hoped he would keep his mind on his guard job.

* * *

Back at the mansion Bert was waiting for them. Tom insisted on inspecting the house before they left the foyer. Dana wearily agreed. It was past midnight and all she wanted to do was crawl into bed and sleep for forty-eight hours.

When Tom returned he assured them the house was safe and that Dana might consider installing decorative bars on the windows the following day.

"Like a prison?"

"No, ma'am. Those curly que type of metal bars. White ones, maybe."

"On a Queen Anne Victorian?" Dana shook her head to prevent her eyes from closing. "I'll think about it tomorrow."

Sarah followed her upstairs and Dana felt asleep as

soon as she reclined. The digital clock said 2:28 when she awoke worrying about Gus. Was he going to make it? Would he live long enough to tell who kidnapped him and held him prisoner? And where were the other two missing men? She finally fell asleep but was so restless that she woke both herself and Sarah, who usually slept like a hibernating bear.

"You think Gus's gonna be all right?" Sarah asked, yawning.

"I've been praying for him half the night."

"Whoever did that to him is a monster, Dana."

"You're right and I'm worried he may try the same thing with us."

"Maybe we should take Tom's advice and install bars on the windows and doors."

Dana sat up in bed. "I've been thinking about that. Who cares if it offends the neighbors. "We'll pretend it's Queen Anne's dungeon."

"Better safe than murdered."

"Amen. Let's get some sleep."

The following morning Tom greeted them in the kitchen with a freshly brewed pot of French vanilla coffee. The aroma had lured Dana out of bed long before she wanted to leave. She then thought of Gus and woke Sarah, telling her to get dressed. The four of them were on their way to the hospital within the hour.

Gus's son Charley was in the waiting room. He'd recently arrived from south of Denver. Small like Gus, his short cropped hair seemed to have been styled by a military barber and he appeared to have had little sleep. When asked how Gus was doing, he said he was holding his own.

Dana sat down next to Charley. "Did the doctor say what's wrong with your dad?"

"Dehydration and a slight stroke. They think he's going to pull through."

Everyone exhaled and smiled.

When Dana told him what had happened before his arrival, Charley said he'd been worried because he hadn't heard from Gus in three days.

"Dad always emails me every night to let me know how he's doing and if he's got another wolf patient."

"Did he tell you about the fire and that someone's shooting at people who drive up the mountain?"

"No, all he told me about were his wounded wolves. I told *him* to be careful but he's too stubborn to listen."

"That we know. I think you need to take him home with you for a while when he recuperates," Dana said.

Charley smiled. "That's like inviting a whale to swim in a kiddie pool. Dad refuses to leave the mountain."

Tom asked if Gus had any enemies or other antagonists who would want to harm him. Charley replied that Gus was well-liked by everyone and he couldn't imagine someone tying him up and leaving him to die.

At least Gus was alive. Dana prayed he would live long enough to name his assailant and tell what had happened to the Tolivers.

Chapter Seventeen

Kerrie had to fly back to Denver that morning, with a promise to return the following weekend. She wasn't about to give up on her feature story. Tom drove her to the airport and saw her off on the early flight. Kerrie had insisted that her mother and Sarah leave for the hospital instead of going to the airport. "If Gus dies, we're back where we started."

* * *

"Gus is too ornery to die." Marietta wiped a tear from the corner of her eye. "Charley being here is good for Gus."

Dana started the Jeep for the trip to the hospital. "We could have made room for Charley at the mansion but he insisted on staying with his dad."

Sarah said, "You don't think the killer knows where Gus is, do you?"

"Surely not this soon, but who knows how he or she gets their information."

"I wonder if it could be that nasty woman deputy."

"What earthly reason could she have to kill Rhonda Bailey and kidnap the men?"

Light rain splattered the windshield and Dana triggered the wipers. "There's something going on besides wolf killings. I think the wolves are a smoke screen to disguise what's happening below the surface."

"What could it be?"

"Drugs or human trafficking. Gun running. Terrorist activities—"

Marietta snorted. "I would have noticed strangers on the mountain."

Dana suggested helicopters but the old woman said she would have heard them. Her hearing was still quite good. What about pack mules? Sarah said grinning.

Marietta shook her head. "I guess that leaves spaceships and I haven't seen any of those."

They pulled into the parking lot and climbed from the Jeep. It was too early for visiting hours but they would find Charley and ask if he'd learned anything. They found him asleep in a lounge near ICU. He appeared so tired that they decided not to wake him. Dana walked down the hall to inquire about Gus at the nearest nurse's station. Told he was in stable condition, she looked about for Jeff, who seemed to be missing. A few minutes later she spotted him walking down the hall with a Styrofoam cup in hand. She could smell the coffee before he reached her.

"The old guy came to about four this morning. He looked around and went back to sleep. I think he'll be ready for questioning later this morning."

"Did you get any sleep, Jeff?"

"I had a catnap after Gus went back to sleep."

When are they sending a deputy to replace you?"

"Should be here any time." As he spoke, someone appeared in the muted hallway behind him. The swagger was familiar but Dana didn't recognize the deputy until she reached the lounge. Her name tag said, D.A. Luvlie. Dana suppressed a grin. Why hadn't she noticed the name before?

Jeff pointed out Gus in the glassed-in ICU to the deputy, leaving Dana to worry that Sarah might be right. Was Jeff leading the fox into the henhouse? A cold chill made her shiver as she retraced her steps to the lounge.

Sarah looked as though she'd seen the Boston strangler. "That's not who I think it is."

"I'm afraid so. She'll be guarding Gus."

"Then we need to take turns watching her."

"My thoughts, exactly. Jeff needs some sleep. I'll suggest that he go back to the mansion."

When Jeff returned, his expression mirrored her own concern. "Stanton County must be desperate for deputies. D.A. Luvlie is the closest thing to a law enforcement bully I've ever met. She told me in no uncertain terms that I was no longer needed."

"Then who's going to replace her for the night shift?"

"I have no idea, but I'll call the sheriff to request a replacement."

"For the night shift, Jeff?"

"No, ma'am. Gus doesn't need her around when he wakes up. She'll cause him to have another stroke."

Dana admitted she was worried. She then asked who would question Gus.

"As it stands now, it will probably be Deputy Luvlie."

Sarah sneered. "Lovely she's not. She looks more like a linebacker for the Denver Broncos."

"We need permission to have someone else present."

Dana placed a hand on Jeff's shoulder. "Can you do it, Jeff? Or shall I call Walter?"

"I'll try but Walt might have better luck."

Dana retrieved her cell phone and walked out on a balcony to call. Walter wasn't answering his cell phone. She tried the sheriff's office to leave a message and his secretary Jody answered.

"Sheriff's out on a manhunt," Jody said. "I don't expect

him back till they catch the bugger." She briefly told Dana about the man who opened fire in a bakery because the store was out of cinnamon rolls. "Pure craziness, if you ask me."

"A lot of that going around." Dana asked that the sheriff call as soon as he checked in.

"He's still mooning over you, Miz Logan. He keeps your picture front and center on his desk along with the portrait of his hounds."

Dana sighed. There was no dissuading Sheriff Grayson once he made up his mind. Their only hope was Jeff Mailer. Without sleep, would he be able to convince the sheriff to allow him to be present for Gus's interrogation? She winced, imaging the large woman bullying Gus.

Jeff had a conversation going of his own. When he clicked off, he said that his police department friend had a contact in the Stanton County sheriff's office who could hopefully intercede. In the meantime, he needed a nap. He asked that Dana keep an eye on the deputy and to wake him if she made a move on Gus. She agreed but had little confidence they could prevent Deputy Luvlie from doing anything.

Between them, Dana, Sarah and Marietta watched the deputy pace the hall outside the ICU. Thank heavens Gus wasn't in his own room. They hoped the nurses could keep Luvlie out. She was probably all bluster and had nothing to do with the killings. But at this point, it was hard to trust anyone.

Sarah brought them back sweet rolls from the cafeteria. Jeff was with her, both laughing although their bodyguard was bleary-eyed. Dana had never seen her friend so happy. Jeff told them that the sheriff was coming at two that afternoon to question Gus himself. The news had everyone smiling.

"Will he tell us what Gus has to say?" Dana asked.

"Depends. If anyone in his department is implicated,

you can be sure he'll keep it close to his chest."

"Is there any way you can be present, Jeff?"

"I doubt it, but I'll try. I first need a shower and a change of clothes." Rubbing his face, he admitted he also needed a shave.

Sarah's expression said she wanted to accompany him but Dana gripped her arm. "Not now Cafferty. There's plenty of time later. I need you here."

Dana took her own sweet roll to the deputy and offered to buy her a cup of coffee. She was surprised by the woman's grateful smile. Maybe she wasn't so bad, after all. It must be difficult competing in a traditionally male occupation. The men probably gave her a bad time.

Charlie waylaid Gus's doctor as he walked past the waiting room. Dana and the others joined them in time to hear the doctor say that Gus was progressing well and would be moved to his own room that afternoon.

"Will Gus be up to questioning?" Dana asked.

The doctor screwed up his face before answering. "Depends on whether he wants to be questioned. We don't want him to get excited and have a possible setback."

Charley said, "Maybe I oughta talk to Dad first."

They were all in agreement. Jeff could brief him on what to ask before the sheriff arrived—*if* the doctor would permit Charley's visit. At the moment he seemed undecided. Charley told him that he and his father were close and that Gus would be cheered by his visit. The doctor reluctantly gave permission, but said the visit should be kept to five minutes.

Dana frowned. As slowly as Gus talked, it could take an hour to get the answers they needed. She pulled a notepad from her purse and jotted down the most pertinent questions. Number one was who kidnapped him and two: where were Frank and Pete Toliver? They also needed to know if Gus was aware of Rhonda Bailey's death and the reason for it. And how did the wolf killings tie in?

Dana knew that Gus would probably experience some confusion. She hoped his son could get the answers before the nurses ran him out of Gus's room. Jeff doubted that Gus knew anything more than who kidnapped him, if he even knew that.

Tearing the page from the notepad, Dana handed it to Charley and they went over it together. Nodding, he said he would do his best without overexciting his dad. He didn't look any more hopeful than Jeff had. Crossing his fingers he leaned back in his chair and closed his eyes. Dana knew he was as tired as she was. Stress and anxiety were taking their toll on everyone.

Gus's gurney moved past the waiting room just before noon. He managed a weak smile and slight wave of his hand when they stood and called his name. Charley hurried to walk alongside the gurney and grip his father's hand. Smiling at Dana, he nodded his reassurance that he would elicit some answers. She crossed her fingers and sat back down heavily in her chair. From the corner of her eye, she noticed Sarah doing the same. Marietta had walked to the door and still had her hand in the air, tears streaming down her lined face. Dana rose to comfort her.

Charley returned nearly half an hour later. Shoulders slumped, he was gazing at the floor as he approached. Sitting down next to Dana, he said, "Dad doesn't remember much and doesn't know who kidnapped him. He said somebody threw a dark bag over his head from behind and tossed him into the back of a pickup. It was dark when they took the bag off and blindfolded him, so he didn't see a thing."

"Does he know how long he was in the truck?"

"He thought about an hour but wasn't sure."

"What about the Tolivers? Was anyone else with him in the truck?"

"He thinks he was alone."

Dana closed her eyes to think. "Did he hear anyone's voice that he could identify?"

"He didn't say, so maybe the kidnapper was alone."

"Does he think they left him there to die?"

Charley's expression grew angry. "They didn't even give him any water, so he's dehydrated."

"I wonder if he knows anything about Rhonda Bailey."

"He said he's never heard of her."

Dana sighed. How she wished they could vacate square one. "Can we visit Gus for a few minutes, one at a time?"

"The doctor said he needs to rest up before the sheriff gets here. I think he's wasting his time. Dad doesn't seem to know much of anything."

Sarah leaned to pat the young man's back. "You're a good son. You remind me of my own son Charley."

He briefly smiled and hung his head. "Why would anyone do this to a nice old guy like Dad?

Dana assured him they would solve the mystery, no matter how long it took. Watching and listening to him, she wondered how he'd learned to speak proper English. Certainly not from his father. Charley was in his late 30s and probably the son of Gus's third wife. His mother might have been a teacher who insisted he learn the language. She would ask Marietta after they left the hospital.

Jeff returned in time to join them for lunch in the cafeteria. He appeared refreshed and eager to wade back into the case. His friend at the police department had contacted someone at the Stanton County sheriff's office, who said that Rhonda Bailey's body had been recovered from the mountain and an autopsy was scheduled for the following day. No further information was available.

"Looks like we're currently up the creek without the proverbial paddle," Dana said.

Jeff smiled. "Not necessarily. Tire tracks are visible in the ashes in Gus's yard, along with yours, mine and Gus's old truck. Whoever planned the kidnapping doesn't know much about police investigations. If we can match the tracks with those at the Toliver ranch and the cabin where Gus was found, we'll have a running start on knowing who's involved."

Tom surprised them when he walked into the waiting room. With Kerrie out of state, he wondered whether he still had a job. He also wanted to know Gus's condition.

When they had filled him in, Tom said, "Kerrie'll be disappointed if we don't come up with some answers while she's gone. She's going to check into other wolf killings from Denver."

"I think the wolf killings are a subterfuge designed to keep us off balance," Dana said. "There's something even more sinister going on."

Jeff nodded. "I'm inclined to agree."

Sarah moved closer to Jeff. "If Gus can't help us, who can?"

Jeff's cell phone rang and he moved to the balcony. He was biting his lip when he returned. "Frank Toliver's body turned up in the same stream as Rhonda Bailey's. I don't know the details, except that he was fully clothed, bound and blindfolded like Gus."

Dana collapsed into the nearest chair, wondering whether the killer had planned to kill Gus as well. Tom and Kerrie had probably saved his life. Was a similar fate in store for Frank's son? She turned to Marietta who seemed in shock.

The tiny woman mumbled to herself, "Am I next?"

Dana tried to reassure her. Turning to Tom, she said, "You're on the payroll until the killer's in custody."

Jeff said that he'd checked on Deputy Luvlie. She was new on the job from her previous position in Kansas, and had an unblemished record. Obviously, no one had complained about her tactics. Dana speculated that everyone had been afraid to report her. Jeff also said that he'd had a talk with her about Gus and warned that upsetting him could trigger another stroke—not a mild one like the one he'd recently suffered.

"I don't think we'll have to worry about her from now on. I promised to blemish her record if she tried to bully Gus." Jeff rose from his seat. "If you ladies are up to it, we'd better drive to the mountain to take some tire track samples. We can match them with the tracks at Elk Creek. Safety in numbers."

Marietta's shoulders slumped as she sat staring at the floor. Worried, Dana wondered if she were up to the trip? When asked, the old woman said, "I don't trust that deputy. I'll stay here with Gus. When you find the monster, fill his hide fulla buckshot for me."

It felt good to laugh after so much stress. Smiling, they left the hall outside Gus's room. Relieved that someone besides the deputy was guarding Gus, Dana glanced at her companions and said, "Let's go."

Chapter Eighteen

They drove to the mountain in Jeff's car, hoping the killer wouldn't recognize his plain off-white sedan from the previous night. Marietta had told them about a shortcut to the stream and they parked in the area where Rhonda Bailey's body had been found. No one was around so they used binoculars to scan the bushes and trees along the stream, which was still swollen with spring runoff.

Jeff cautioned them to be quiet as he led the way down the bank searching for tire tracks. When no tracks were found, they returned to the car and drove farther east.

Sarah yelled for Jeff to stop when they had gone less than a half a mile. Seated on the passenger side, she had been leaning out the window. "I saw some tracks a second ago."

Jeff backed the car until she told him again to stop. He told them to stay put while he checked them out. He returned smiling. "I think we found the right truck but I'll have to compare the tracks with my photographs."

Everyone left the car when he popped the trunk. Retrieving a folder from his brief case, he handed it to

Dana while he removed his camera's lens cap. Returning to the tracks, he motioned everyone to stay back as he clicked off a dozen frames. He then stooped to compare the tread design with the photos in his folder.

"Bingo. I think we've found the right truck."

Dana asked how he knew the tires belonged to a truck. Jeff explained that the tires were wider than the average car and an off road, heavy duty tread. The owner probably lived on the mountain. They all wanted to know how they could match the treads to the right pickup truck.

Jeff smiled. "Leave that to me."

The others shrugged and said okay. Now what? He cautioned them not to disturb the tracks while they searched along the bank for other clues. The investigating officers had probably done a thorough search when they found the body but something might have fallen into the water and beached itself downstream. He decided to drive another quarter of a mile farther down the bank.

Tom spotted something shining along the edge of the water in the early afternoon sun. He pointed it out to Jeff, who pulled on a pair of latex gloves. The light blue cigarette lighter was placed in a plastic evidence bag before they were allowed to examine it.

"Ever see this?" Jeff asked.

Dana thought it looked rather ordinary. A lighter purchased at a convenience store. There was nothing special about it until Jeff turned it over. A large gold crest nearly filled the entire surface. When he looked closer he noticed the initials FT embossed on the lower left corner. "It must be Frank Toliver's lighter. I'll show it to Gus and Marietta before I turn it over to the sheriff's office."

"His body must have been found near here," Sarah said.

Dana took the packaged lighter from Jeff to look it over. "If that were true, the police would have found the lighter when they retrieved Frank's body."

Jeff agreed. "From the footprints leading away from the tire tracks, I noticed drag marks as though the body was pulled from the pickup bed. I think we need to go back to the area where Frank's body was found."

Pete Toliver will be next if we don't discover the killer's whereabouts soon. Dana wondered whether there was anyone on the mountain with a grudge against Gus or the Tolivers. She thought again about Rhonda Bailey's connection and the reason both bodies were dumped in the same stream. The killer must live nearby.

"How far are we from the cabin where Gus was found?" she asked Tom.

He turned to survey the area to get his bearings. "About a mile as the crow flies, I'd say."

"I wonder if the sheriff's deputies have searched the cabin for clues to the killer's identity."

"I'm sure they have."

Dana thought for a moment. "Why didn't the killer bury the bodies instead of bringing them here? He obviously wanted them found. A warning to others to stay away?"

"Looks that way," Jeff said.

"Why is he leaving clues?" Dana said to no one in particular.

"He may consider it a game like hide and seek. Psychopaths are usually intelligent people who consider themselves superior to others. I think he might be taunting the rest of us."

When nothing else was found, they drove back to the original site, where Jeff showed them the drag marks and probable site where the body had been found. The footprints were narrow at the heel and pointed at the toe, indicating a pair of western boots of average size. They could belong to a man or a woman. Because the boot impression wasn't very deep in the sand, the killer probably didn't weigh more than 150 pounds. So how could he or she manage to toss a body into the bed of the pickup? Especially someone Frank Toliver's size? Unless there were one or more of them working in tandem. Dana shivered at the thought.

Jeff suggested they drive by the cabin where Gus had been found. If no one was present, they would look for tire tracks and open the garage door, if it wasn't locked.

"What if we're caught?" Dana asked.

"We'll claim we made a mistake and found the wrong cabin. We look like a family on an outing."

"Sounds risky," Tom said.

"The women'll stay in the car while we make a quick inspection. Then we'll get the hell out of there."

Jeff said they needed to check on the Tolivers. Had they been involved in any illegal activities?

Dana said she had already checked them out and found no criminal activities. She would try calling Marietta at the hospital. They were fortunately in a cell service area.

"Ask her about Frank's home life. Was the marriage happy?"

Dana's phone rang a few minutes after she tried calling Marietta. The old woman said her cell phone twittered whenever she had voice mail and that she was out on the balcony with an eye on Gus's room. Why had Dana called? When Dana asked about the Tolivers, she said, "Jenny was a lovely woman and she and Frank seemed happy. But there was that terrible accident that killed her. Frank was driving and he never got over her death."

"What about their son?"

"Pete was Jenny's son by her first husband. Frank adopted the boy and loved him like his own. I have no idea why anyone would want to kill them. Such nice people."

"Were they ever involved in any questionable activities?"

Dana asked.

"Never. I would have known if they were."

Marietta must have been the mountain busybody, Dana thought when she disconnected the call. She seemed to know everyone and everything they'd ever done. After she repeated what Marietta had said, Jeff suggested they leave for the vacationers' cabin to check for tire tracks.

* * *

The cabin appeared deserted when they drove past, so Jeff made a U-turn and pulled alongside the garage on the lower level. No tire tracks were visible on the short concrete driveway and they made a quick inspection of the dirt approach. Jeff gave them a thumbs-up and motioned for Tom to help him lift the garage door. Inside was an older model Silverado pickup with treads that matched the ones Jeff had photographed. When he checked, he discovered that the last number of the license plate was a seven. Could it be a coincidence? He didn't think so. To the right of the pickup was a come-along attached to the rafters with a sling that dropped to the floor.

"So that's how the bodies were hoisted into the truck bed," Jeff said. "Let's get out of here."

"Stay where you are," a man's voice said from the doorway into the house. The shotgun pointed at them seemed as large bored as a cannon. "Toss your keys on the floor and tell the women to come in the garage."

When the man stepped from the darkness of the house, Jeff noticed a dark hood worn over his head, which reached to his shoulders. He resembled a terrorist holding an AK-47.

"Set your guns in the pickup bed and don't do anything stupid. I have a touchy trigger finger." His voice alternated between tenor and baritone, tempered by a strange accent.

They placed their revolvers in the bed of the truck and

Jeff dropped his keys on the concrete floor. Why hadn't he left them in the ignition? The women could have escaped. Why had he been so stupid? He should have checked to make sure that no one was home. He could make a run for it, but the killer would probably take his escape out on the others by shooting them.

Standing under the overhead door, he signaled for Dana and Sarah to join him. As soon as they left the car, he apologized. Sarah shrieked when she spotted the gunman and Jeff pulled her into an embrace, telling her to remain calm.

The man holding the gun motioned for them to walk into the house single file. Jeff's eyes looked for something he could use as a weapon. He knew Tom was doing the same as they passed through the kitchen. But the counters were clear. Herded into the living room, they sat on the floor with hands behind their heads as ordered. He thought the gunman's strange manner of speaking was designed to disguise his voice, so he must be someone they had met. From Jeff's seat on the floor, he estimated the gunman to be five feet six and a hundred and forty pounds. If he were close enough, he could lunge at his legs and throw him off balance. But would any of the captives die of a gunshot in the process?

Dark eyes glaring at them through slits in the hood, the guy with the gun groped with his left hand to retrieve a rope coiled in a nearby chair. He seemed prepared for their arrival, or had he used this same rope to tie up his previous victims? Jeff watched him toss the rope to Tom, telling him to tie the women's hands together and link them to their feet. Sarah was sobbing but Dana sat glaring back at him with murder in her own eyes.

What did he have planned for them? Jeff realized that his heart was pounding and breathing was becoming difficult. When Tom had finished tying the women, he slumped back on the floor facing the shooter, who tossed him a roll of duct tape, telling him to tape Jeff. Tom complied. He was then told to lie on his stomach with his wrists crossed behind him. Jeff wondered when Tom was going to put his army training to work to take the killer down before he became the first shooting victim.

Jeff's mouth was so dry that he thought he was going to heave. He held his breath as the gunman walked over to hit the back of Tom's head with the butt of his gun. The women cried out and Jeff shook his head and glared at them. He was afraid they would excite the man enough to shoot them all.

The shooter set the AK-47 aside, grabbed the duct tape and tore off strips long enough to wrap Tom's wrists and ankles. Jeff hoped that Tom's head injury wasn't fatal. Laughing, the only man standing retrieved his gun and left through the kitchen, without a backward glance. A few moments later Jeff heard a truck start in the garage and back onto the driveway. He envisioned a rooster tail of dust as the Silverado left on the dirt road.

Sarah was crying and he asked that she calm down. "Is he going to kill us when he gets back?" she asked between sobs.

They were relieved to hear Tom groan. Jeff hoped all he had was a concussion. Twisting his wrists, he found that the tape had loose spots not attached to his skin. Tom had done a good job wrapping his wrists loosely although unnoticeable from the shooter's vantage point. He told the others to twist their wrists until they were free of the rope.

Why hadn't the gunman killed them? Maybe he wasn't the killer but an underling working with him. To his surprise Sarah was the first to pull free. When she had managed to untie her ankles, Jeff told her to help Dana, who was still struggling to free herself.

The end of his tape was loose so he bit into it, jerking it free with his teeth. He then reached to untape his ankles. Crawling on hands and knees to Tom, he quickly set him free, but Tom wasn't responding. Blood covered the back of young man's head. Jeff knew there were hundreds of tiny blood vessels just beneath the skin's surface.

Rolling the big man over, he slapped his face and repeatedly called his name. From the corner of his eye, he noticed Dana and Sarah getting to their feet and he told them to wet a kitchen towel. Dana hurried back with a dripping towel and he applied it to Tom's face. A few moments later Tom groaned and his eyes gradually opened.

"Think you can stand?" Jeff asked as he pulled him into a sitting position. "We need to get out of here." He glanced at the large blood spot on the carpet and knew the cabin owners would be upset. There was no time to clean the carpet.

Pulled to his feet, Tom stood unsteadily for a few seconds before he took a step toward the kitchen door. "I'm good," he said. "Let's go."

Sarah brought up the rear with a handful of ice cubes wrapped in another kitchen towel. As soon as they were seated in Jeff's car, she held the ice pack to Tom's head. Jeff crouched to retrieve the magnetic box containing his spare key. He listened as the gunman had driven west, so he drove east, hoping to find the route Marietta told him would take them down the mountain. The blue and white Silverado might be on its way to town.

Jeff managed to locate the little used trail and they bounced about like ping pong balls in their seat belts. Jeff slowed to a crawl when Tom yelped several times when he hit the headliner. The second order of business was to get him to the nearest hospital. Jeff would never forgive himself for placing them all in the deadly situation. He must be getting old.

* * *

Jeff's call to the sheriff's office produced what he hoped was an all-points bulletin for the gunman. He kept a constant watch for the Silverado in his mirrors while rushing Tom to the hospital. The drive to town seemed to take forever although he was ten miles over the speed limit once they reached the Interstate.

Tom was holding his head and groaning when they pulled into the emergency room parking lot. Jeff hurried through the admittance door to grab a wheelchair, berating himself for not calling ahead. When he had helped Tom into the chair, he pushed it inside the building and explained to a receptionist that it was a serious head injury. From the corner of his eye he could see other patients in the waiting room and hoped that none of their complaints were life threatening. He knew from experience how long most ER patients had to wait.

Tom's head was so bloodied that he was immediately taken in. Jeff realized that if the gunman had hit *him,* he probably wouldn't have survived. Tom was at least thirty years younger and Jeff wasn't in the best shape since he'd retired from the police department.

Dana placed a hand on his arm. "Would you mind if we borrow your car to go home to change clothes? We'll bring you something to eat."

Jeff hesitated before he handed over the keys. "The gunman's out there somewhere. If you see the truck, call 911 and head back here."

Sarah smiled as she waved goodbye from the door. Nice woman but if he had his druthers, he'd choose Dana Logan to keep him company. Unfortunately, Sheriff Grayson had already spoken for her. If only Alice hadn't died shortly after he retired. They'd be traveling the country in their RV instead of him standing here in ER. Jeff took a seat opposite the door leading to the treatment rooms. Frowning, he bit his lip as he replayed the scene that had happened in the cabin.

Chapter Nineteen

They looked in on Gus before they left the hospital. Gus was sleeping, so they talked Marietta into accompanying them to the mansion. The sun would soon set and Dana's stomach growled. She knew her companions must be hungry as well. Glancing at Sarah, she noticed she was smiling. She must be thinking of Jeff. Raising her chin, she looked for Marietta in her rearview mirror. The tiny woman had fallen asleep in the back seat.

Dana spotted a blue and white Silverado parked two houses down in her unpaved rural subdivision when she pulled into her driveway. Frightened, she backed slowly onto the road and told Sarah to call 911. The gunman was probably in the mansion. A lump formed in her throat, threatening to throttle her when she thought of their German Shepherd. Had the hooded man killed Bert?

There was nowhere to go except the hospital. Jeff would need his car. It was too risky to try driving the Jeep from the garage. The earlier incident that had taken place in a garage flashed through her mind. When Sarah completed her 911 call, Dana told her to call Jeff to warn him they were on their way. She stepped down on the accelerator, knowing that the gunman would follow if he noticed them in the driveway. She remembered an incident in Arizona, when a terrorist in a pickup had rammed their SUV. This time the Silverado could destroy Jeff's car and them along with it.

Glancing constantly in the rearview mirror, she listened as Sarah talked to Jeff at the hospital. When she clicked off, she said, "Tom's still in ER and Jeff said to take evasive action if the gunman comes after us."

"What does that mean? This is the only road into town and we're in a car, not the Jeep. We can't take off cross country." Dana glanced into the mirror and what she saw nearly stopped her heart. A fast moving vehicle was closing ground behind them.

Marietta said, "I'll take care of it." Unbuckling her seat belt, she removed the revolver from her purse and perched on her knees on the back seat. Thrusting her arm out the window, she fired at the pursuing pickup. The pickup swerved and ran off the road. A moment later, the truck pulled back onto the pavement and picked up speed.

"There's more where that came from," the old woman said, firing again.

Pulling off the side of the road, the Silverado made a U-turn back toward the mansion.

Hands shaking, Dana slowed Jeff's car and asked if Marietta was all right.

"Right as rain. I haven't had so much fun since our mule kicked Elmer in the butt. Elmer was my last husband, in case you didn't know."

Dana thought she heard a siren. A moment later a patrol car screamed past, its lights flashing. She wondered whether they should return home to check on Bert or proceed to the hospital. Her worry about the dog made the decision for her. Turning around she headed back to the mansion.

"Careful," Sarah warned. "We don't want to get caught

in the middle of a crossfire."

"I hope the deputy called for backup. Better get in touch with Jeff again and tell him what's happened."

Sarah called and relayed Jeff's message. "He says not to go home. We might get caught in the crossfire."

"What about Tom?"

"The ER doctor released him and they're waiting for us."

Dana made another U-turn and drove to the hospital. The men were waiting for them in the parking lot, Tom in a wheelchair. Marietta beamed when Jeff said he appreciated her marksmanship. It had probably saved their lives. Dana and Sarah got in back as Jeff helped Tom into the passenger seat.

Once they were on their way, Jeff warned them of the dangers of getting too close to home. They heard sirens as they approached the subdivision and saw a battery of flashing lights as they drove near the mansion. Jeff pulled off the road and parked. Telling them to stay put, he left the car and walked toward the first patrol car in the fading light. He was gone for nearly half an hour before he returned with the news that the gunman had eluded deputies, but an APB had been issued for the blue and white Silverado with a license number ending in seven.

Dana asked, "Did he break in the house?"

"I'm afraid so."

"Is Bert—?"

"He's alive but he needs medical attention. I'll take him to the vet as soon as they let us in the house. The bomb squad's checking the place out now."

"Bomb squad?" Sarah cried.

"They're not taking any chances."

Tears streaked both women's cheeks as Dana asked how badly Bert was injured. Jeff said he had been hit in the head and lost some blood, like Tom. She then recalled the first time Bert had sustained a head injury when crazy Jack struck him a glancing blow with a club on the mountain when they were investigating the drug gang. Poor Bert! Would he recover?"

* * *

The veterinarian wasn't optimistic when he examined the German Shepherd, who was still unconscious. The x-rays showed a brain injury and he advised euthanizing him.

"If Gus was here, he'd nurse Bert back to health," Marietta said. "He doesn't give up on any animal."

Dana asked if the dog would be in pain when he regained consciousness and was told that pain medication would keep him comfortable.

"Then let's give him every chance, Doctor. Bert means a lot to us."

The vet nodded and placed Bert in a padded cage. Blowing the dog kisses, the three women followed Jeff back to the car. Dana was seriously considering selling the mansion and returning to her native California. So much had happened in their rural subdivision and she knew the neighbors blamed her for everything.

Jeff called his friend at the police department to check on the APB. Sighing, he clicked off and reported no progress in apprehending the suspect. How the blue and white Silverado had eluded police was as big a mystery as why Rhonda Bailey had been killed and the three men kidnapped. Not to mention the wolf shootings. Was it safe to go home?

Jeff suggested staying in a hotel until the house damage was repaired and the property fortified. When Dana agreed, he made reservations at the Frontiersman before driving them back to the mansion to gather a few clothes.

Tom sat dazed on the couch in the midst of the vandalism.

The destruction appeared as bad as the one at Marietta's house, but on a larger scale. A tear hesitated on Dana's check as she climbed the stairs to her room. The intruder had probably been scared off before he climbed upstairs, for nothing seemed out of place. She sat down heavily on the bed and cried. Why did she and Sarah attract so much trouble?

Sarah followed her into the bedroom. Setting her suitcase down, she hugged her friend. "Marietta will be ready to leave soon. Why don't I help you pack?" Dana nodded and watched as Sarah filled a suitcase with lingerie, tee shirts and designer jeans. She then filled her own.

"I'm really tired of all this déjà vu, Sarah. I've decided to sell the mansion and move back to California."

"Can't say I blame you. But who's going to buy this place when they know it's been vandalized so often?"

"Maybe I'll donate it to the county for a museum."

Sarah smiled. "I hate to say this, but it does look like an English museum. Wouldn't the neighbors love that?"

"They'd tar and feather us," Dana muttered. Rising from the bed, she tossed several pairs of shoes into an overnight bag.

Jeff called from downstairs. "You ladies ready to leave?"

"Isn't he the most—?"

"I don't know what we'd do without him." Dana picked up two suitcases and started downstairs. The mansion was well insured so it wouldn't be a total loss if the killer set fire to it. But why was the gunman determined to punish everyone who had come in contact with Gus? He was obviously insane.

They arrived at the Frontiersman half an hour later. Dana thought the western decor was charming and understood why Jeff had selected the hotel. The three-bedroom suite was located on the top floor with a view of the North Platte River. Although it was dark, moonlight highlighted ripples in the water. The effect was calming and she stood at the window until Jeff told her that Tom was resting comfortably in the bedroom the two men shared. Each room had two queen-sized beds and Marietta had an entire room to herself.

Jeff suggested they call room service for dinner. They could then brainstorm, if anyone was up to it. Halfway through her chef salad, Dana asked Tom if he had noticed anything unusual about the gunman. Did he think he had any military training?

"None that I could detect. He seemed young—mid to late twenties—and a bit clumsy with his gun."

Jeff said, "I noticed that too. I also noticed a tattoo on his right am. There was a vertical M, but the rest of the word was covered by his sleeve."

Sarah's fork clattered to her plate. "He was wearing beat-up hiking boots and the cuffs of his chino pants were frayed. He wasn't wearing jeans like you'd think he would in the mountains."

Dana smiled, grateful for the group's fashionista. "What about his hands? Did anyone notice whether he was wearing a ring?"

Jeff said he had a large pinky ring on his left hand, but that he didn't notice a wedding band. "It could have been a class ring, either high school or college."

"A military or sports ring, maybe?"

Sarah laughed. "I doubt he played in the super bowl, Dana."

"He wouldn't be the first athlete to commit murder."

"He's not big enough," Tom said, "unless he's a gymnast or speed skater. And he didn't seem to be all that coordinated."

Dana crossed her arms. "So where's that leave us? A klutzy young man with a vendetta, who can't afford new clothes?"

"That hood he was wearing seemed to be a canvas

sack with holes cut out for his eyes and mouth," Jeff said.

Tom wondered where the gunman found a black canvas sack.

Jeff smiled. "Probably at Terrorists.com."

Dana wasn't amused. "What kind of terrorist kills wolves?"

"He must have his own thing going." Marietta had been silent until now. "Trashing houses and killing people and wolves don't seem to go together. You know what I mean?"

"A smoke screen to confuse the issue," Dana said. "I think he's laying land mines to keep us guessing and warned away from the mountain."

Sarah scowled. "You really think he's toying with us?"

Jeff said the gunman probably thought of it as a game. Why didn't he just kill them when he had the chance?

Dana laid her fork aside. "Maybe he's not the killer but someone hired to throw us all off track."

Jeff agreed that more than one of person was involved. He also suggested that Rhonda Bailey's death could be attributed to rivalry between the wolf killers. "Or maybe she threatened to turn them in."

Dana checked her watch. "We need to visit Gus at the hospital. Maybe he remembers something that happened while he was held captive."

"I think I'll pass." Tom carefully touched his head. "I'll keep my gun handy while you're gone."

Dana looked to Jeff who seemed undecided until Marietta picked up her purse and headed for the door. They didn't have much time before visiting hours were over.

Jeff opened the door little more than a crack and peered into the hallway. When they had all slipped from the room, they heard the dead bolt slide into place behind them. Dana didn't think the gunman had followed them to the hotel. He'd done his work and probably gone home to watch his favorite TV show, unless he was lurking at the hospital.

She should have hired an extra guard. Was Gus in danger? Dana dug her nails into her palms during the ten minute drive across town to the hospital. They found Gus asleep in his bed without a guard at the door. Jeff volunteered to stay before remembering it would leave his charges unprotected. While the women entered Gus's room, their bodyguard walked out onto the balcony to call the sheriff's office.

Gus's face seemed to have gained more wrinkles, his cheeks sunken and skin pale. He could have been mistaken for a hundred years old as he lay on his back on the pillow. Marietta gripped his hand and stroked his arm, softly calling his name. When his eyes flickered open, a faint smile played across his face when he recognized her. "Will you marry me?" he asked slightly above a whisper.

"You bet I will when this is over."

"Am I dreamin' or did you just say yes?"

She patted his face, telling him they would talk about it later. They needed to talk to him about the wolf killers.

Gus screwed up his face, trying to remember. "I told the sheriff that the guy who tied me up tried to change his voice so's I wouldn't recognize him."

"And did you?" Marietta prompted.

"It'll come to me, but right now I can't think of anything but a nice juicy steak. They been feedin' me baby food."

Dana took her place on the other side of the bed. "Was there anyone with him, Gus? Did you hear anyone talking?"

"No, ma'am. The guy that hogtied me only said a coupla words before he conked me on the noggin."

Dana noticed a bruise on Gus's bald spot and vowed to pay the gunman back in kind. She asked if he'd been unconscious until he arrived at the vacation cabin. Gus said he had and wondered why he hadn't been killed like his neighbor Frank Toliver. When asked how he knew about Frank, he said Deputy Luvlie had told him.

Bless her little black heart. "Where is the deputy?"

"Said she was goin' for coffee."

"How long ago?"

"Don't know. I fell asleep after they took my supper tray."

"That must have been hours ago." Dana walked from the room to search for Jeff, who still stood on the balcony listening to his cell phone. When he noticed her, he held up an index finger. She returned to Gus's room, where Sarah stood at the foot of the bed, tears glistening in her eyes.

Dana realized that someone was missing. "Where's Charley?

Gus said his son left for home as soon as he knew his dad would survive. "He didn't wanna leave but I told him he'd lose his new job if he didn't. No sense him hanging around here."

Jeff entered the room with his mouth set in a grim line. "No one ordered a night replacement deputy, and it seems that Luvlie walked off the job at her usual quitting time."

"I hope you don't mind spending the night here, Jeff."

"I don't but I'm worried about the three of you returning safely to the hotel."

"Don't worry about us. My Smith and Wesson's in my purse."

"I'm packin' too," Marietta stood as tall as her small frame allowed.

Jeff's worried expression dissolved into a grin. "Call as soon as you reach the hotel. I'll have a talk with Gus when visiting hours are over."

Less than five minutes later a nurse ushered them out of the room and they trouped to the elevator. Jeff gave them a high sign and told them to be careful.

"I want you both to watch everyone when we leave the elevator," Dana said, pushing the down button. "We'll take the back way out and walk single file around the building to Jeff's car."

They nodded and rode silently down to the first floor. Marietta walked out first to casually look around before she motioned to her companions. They followed the exit sign and were soon in the parking lot. Jeff's car sat under an overhead light and they studied each of the other cars in the lot before walking to it. Dana noticed movement from the corner of her eye and ran the few remaining steps.

When Sarah and Marietta caught up with her, Sarah said it had been someone in a white lab coat. Breathing heavily, Dana reminded Sarah of the terrorists dressed in green scrubs who blew up the hospital in Denver. Hurriedly unlocking the car, they climbed in and drove an erratic route back to the hotel. No one seemed to be following, so they parked and entered the hotel by the back entrance. They found Tom asleep on the living room couch with the television playing an old war movie.

Chapter Twenty

It was cleanup day at the mansion. Whoever vandalized the first floor had been thorough. Nothing was salvageable. They filled the dumpster and stacked a row of plastic lawn bags around it.

Dana tied the last of the trash bags. "Three strikes and we're out. I can't go through this again."

"At least the drug gang who did this months ago are all in prison," Sarah reminded her. "Along with your former brother-in-law."

Dana held her hand as though it were a stop sign. "I thought this destruction was behind us, like a bad dream."

"Kerrie will be flying in tomorrow. Are we going to stay at the hotel or here when we finish cleaning up."

"I haven't decided. I don't have the heart to buy new furniture just to sell the house."

"We can rent some, Dana, like they do on that house and garden channel."

Dana's cell phone rang and she handed the vacuum cleaner to Sarah. Walter was on the line. He had called the Stanton County sheriff to check on his progress and was told that Dana's house had been vandalized. He was flying in the following morning and would arrive an hour before Kerrie's flight. She tried to talk him out of coming but he refused to listen.

"It's good he's coming to help," Sarah said when the phone conversation ended. "Things have gotten out of hand."

Dana shrugged, embarrassed to admit that Sarah was right. She needed a big strong man to envelop her in his arms. She should have exacted a promise from him that he wouldn't say a word about marriage. That could be accomplished at the airport before she allowed him in the Jeep. Thank heavens Kerrie would be along for the ride.

They had driven Marietta to the hospital after breakfast to spend the day with Gus. Tom rode along and seemed to be feeling better. Still, Dana worried about him. She knew he was looking forward to Kerrie's visit and her fussing over him. Dana smiled, imagining again Tom as her son-in-law.

The land line rang and Sarah picked it up. Her eyes grew large as her mouth dropped open. Pointing to the receiver held to her ear, she mouthed "It's him." Dana took the phone in time to hear an eerie laugh before the line disconnected.

"It was the shooter, Dana. He said if we go to the mountain again he's going to firebomb the mansion while we're asleep."

Dana wondered whether he knew they were staying at the hotel. Probably not or he would have called their suite. Did he have someone watching them? Some of them should probably leave in Jeff's car after dark and the rest later in the Jeep. That ought to confuse the issue long enough for the women to safely arrive at the hotel undetected.

She needed to check on Bert. After the last dustpan had been emptied, she and Sarah changed clothes and Tom drove them to the veterinary clinic in his pickup truck.

Doctor Cavanaugh allowed them a brief visit with Bert, who was conscious but didn't seem to recognize them. He briefly lifted his head and closed his eyes. Dana wanted to see his tail wag in greeting but he almost seemed paralyzed. She would shoot the bastard who had done this to her dog. The brain injury may have completely destroyed his memory. They both left the office in tears.

Jeff came downstairs to greet them when they returned home. He'd left the hospital when Deputy Luvlie arrived, after lecturing her on leaving Gus unprotected. She assured him that a replacement deputy would relieve her that evening.

"I think we should be there to make sure," he said.

Dana agreed. "I'm sure Marietta will be ready to leave. I hope Gus remembered something about his kidnapping that she can tell us about. Hopefully he recognized his kidnapper's voice."

"I talked to him for over an hour last night after you left and he couldn't remember anything but the bag and his head injury."

"Poor Gus," Sarah said. "Why wasn't he killed instead of Frank Toliver? Frank wasn't helping to save wolves, was he?"

Jeff shook his head. "I think the wolf killings are a cover-up for something more serious or illegal. Like drugs, human trafficking or illegal weapons."

Dana agreed. "How are we going to learn what's really going on?"

"Gus said something that has me wondering. He caught a glimpse of the man's hiking boots before he went under. They were old and greasy."

"Did he say anything about frayed chinos?"

"No, but we can ask him this evening. Maybe he remembered something today that he was too fuzzy-brained to recall last night."

183

* * *

Deputy Luvlie dwarfed Marietta as the two stood talking outside Gus's room. It was a heated discussion that ended the moment Dana and company arrived. Both women's faces were red from obvious anger and the deputy immediately packed up her clipboard and left without a word.

"What was that about?" they all asked at once.

"A difference of opinion is all. I don't appreciate the deputy taking so many breaks while she's guarding Gus. Coffee breaks, magazine breaks, potty breaks—She wasn't here half the time. Good thing I've got my .45." They ducked when she pulled it from her purse.

"Put that away before they call security," Jeff said.

She dropped it into her purse as though it had scorched her hand. "By the way, Gus just remembered something important. He said he heard Pete Toliver's voice."

Dana caught her breath. "When?"

"After he was tied up at the cabin."

"What did Pete say?"

"Gus said it sounded like Pete was in another room when he yelled, 'Don't kill my dad.'"

"So they were holding him in the same house as Gus?"

"I reckon he's dead by now, like Frank."

Why the Tolivers instead of Gus? And had they known Rhonda Bailey? Dana thought another phone call to the college student, Annie Woods, was in order. Maybe Pete had dated Rhonda and that would explain the connection. Walter had the number and she'd ask him to call when he arrived the following morning.

Jeff said he would request a replacement for Deputy Luvlie. On second thought maybe a call from Sheriff Grayson would accomplish the transfer. He seemed relieved that Walter was returning.

Jeff suggested they take separate routes from the hospital to the hotel. Dana had left all the lights on in the mansion as well as the yard. If that wasn't enough of a deterrent, an alarm system had been installed that would wake the entire neighborhood.

Next morning they left early for the drive to the airport, after dropping Marietta off at the hospital. Walter's plane was late and Dana wondered why he had worn his uniform instead of civilian clothes. She guessed that it earned him special attention from the flight attendants.

Dana welcomed his embrace. They decided to wait in the coffee shop for Kerrie's flight where Walter filled them in on his latest murder case.

"Cuffed and stuffed," the sheriff said smiling.

"Meaning?"

"We arrested him at his apartment, handcuffed him and stuffed him in a jail cell."

Dana managed a smile although she wasn't in the mood for police humor.

When Kerrie's plane arrived, Tom was the first person she hugged. Dana smiled when she was next in line. She had a feeling the engagement to Roger Brandt had been broken.

During the drive back to town, Walter said he had done some investigative research of his own. He'd come to the same conclusion that something else was going on besides the wolf killings. So they were all in agreement, but what had the Tolivers done to earn them an early grave? They needed to conduct a thorough search of the cabin. Could Walter get permission or would they have to break in? She thought it would probably be the latter.

Jeff drove straight to the sheriff's department and Walter went inside. Nearly half an hour later he returned scowling. "Looks like I've worn out my welcome," he said.

"They're holding their cards closer than I would, under the circumstances."

"They must not have any new leads." Jeff started the engine. "I'll see what I can find out through my contacts."

Walter wanted to talk to Gus so they drove to the hospital. They found Deputy Luvlie reading a romance novel outside Gus's room. She didn't notice them until they reached the door.

"Put that book down and pay attention," Walter said in his gruffest voice.

Noticing the uniform, she dropped the book and stood at attention. Dana thought she was actually going to salute. She obviously didn't notice that Walter was from another state.

Marietta was holding Gus's hand while she watched him sleep. When she noticed the sheriff, she shook Gus's shoulder to wake him. Dana and Kerrie accompanied him to the bed while the others waited in the hall.

"I came to interview you, young man."

Gus guffawed and reached to shake Walter's hand. His face had more color than the night before and he seemed much improved. "What can I tell ya that I ain't told ever'body else?"

"I assume that you know Frank and Pete Toliver pretty well."

"Yep. Knowed 'em for at least seventy years—well, I knowed Frank that long but Pete didn't come along till Frank married Jenny 'bout twenty years ago. She was younger and they was a package deal. Her and six-year-old Pete."

"Was Frank ever involved in any illegal or suspicious activities?"

"None that I knowed about."

The sheriff pulled a notepad and pen from his shirt pocket. "How did Frank earn a living?"

"He grazed sheep and some cows on the land his granddaddy left him. And he raised some alfalfa. His wife taught school on the mountain."

"Did you ever see any strangers visiting Frank?"

Gus chuckled. "Only a coupla his relatives and they was purty strange."

Marietta raised her hand as though she were in school. "I saw two strangers leaving the road to Frank's place."

"When was that?"

"Not long ago."

"Can you describe them?"

"A young man and woman in a gray van."

Dana wondered whether it had been Rhonda Bailey and a friend.

"The girl looked to be a teenager but I didn't get a good look at the boy 'cause he had his elbow on the window ledge and was hiding his face. The girl had long brown hair. She kinda looked like Rhonda Bailey."

Walter asked Marietta if she knew of any illegal activities the Tolivers were engaged in. Shaking her head, she said that Frank was an honest man. Pete, on the other hand, was a little wild, but weren't most boys his age?

"Good people," Gus insisted. "And good neighbors."

Walter scribbled something on his notepad. "Do you have any idea who might have set the fire to burn your cabin?"

"Don't know anybody that holds a grudge agin me."

Marietta assured the sheriff that Gus was well-liked.

"What about the cattlemen and wool growers? Were any of them mad because you were saving wolves?"

"Nobody said nuthin' to me about it."

"And you haven't heard anything about drugs or gun running or other illegal things going on up there?"

"Nope."

Apparently exasperated, Walter pocketed his notebook

and shook Gus's hand before leaving the room. Dana stayed long enough to inquire how Gus was feeling and leaned to kiss his forehead. Kerrie then took over the questioning.

Dana joined Walter in the waiting room. Eyes closed, he seemed deep in thought until she heard him snore. His chin rested on his chest and she knew he was exhausted. Why did he insist on flying to Wyoming so often to help solve the case? He would be bankrupt soon unless the airlines gave law enforcement officers a special rate.

Closing her own eyes, she thought about everything she knew about the case. Although he'd been saving wolves, Gus's life had been spared. Or would he too have been killed if Tom and Kerrie hadn't found him? The voice on the phone sounded like Darth Vader, so it must have been someone who didn't want to be recognized. But why if a stranger made the call? The killer must be someone they had talked to. But who? Gus's friend at Granite Creek? That seemed unlikely. One of the college students? What was their motive? And why was Rhonda involved? Had an evil boyfriend talked her into taking part in something illegal?

Jeff's voice seemed to be calling her from a distance. Had she fallen asleep?

"Pete Toliver's been found."

Dana rose from her seat. "Where? In the stream?"

"No, he's alive and talking to the Stanton County sheriff."

"How do you know, Jeff?"

"My PD contact just sent me a text message."

"We need to talk to Pete. Where's Kerrie?"

Kerrie was still interviewing Gus and they would have to wait outside the sheriff's office to talk to Pete. He might even have a guard.

"I wonder how he escaped."

"We'll have to ask him."

Dana woke Walter and everyone except Marietta left the hospital to drive to the sheriff's office. They didn't have long to wait. Pete appeared with bruises on his face and a slashed left shirt sleeve. He was smiling and running a hand over his shaved head. Jeff was the first to leave his car and call Pete's name. A deputy stepped out of the building behind him and took Pete's arm. He ushered him into his patrol car before they had time to question him. What was going on? Were they taking him into protective custody?

Walter entered the office to have a talk with the sheriff. The determination on his face told Dana that he wouldn't leave without some answers.

Chapter Twenty One

Sheriff Johnston was on the phone so Walter was told to have a seat in the ante room. Looking over his notes, he realized that he would have to lie to get the information he needed. That didn't set well but he didn't know how else to pry the information from his Wyoming counterpart. Moments later he was led into the office by an attractive secretary.

"What is it this time, Grayson?"

Walter studied the aging lawman whom he thought should have already retired. His balding pate gave way to a double chin as well as an oversized belly. He realized that it could happen to him if he spent too much time behind his own desk.

"I have reason to believe that Pete Toliver's been transporting drugs from California," he said.

Sheriff Johnston smirked. "As far as I know the kid's never been out of the state."

"I need to know the real reason he's been missing. I'd also like to check his cabin."

"Somebody kidnapped him and his dad and held them

hostage."

"I'm aware of that. I need to know how he escaped."

Sheriff Johnston's chair creaked when he leaned back with his hands behind his head. "Toliver said he managed to untie himself when the suspect took Frank's body to the stream."

"Why didn't he untie Gus Blake while he was at it?"

"Beats the hell outa me. Maybe he was afraid he was next on the killer's list."

"Sounds suspicious, if you ask me. How'd he get to town?"

"He hiked back to a neighbor's cabin and hitched a ride."

Walter screwed up his mouth in thought. "Where's he now? Protective custody?"

"I thought it best that he spend a few days in PC. One of my detectives will go over his story and get it on video."

"Good idea. Any leads on the Frank Toliver and Rhonda Bailey murders?"

"None yet but we're working on it."

Walter waited for additional information but it wasn't forthcoming. "Mind if I take a look in the Toliver cabin to see if there's any evidence of drugs."

The chair creaked again as Johnston rocked back and forth in thought. "I'll let you know. How long you gonna be in town?"

"Not long. I've got a case pending in Modesto." Walter handed him a card with his cell phone number.

"I'll give you a call later this afternoon."

Walter nodded and left. He found Dana pacing outside the office, a distracted expression on her face. Signaling Tom to follow, they climbed in Jeff's car and drove back to the mansion. Gathered in the kitchen where the only downstairs furniture left were metal stools, Walter filled them in on his conversation with Sheriff Johnston.

Kerrie was busy taking notes. "Why would Pete Toliver lie about his escape?"

"That's the key to this entire mystery," Walter said, "and the reason we need to search the Toliver cabin."

"I'm not sure I understand."

"If someone kidnapped you and someone else, wouldn't you try at least to untie them before you escaped?"

"Maybe Gus was in another room and Pete didn't know he was there?"

Tom said, "We found Gus tied up in one of the bedrooms, so Pete could have missed him when he left."

Kerrie's pen tapped her notepad. "The garage door was closed so he must have left by the front door. We searched the other rooms and Pete wasn't there. And we didn't see him on the road."

"So where's he been for the past two days?" the sheriff asked.

Jeff thought he might have taken a short cut over the mountain until he found someone who could give him a ride into town. Or to his own pickup truck.

"That's very plausible," Dana said. "I can't imagine Pete Toliver taking part in his father's death or the wolf killings. "

"Let's hope my talk with Sheriff Johnston bears fruit."

Dana reached to hug him. "I don't know what we'd do without you, Walter."

The sheriff sighed. "About time you realized that, my dear."

Jeff seemed puzzled. "We don't have many suspects and I don't think any college students were involved, other than Rhonda Bailey." He looked around the group as though to get their reactions.

Tom shrugged, saying it could be anyone.

The kitchen wall phone rang and Sarah answered.

"For you, Walter. It's Sheriff Johnston."

Dana watched as Walter turned to the wall for privacy. A moment later he said, "Permission granted. Let's go before he changes his mind."

"How are we going to get in?" Dana asked.

"Deputy Bachman will meet us there with Pete Toliver's key."

Dana thought Pete must be innocent if he would allow Walter to search the cabin. Unless he removed all the evidence before faking his own kidnapping. They needed to find Pete's picture to show to Annie Woods and the other students. If they recognized him, it might provide the missing puzzle pieces.

"Do we know Frank Toliver's cause of death?" she asked.

"Blow to the back of the head with a blunt instrument is the preliminary diagnosis but his autopsy hasn't been completed," Jeff said.

"Probably with the rifle butt. But how could someone Pete's size drag Frank Toliver off to the cabin."

"He might have tricked him by calling and saying he'd found Gus there."

Dana's heart sank. How could anyone kill his own father?

"Pete might have wanted Gus to provide him with an alibi by yelling from another room *not* to kill his dad."

Jeff shook his head. "Then he should have untied Gus. Dead men don't make good witnesses. He couldn't have known that Gus would be found before he died."

Walter said there were too many holes in the case. "It'll be thrown out of court unless more evidence is found."

Dana grabbed her purse. "Then let's go."

Forty minutes later they met Deputy Bachman at the Toliver cabin. Tall and stocky, his dark crew cut resembled a hog bristle brush. He seemed surprised that Walter had so many assistants, but his smile put them immediately at ease. When he unlocked the door they saw that the cabin was in the same vandalized condition. Dana found it hard to believe that Pete would have demolished his own home.

Sarah had already begun sifting through the debris, piling the non-suspected items against a far wall. An old photo album had pictures missing, leaving only images of Frank, Pete and their wolf dog. Sarah wondered aloud whether the missing photographs had been taken after Jenny Toliver's death. Dana walked over to see for herself.

"Pete doesn't look more than ten years old," she said. "I wonder when his mother died."

Sarah pursed her lips. "I think Marietta said she died a couple of years ago."

"Then why would all her pictures disappear from the album?"

"Good question. Do you think Pete took them after his mother died?"

"Why don't we look in his room?"

The deputy cleared his throat. "I thought you people were looking for drugs."

"We are," Walter said. "You never know where you'll find them."

They'd have to hurry. The deputy seemed suspicious. Locating what looked like a young man's room and the only one that had not been vandalized, they searched his dresser and night stand. Buried in the bottom drawer under a stack of T-shirts was a box filled with pictures of his mother.

"Dana, are you thinking what I'm thinking?"

"Pete idolized his mother and blamed his father for her death. He could have created this elaborate smokescreen to hide his motive for killing Frank Toliver."

"The wolf killings, fire, vandalism, and kidnappings? All planned to throw everyone off his trail?" Sarah sat down heavily on the bed. "But why kill Rhonda Bailey?"

"Pete might have been the boyfriend who convinced her to stage the wolf rally and later helped her escape from the hospital. Maybe she found out that he planned to kill Frank and threatened to turn him in. So he killed her."

"That's quite a theory," the deputy said from the doorway. "I think Sheriff Johnston would like a word with the two of you." Taking each of them by the arm, he towed them into the living room where Walter, Tom and Kerrie were sifting through mounds of trash.

Walter had a bloody hiking boot in hand and Dana waded through the debris to take it from him.

"This," she said, "is the clincher. If you test the boot for blood type you'll probably find that it belonged to Pete's mother. Why would Pete keep the boot unless he harbored a deep-seated grudge against his adoptive father?"

"Stay put while I get an evidence bag from my patrol car." Bachman promptly left the cabin. While he was gone Dana filled the others in on the pictures Sarah had discovered as well as their own conclusions.

"I think that if they test Rhonda Bailey's body for fibers, they'll find they match the carpet in the vacation cabin the killer was hiding in."

Walter gaped at her, obviously surprised. "When did you figure this all out?"

"Over time. We found that bloody boot the first time we were here. Then there was the fire that he must have started on his day off from work. The fact that he didn't help Gus escape raised some questions as well as the time frame from when he claims to have escaped from the cabin and appeared at the sheriff's office. And now all those pictures of his mother we found in his chest of drawers. I'll bet if we search out back in the trees, we'll find that blue and white Silverado."

Walter pulled her close. "My favorite amateur sleuth. I wish you were one of my detectives."

"Don't forget me," Sarah made it a group hug and the others joined in.

"Don't count your chickens just yet," the deputy said from the doorway. "I just contacted Sheriff Johnston on my radio. Toliver insisted on leaving protective custody, so he's probably headed back this way. There'll soon be an APB out on him as well as another deputy for backup."

Sarah wanted to know how Toliver was returning to the mountain. "I thought he said a neighbor drove him to town."

"Another one of his lies," Dana said. "He must be driving his pickup truck."

"Figured it out, did ya?" a male voice said from the open doorway. The AK-47 he held waved them into a corner after he relieved the deputy of his gun. "This mess will make a great bonfire, but if you'd rather die of a bullet wound, I'll oblige you."

Pulling a cigarette lighter from his pocket, he flipped the roller with his left thumb and tossed it into the middle of the debris. "A friend's out back with his gun trained on the door, so I wouldn't try to escape. I'll shoot anybody who comes out after me."

Laughing, he closed the door as the fire blazed as high as the ceiling. Shielding her face from the heat, Dana felt Walter's arm around her.

"He's alone," Tom said, taking Kerrie's hand. "I'm betting my life there's no one out back and I'm gonna prove it. Follow me."

Everyone crept after him, including the deputy. Easing the back door open, Tom crouched to half his height and ran a zigzag route into the trees. He then motioned to Kerrie, who did the same. The others followed. They heard a volley of shots and Dana guessed that Deputy Bachman's' patrol car had four ruined tires. Overkill, she thought, if

Toliver expected them to die inside the cabin. Or maybe he knew they would escape and wanted to insure they couldn't follow him. Four more shots convinced her that Jeff's car was Toliver's latest victim.

Moving well back into the trees, they waited until they heard his engine start and noticed a dust cloud fill the air.

"Looks like he's headed back down the mountain," the deputy said. "I've gotta radio headquarters to let them know his location."

Jeff groaned. "If that maniac has any brains at all, he shot up your radio."

The deputy led the way as they crept past the burning cabin. No one else was in the area and Jeff had been right. The patrol car's dashboard was a tangle of wires and metal.

"I don't think we'll make much time driving on our rims," Jeff said. "The bastard ruined my brand new set of tires." He apologized to the ladies for his language and was told they agreed with him.

"I think we'd better hose down the place before we have another forest fire," Tom said. After a quick inspection, he reported no hoses hooked to the outside faucets.

Jeff cursed beneath his breath. "Toliver must have planned this—knowing we would be here—and took the hoses with him."

"Now what?" Kerrie said as she retreated from the flames.

"I hope my backup officer notices the Silverado—if that's what Toliver's driving. Problem is the steep, narrow road leading up here doesn't have many turnouts. And radio reception isn't always available."

"That we know," Sarah said. "But we won't be stranded once he gets here."

Behind them flames roared, destroying evidence of Pete Toliver's crimes. At least there were credible witnesses to testify when he went to trial.

Tom and Kerrie stood talking near the road. Dana watched them, thinking that Tom would soon be out of a job. She could keep him on as a guard until Pete Toliver occupied a jail cell, but Kerrie would be returning to Denver soon. Maybe he could find a job there as well.

While thinking over the events of the past few days, Dana said, "Who were those two young men we saw leaving Gus's cabin with his notebook computer?"

Sarah thought that Pete must have been one of them.

"But how does that tie in with Frank Toliver's death, other than the email message warning us to stay off the mountain?"

"What else could they have been up to? Maybe somebody hired them to kill the wolves?"

"With an AK-47? That's seems like overkill."

"It might be a good idea to search the ranch for a hidden cache," Jeff said.

The deputy thought it was a good idea and left a note under his windshield wiper telling the backup deputy they were searching the property. They then spread out, each searching for mounds of freshly excavated dirt, old sheds or anything out of the ordinary. Rusting, abandoned vehicles or farm machinery were also suspected places to hide contraband.

The women stayed within sight of each other, glad they had worn boots and jeans. The ranch was generously peppered with knee high sagebrush, which made their search more difficult. Each had armed herself with a hoe or shovel, which served as a digging tool as well as a weapon. When they left the trees, progress was slow in the hot summer sun as they searched half a section of land. Huge white clouds graced the horizon and a small herd of cows grazed in the distance. Dana hoped no bulls would come to investigate them.

Half an hour into their search, Sarah shrieked, dropped her hoe and took off running. Dana and Kerrie rushed over to discover what was wrong and spotted a badger crawling back into its hole. Sarah's scream must have frightened the low slung animal as much as the badger frightened her.

Kerrie picked up the hoe telling her companions that the badger was a dangerous animal and they needed to be careful. Tom had warned of possible diamondback rattlesnakes in the area and had demonstrated the technique of killing one, using a narrow fallen tree limb as the reptile.

Wiping sweat from their brows, they took up their original positions and paid more attention to crawling critters. Sometime later Dana discovered a small stream and wondered if it were the same one where the bodies had been found. Calling to Sarah and Kerrie, she showed them boot prints along the bank, suggesting they follow them without disturbing the imprints.

Before long a duck blind came into view and they scrambled into the water to look inside. The camouflaged canvas was pulled aside and they discovered brick-shaped, plastic wrapped packages hidden beneath a tarp. They weren't heavy enough for gold or silver.

Sarah picked one up and shook it. "What's this?"

Kerrie took it from her. "I wouldn't do that. It's probably cocaine. We need to find the deputy." Handing the package to her mother, Kerrie jogged in the direction the men had taken.

While she was gone, Dana counted the number of packages, which added to twenty-four. If they were drugs, the stash was worth a fortune. No wonder Pete and his one-man gang were attempting to scare people off the mountain. She needed to talk again to Annie Woods.

The student must have some idea of Rhonda Bailey's involvement and the identity of the other masked man.

Dana shivered in the afternoon heat. Pete wouldn't stay away long with all this contraband on the property. She had to admit that the duck blind was a clever hiding place. She wondered when and where he was planning to sell his stash. And where he got the money to buy the drugs? Drug dealers didn't sell on consignment, did they?

Kerrie led the men to the stream where Dana handed the package to the deputy. "If Bert had been with us, he would have sniffed out this cache in short order."

"Bert?" The deputy's brows rose.

"Our drug sniffing retired police dog."

Bachman looked the package over carefully. "This may not be what you think."

Sarah lifted the canvas flap to reveal the other packages. When the deputy looked inside, he said, "Then, again, you could be right."

Crawling inside the blind, he handed out four packages to each of them. "Let's get back to the cabin. My replacement should have been here an hour ago."

Smoke from the cabin spiraled skyward but there had been no wind to spread the flames to other areas. The cabin's logs still smoldered although there wasn't much left to identify it as a ranch house. When they found no deputy waiting, Tom offered to hike down the dirt road to determine whether he had gotten lost. Kerrie decided to go with him.

Jeff said he'd located a cell signal and called the sheriff's office. He reported what had happened at the cabin as well as the missing backup deputy. Dana knew no one relished spending the night on the mountain. Pete Toliver could return at any time with his AK-47 to reclaim his property.

Tom and Kerrie arrived ashen-faced some forty

minutes later. What they had seen still had Kerrie trembling and clinging to Tom, despite her previous journalism background.

Tom said, "Toliver must have opened fire on the deputy while he was driving up the mountain. The patrol car went over a steep embankment and exploded on the rocks below. That started a brush fire that's still burning."

"Horrible," Kerrie whimpered and Dana rushed to embrace her.

Deputy Bachman sagged against his ruined patrol car, swearing beneath his breath. "Three young kids at home and another on the way."

Dana's guilt was overpowering. If only she hadn't insisted on returning to search the Toliver cabin. A lump the size of a golf ball seemed to have lodged in her throat.

Nearly an hour later a patrol car pulled into the yard. When the deputy opened his door they heard a dispatcher's voice calling for volunteer firemen to extinguish the canyon blaze. There wasn't enough room for all of them to ride in the patrol car so Bachman volunteered to stay behind. He was advised to make himself as invisible as possible to get the drop on Toliver, if he returned that night.

The young deputy, whose name tag said G. B. Sterns, opened both doors to his patrol car and waved them all inside. During the trip down the mountain, he told them about the large area he and a handful of other deputies had to patrol. Thousands of rural roads in an agricultural county made it impossible to keep an eye on everything and everyone.

Kerrie asked which types of crimes happened most often and if he had any idea why someone would have a wolf vendetta.

"You'd be surprised by the number of theft reports and drugs in a ranching area, most of them originating in small towns. We had a gang of young men stealing the ranchers'

ATVs that they use for cattle herding. The money usually buys them drugs."

"Seems strange in small communities. What about the wolves? How long have the shootings been going on?"

"Wolf shootings have been taking place since ranchers have grazed sheep and cattle. But reports of vehicles getting shot at started about six months ago. The shooter disappears like a ghost and we haven't been able to find him. Whoever's doing it must live on the mountain."

Dana asked if Pete Toliver had been a suspect.

"He is now but I don't think anyone suspected him earlier. Especially after his father was killed."

The deputy dropped them off at the mansion, warning them to lock their doors and windows and to keep the yard lights on. He then left to return to the mountain. Tom walked over to pat a fender on his truck, obviously glad that he'd ridden with Jeff. At least he and Dana had transportation, but there was no guarantee the killer hadn't reached the mansion before them.

Walter drew his gun while Tom retrieved a rifle from his pickup. Tom crept toward the back of the property to check out the area as the sheriff entered the foyer. Minutes later, Walter declared the house safe to enter.

They all missed Bert and his wagging tail. It was time to check on him. Dana reached for the phone to call the clinic. A moment later she clicked off with tears in her eyes.

"Bert didn't make it," she said, choking on her words. "The vet tried to call while we were gone. Poor dear Bert."

Walter pulled her into his arms and held her while she cried. Jeff did the same for Sarah. The dog's death was a terrible blow and an end to a distressing day. Dana knew if the men present caught Toliver before the local deputies arrived, he would sport multiple bruises in his jail cell. Bloodied even and she would help them.

Tom arrived from the back entrance and Kerrie went into his arms. "What happened? Another break-in?"

When Kerrie told him that Bert had died, Tom's face mirrored his fury. "We've got to stop that maniac— somehow." Turning to Dana, he said, "I'm staying here until Toliver's arrested, if you don't mind, Miz Logan. I can use a sleeping bag until you buy new furniture."

She had been undecided until now but would acquire at least a sleeper sofa the following day.

Pulling herself from Walter's embrace, she said, "I'm relieved you offered. I have a feeling we haven't seen the last of Pete Toliver. He threatened to firebomb this house."

"I'm not going to let it happen, if I have to camp out in the flower bed."

Walter appeared crestfallen when Dana offered him the daybed in her office. The Logan-Cafferty hotel had no more vacancies.

Jeff advised Tom to park his pickup in the garage. They'd need to stand alternating night watches until Toliver was arrested. Kerrie reminded them of his accomplice and wondered why he hadn't been along when Pete tried to cremate them in the cabin.

"I have a feeling he's a student at the university," Dana said. "He may have thought playing a masked marauder was fun but balked at the killings. Pete Toliver is probably on his own."

Sarah wiped remaining tears from her eyes. "I hope he didn't kill the other young man to prevent him from talking."

"I wonder if Rhonda Bailey was his accomplice until he killed her. That would explain no shooter out back at the Toliver cabin. If he's crazy enough to kill a sheriff's deputy, I'm afraid *he's* gone over the edge. And we're apparently his last intended victims."

Jeff suggested protective custody for the women while he, Tom and Walter protected the house. Dana vetoed that idea but turned to glance at her companions. Kerrie and Sarah both shook their heads and she suspected that Marietta would insist on guarding the place with her own gun, if she were present.

"So it's settled," Dana said. "We'll either sleep in our clothes or keep them handy in case we have to evacuate the house. With all the security devices in place, I don't know how much more we can do."

Jeff smiled. "Keep the coffee pot plugged in. Tom, Walt and I can take three hour shifts during the night and you gals can watch from the windows during the day. There's no way Toliver's going to get by us."

"I wouldn't be too sure," Dana said. "He's already made some sneaky moves."

Apparently weary, Jeff sank into the nearest chair. "We know he's capable of just about anything, so we'll have to be prepared."

Dana checked her watch. "We need to pick up Marietta at the hospital and spend a little time with Gus. Who's going and who's guarding the house?"

Jeff glanced at Tom who nodded. He asked Kerrie if she would like to stay behind but she surprised everyone by saying she needed to talk to hospital authorities before she returned to Denver.

"I've got an extended cab," Tom said. "I think we can all fit comfortably inside."

"I'll stay," Jeff said. "Just make sure there's a replacement deputy on duty before you leave. I wouldn't put it past Toliver to take Gus out to prevent him from talking. Gus doesn't remember much but Pete doesn't know that."

Dana shivered, envisioning Pete attacking Gus in his hospital bed. "We'll alert the hospital about the danger,

Jeff, and I'll call you before we leave."

Jeff walked to the large bay window. The sun was setting which made it difficult to determine whether anyone was out there. He told them to stand by while he checked the yard. Tom took his cue and scanned the garage. Ten minutes later Jeff assured them the area was safe to leave.

"I'm beginning to feel that we're living in a war zone," Kerrie said. "All this because of one man."

"There could still be two of them," Jeff warned. "We don't know what's happened to Toliver's accomplice."

Another trip to the university seemed in order.

Chapter Twenty Two

Deputy Luvlie appeared to be dozing when they reached Gus's room. Walter used his night stick to tap the floor near her foot, causing her head to snap back from her chest.

"If you were one of *my* deputies, you'd be standing in the unemployment line."

"Do you know how boring this guard job is, Sheriff?"

He leaned to whisper, "Find another job."

They found Marietta sleeping in the chair next to Gus's bed. Dana thought someone must have sprinkled fairy dust over the entire area because the patient was also asleep with his hand firmly held in Marietta's.

Sarah smiled and Dana knew she was thinking how sweet they looked, although unprotected from a surprise attack from Pete Toliver. They couldn't depend on Luvlie to ward off a killer. Their only hope was that Pete liked Gus enough to spare his life. He could have killed him in the cabin and she didn't think he would risk arrest by attacking him in the hospital. He was probably searching for his drug stash—if that's what it was.

Dana feared that Pete would lose control when he found

the packages missing. She knew he would come looking for them when he found no bodies in his burned cabin. They should leave the hospital when Luvlie's replacement arrived.

Gus opened his eyes when she touched his arm. "Good to see ya, Miz Dana. You come to take Marietta home?"

"She needs some rest, Gus."

He turned his head to look at Marietta. "I wish I could convince her to marry me."

"I think she might be willing once this case is closed."

Marietta opened her eyes to smile at Gus. "Don't go getting your hopes up, old man. I have other suitors, you know."

Gus chuckled and winked at Dana. "Take care of her for me till I get outa here."

Marietta muttered, "I can take care of myself."

Walter appeared in Dana's peripheral vision. "The replacement deputy's here. I think we'd better get back to the mansion, don't you?" He shook hands with Gus and wished him well. Offering his hand to Marietta, he escorted her out of the room after she had planted a kiss on Gus.

Dana spotted Kerrie at the end of the hall talking to a doctor. She waved when her daughter looked up from her notes. Dana hoped the interview wouldn't take long. She was nervous about Jeff guarding the mansion alone. Walter held her hand as they strolled down the hall together. When they reached Kerrie, she was dropping her notepad into her purse. The doctor had just turned and walked away.

"Gus will leave the hospital in two days, if he continues to improve."

"Where will he stay, Kerrie? Certainly not in his cabin."

"We need to contact his son. Maybe Marietta knows

how to get in touch with him. He needs to convince Gus to stay with him when he leaves the hospital."

"Marietta mentioned that Charley didn't call today as he usually does to check on Gus's progress. I hope nothing's happened to him," Dana said.

"You don't suppose that Pete was able to track Charley down through Gus's computer. He might have emailed him and asked to meet somewhere. If he knows his stash has been confiscated, he might try to trade Charley for it."

"I doubt Toliver has had time to set up a meeting," Walter said. "But you're right. We need to call Gus's son to warn him."

Kerrie agreed. "But unless Toliver's a computer hacker, I doubt he could have accessed Gus's messages."

Marietta had walked down the hall to join them. Overhearing the last part of their conversation, she said, "Frank used the last of his savings to send Pete to college. That boy's a computer whiz. That is, he was before they kicked him out of school."

"Kicked out? Why?" Kerrie asked.

"Something to do with drugs."

"That settles it." Walter took out his own pad and began writing notes, as did Kerrie. "When did this happen?"

"Not long after his mother died."

Dana had felt sorry for the young man, but his later actions hardened her heart against him. Who was he going to kill next? She prayed it wasn't Gus's son.

Marietta didn't know Charley's email address or his phone number so she hurried back to Gus's room. The deputy stopped her, telling her that visiting hours were over. Walter went to her rescue although the night deputy wasn't impressed with Walter's out-of-state uniform.

"It's a matter of life and death," Walter said, his anger apparent. Fortunately, he towered over the younger man and outweighed him by at least fifty pounds. When the deputy relented, Sheriff Grayson entered the room and returned moments later with the information they needed. He punched in Charley Blake's number as soon as they left the hospital.

When Charley didn't answer, Walter left a message telling him not to respond to any messages from Gus's computer. He also asked that he return his call post haste. When he clicked off, the sheriff sighed. "I'm afraid you may be right, Dana. Toliver might have already reached Colorado and taken Charley hostage."

Marietta leaned from the backseat to say, "Those two never got along. I recall a time or two when they had bloody fist fights. Gus and Frank had to break them apart."

Dana winced. Poor unsuspecting Charley. "Shouldn't we call the highway patrol in both states to keep an eye out for Pete Toliver?"

"There's already an APB out on him," Walter said, "I'll call Sheriff Johnston and tell him what we suspect so they can alert everyone in the area."

A feeling of doom seemed to fill the car's interior. Were they too late? Dana stared into the darkness, her imagination gone wild.

"I almost forgot," Marietta said. "Charley married Amelia, Pete's high school sweetheart."

"That cinches it." Walter whipped out his cell phone and punched in a number on his contact list. When he finished filling in someone on the other end, he called Jeff and asked that he get in touch with his friend at the police department.

"Now what?" Marietta wanted to know.

Walter turned in the front seat to say, "We'll take you women home and drive down to Colorado."

"Oh, no you don't," Dana said. "We're going along."

Marietta begged off the trip. Claiming exhaustion,

she said she would keep Jeff company or take his place at the mansion. She reminded them of her excellent marksmanship.

Walter said, "You need your rest, young lady. Jeff won't mind holding down the fort while we're gone."

"You're a charmer," Marietta said. "I hope you're as good with your gun."

"Let's hope I won't need it."

"I think you ought to leave this to the Denver police."

The sheriff glanced at Dana. "I don't think I can talk Logan and Cafferty into sitting on the sidelines. And Kerrie needs to wrap up her news story."

When they reached the mansion, Kerrie returned her camera equipment and they left within minutes for Colorado with Jeff's warning to be careful echoing in their ears.

Sarah fell asleep shortly after they left but the others were too keyed to relax. They were already tired of traveling when they reached the Colorado border almost three hours later. Tom said it was another hour and a half to Charley's home. He still wasn't answering his phone and the sheriff stopped leaving messages. If Toliver was holding the family hostage, Walter didn't want to give him advanced warning.

"Do we have a plan?" Dana asked.

The two men exchanged glances before Walter lifted his cell phone. "The local police must have entered the house by now. I'll try calling the Denver County sheriff's office to get some information."

Dana held her breath until the call went through. She then listened as Walter questioned someone on duty. Offering his sympathy for the shootings at the Aurora movie theater, he asked whether Pete Toliver had been taken into custody. When he clicked off, he reported that Charley and his family were not at home and only one car was parked in the garage. There was no word on Toliver.

"Could Pete kidnap the entire family and leave with them?" Sarah asked.

"It's possible," Walter said. "If it were me, I'd ditch the Silverado that everyone's looking for and take one of Blake's vehicles."

Dana was worried. "You don't think he killed them and threw their bodies in the basement, or buried them down there, do you, Walter?"

"I'm sure the officers checked the basement, if they were able to get inside. And that many gunshots would have alerted the neighbors."

"What if the police couldn't get inside the house?"

"They'll get a search warrant and a locksmith. Or force their way in."

"Maybe Charley's taking his family to the hospital to surprise Gus."

"That's a distinct possibility but why isn't he answering his cell phone?"

The sheriff grumbled about making an unnecessary trip, but conceded that since they were nearly there, they might as well check things out. Finding the address in the dark was no small feat but they finally located the older frame house on a tree-lined avenue. Several cars were parked at the curb on either side of the street and Walter thought they were probably undercover agents.

When Tom parked his pickup, the sheriff walked over to the nearest car. He returned a few minutes later, reporting that there had been no activity since six o'clock when Denver police received a call to look for Toliver. There were two possibilities. Either Toliver tricked them into meeting him somewhere or the Blake's were on their way to see Gus.

"Actually, there are three things that could have happened," he said. "No one's been inside, so there could be bodies littering the place."

Dana's heart sank. "Why would he kill Charley's family?"

"Revenge," Walter said. "Who knows what motivates a psychopath?"

Should they sit and wait for a team of officers to enter the house or drive back to the mountain?

Walter flipped open his cell phone and called the Stanton County sheriff's office to report what he suspected. He then called Jeff at the mansion to fill him in on the latest developments and asked that he call his contact as soon as possible. Charley might be driving into a death trap, if Toliver wasn't already with him.

Dana wondered whether Pete would kill Charley's wife and children. His simmering hatred could erupt at any moment. He'd already killed a number of people and perhaps his partner, so Pete had nothing to lose.

"I think we'd better go back," Dana said. "There's nothing we can do here, but we may be able to intervene if Charley's family's held hostage."

The sheriff checked his watch. "I wouldn't think Blake would keep his kids out this late during the week, especially after that massive theater rampage. So they're either dead or held hostage." He nudged Tom who started the engine.

"Hold on a minute." Walter opened the pickup door and rushed over to hand a card to the nearest lawman. A moment later he was back telling Tom to drive to the interstate. There was no time to lose.

Dana settled back in the seat with a sigh. Another five hours of riding meant arriving home in the middle of the night. A pit stop at a service station and a good leg stretching was all that was going to save her and Sarah, who was already complaining of feet cramps. How did they get themselves into these situations?

Five hours later to the minute they arrived at the

mansion where they disembarked for a few hours' sleep. Tom was in favor of continuing on to Gus's cabin but Walter vetoed that notion, claiming extreme exhaustion. Their assault on the mountain cabin would have to wait a few hours.

At daybreak someone tapped at Dana's door. Grabbing her robe, she peered around the frame to find Walter fully dressed and ready to go. He said he understood if she was too tired to go along. She promised to be ready in minutes. She couldn't wake Sarah and reasoned that she'd be happier staying behind with Jeff. Hurrying into a pair of jeans and a tee shirt, she pulled on a pair of boots and rushed downstairs to find Kerrie sipping a cup of coffee. Tom was seated on a stool beside her with a mug of his own.

"I poured your coffee in the thermos, Mom. We'd better get going."

Walter beckoned to them from the doorway and they followed him into the garage. When they were seated in Tom's truck, the sheriff said he'd talked to someone at Stanton County who said a deputy had spent the night at Gus's cabin but they hadn't been able to reach him by radio or cell phone.

"I told them there's no cell or radio service at Gus's place although there is at the Tolivers. I think we'd better get up there to check it out."

Dana thought about the deputy Pete Toliver had already killed and worried that the current one had suffered a similar fate. Deputy Luvlie didn't know how lucky she was to be sitting guard duty.

She noticed that Kerrie was sitting unusually close to Tom on the front beach seat once they were on their way. Dana's smile evolved into a yawn. Walter had scooted close to her in the back seat and she leaned her head against his shoulder and promptly went to sleep. She awoke with a start when they pulled off the side of the road not far from Gus's cabin. Walter had eased her head from his shoulder and prepared to leave the truck. Tom did the same with Kerrie and warned them both to stay inside.

Dana pulled the Smith and Wesson from her purse and told Kerrie to climb into the back seat where they could watch the men's progress without being seen. The sun had cleared the mountain peaks and long shadows made it difficult to watch anyone moving about. So if Pete Toliver were standing watch, he would have the same problem. Fortunately, both men wore jeans and dark tee shirts.

They were back within fifteen minutes, reporting no vehicles or people in the area, including the deputy. Toliver might be hiding near his burned cabin.

Dana and Kerrie followed them when they hiked across country to the Toliver ranch. Crouching low in the underbrush, they waited while Tom and Walter checked out the area. They returned shaking their heads.

"Where's the deputy?" Dana said. "We didn't pass anyone on the road coming up the mountain."

Tom shrugged. "Maybe he went off duty and took another road out of here."

"Without a replacement?"

Walter reminded her that a deputy had been lost the previous day and that there had only been nine original deputies to patrol the entire county.

Dana stood to stretch to her full height. Where had everyone disappeared to? She then thought of Marietta's house and the vacation cabin where Pete Toliver had held his victims. She voiced her concerns to Walter.

"I guess we'd better check them out," he said, climbing back in the pickup. "Keep watch on both sides of the road on the way over there."

Tom's truck crept along the dirt road to prevent a billowing cloud of dust that would announce their approach. If Toliver *were* in the vicinity, he might be standing watch with binoculars.

Chapter Twenty Three

Marietta's ranch was several miles from the Toliver's, and it was full daylight when they pulled into the yard. The drapes were drawn and no other vehicles were in sight. Walter walked with gun drawn to the garage to determine whether any cars were inside. Tom served as his backup.

Marietta's marigolds were trampled beneath the window and her daisies were wilted and drooping. Dana noticed slight movement in the drapes at the broken window but attributed it to the wind. If Pete were inside, he would have opened fire by now. The men found the garage door locked and circled the house, both scowling. The front door was also locked so Walter followed Tom around back.

Dana rolled down the pickup window and listened but the only sounds were the songs of meadowlarks and snapping noises of grasshoppers.

Tom stood on his toes to peer through a side window. Shaking his head, he motioned to Walter to follow him to the pickup. When both men were seated, they decided to continue on to the vacation cabin.

"Do you think Pete returned to the place where he

killed his father?" Dana asked.

"I can't think of anywhere else he might have gone."

"Too bad Marietta's not along," Dana said. "She knows the mountain better than anyone."

Walter grimaced. "If Toliver's not at the next cabin, we'll find a high spot where we can reach her by cell phone. She might have some idea where he's gone."

Tom drove slowly along the dirt road so as not to raise a noticeable amount of dust. It took forever to reach the eastern slope of the mountain and it was nearly nine o'clock when they drove in sight of the cabin. Dana wondered whether the owners knew what had taken place at their vacation home while they were away.

The pickup parked in a copse of trees well off the narrow road. Tom and Walter then quietly left the truck to watch the cabin for several minutes before they crept across the road into tall buck brush. Walter signaled Tom before they crouched low and moved in opposite directions to circle the cabin.

"What'll we do if Toliver shoots them, Mom?"

"You'll find a place to call 911 while I go to help them."

"I won't let you get yourself killed. He's already murdered two deputies, three civilians and probably Charley and his family."

"We don't know that, Kerrie. The deputy may have followed him here and is in hiding watching the cabin."

"You're an incurable optimist, Mom."

A shot rang out and both women ducked. Dana felt she couldn't breathe as Kerrie screamed Tom's name. She held onto her daughter, preventing her from leaving the truck.

"Wait. We don't know who fired the shot. It could have been one of our guys."

"And if one of them's been killed?"

"The other will come back here."

Kerrie wrestled free of Dana's grip to climb over the seat and slide behind the wheel. Backing the truck further into the trees, she positioned the pickup so they could attempt escape, if Toliver appeared with his gun. She then pulled Tom's binoculars from the glove compartment and trained them on the cabin.

"What's happening?" Dana whispered.

"I can't see anything moving."

Dana rolled down her backseat window. "Keep watching. Someone has to make a move." She heard a rattling sound and noticed the garage door rising before a silver Honda SUV backed down the driveway.

"He's making a run for it." Kerrie started the engine and pulled forward.

"Wait for the men to return," Dana said.

"But he'll get away."

"We only have one handgun against his AK-47, Kerrie. We'll find a hotspot and call the sheriff so he can set up a roadblock."

Tom's pickup stopped and Kerrie shut off the engine. She was immediately out of the truck and running toward the cabin, her mother in close pursuit. When they found the front door open, Dana drew her gun. Calling Tom and Walter, she cautiously crossed the threshold. She found them in one of the bedrooms kneeling over four bodies. Tied and bound, they weren't moving.

"This one's got a pulse." Walter carefully pulled a strip of duct tape from the child's face.

"So's this one." Tom lifted a small girl with blond hair from the floor and placed her on the bed. Carefully untying her, he pulled the tape from her mouth. Sobbing uncontrollably, she shrank from his touch.

Dana and Kerrie crouched to help the two remaining victims, which they assumed were members of Charley's family. There was no sign of Charley, so Pete Toliver must have forced him into the Honda.

The woman was nearly incoherent when Walter removed the tape from her mouth. Her nose dripped blood as though it were broken. What had he done to her and the children?

"Help us," she pleaded.

All three children were crying, the small girl shrieking. Dana lifted her from the bed and placed her in her mother's arms. She and Kerrie then tried to comfort the two small boys.

While Tom left to call the local sheriff, Walter tried to question the woman, who confirmed that she was Amelia Blake After she had quieted her daughter, she told them what had happened.

"Pete called to tell us that Charley's dad was dying in a hospice and that he would meet us at the truck stop in Cheyenne. Charley doesn't trust Pete but before he could ask what had happened and where Gus was, the call was disconnected."

Dana asked, "So you left right away?"

"We were on the road within half an hour after packing a few clothes. When we got to Cheyenne, Pete was parked out back of the station and he pulled a gun and forced us to drive him here."

"How did he manage that?"

Tears streamed down Amelia's face as she held a tissue to wipe blood from her nose. "He made Charley drive with me holding Melissa on my lap in the front seat. He sat in back with the two boys holding a gun on all of us."

"Mean man," one of the boys said. "He was gonna shoot us."

"When we got here he made Charley tie us up and tape our mouths."

"Did Toliver hit you?" Kerrie asked.

"My own fault. I screamed at him to leave the children

alone and he backhanded me. I was afraid he'd kill Charley for trying to defend me, but he hit him on the head with the gun after Charley tied us up. Charley came to after Pete taped his hands behind his back."

"Lousy creep," Kerrie said. "That's obviously Toliver's MO."

Dana hugged the small boy who sat in her lap. "Thank the Lord we got here before he did anything worse."

Amelia looked about the room. "Where's Charley?"

Walter said, "I'm afraid he's with Toliver, ma'am, but we'll track them down."

"What happened?"

"I took a shot at Toliver through the window but I missed, so he took off with your husband in the SUV."

"Tom's calling it in to the sheriff's office," Kerrie told her. "They'll be waiting for him when he leaves the mountain."

"But what if he stays?"

Dana glanced at Walter. "The fishing lodge. I'll bet that's where he went."

"You're probably right, but we need to take them to the hospital before we go after Toliver."

Amelia insisted they were fine and would stay put while the sheriff rescued her husband. "Please hurry before he kills Charley."

Kerrie volunteered to stay with them while Dana accompanied Tom and Walter to the fishing lodge. Walter protested until she reminded him of her expertise in previous murder cases. Tom was back within fifteen minutes and they climbed into the truck as soon as he arrived.

Worried about Kerrie and the Blakes, Tom pulled a shotgun from behind the backseat and rushed into the cabin to leave the gun. After a brief demonstration on how to use it, he sprinted back to his truck.

Once he was seated, Dana asked if he remembered

how to find the fishing lodge. Tom's grim expression broke into a grin. "I used to camp in the area with my parents. It's about a twenty minute drive from here."

Walter asked if there was a way to sneak up on the lodge and was told they could hike along the bank until they reached the back porch, if they parked downstream. There were enough trees, undergrowth and buck brush around the lodge to hide a herd of deer.

The sun was nearly overhead and the temperature was rising. It was noon when Tom parked the truck under a stand of cottonwoods. Reaching into the glove box he handed them each a bandana for their foreheads to prevent perspiration from blinding them. They then started off single file with Tom in the lead.

The climb upslope was tiring but Dana's body was pumping enough adrenalin to scale a mountain. Gripping her Smith and Wesson, she wondered how much farther it could be? A moment later Tom dropped to his knees. Twisting toward them he held a finger to his lips and pointed into the distance. When they reached him, they crouched beside him and squinted toward the area he had indicated.

Sun glinted from a small patch of silver visible through the trees and Dana realized it was the Blake's SUV. They had discussed a plan of action once they reached the lodge but she wondered how they could actually pull it off, without putting Charley at risk. She had no doubt what Pete Toliver had in mind. His elaborate scheme had obviously been planned to kill not only his own father but Charley Blake as well. No wonder he hadn't killed Gus. He'd been using him as a decoy.

Walter signaled for Tom to circle around to the back of the lodge and for Dana to hide in the brush some hundred feet from their current position. He would then plant himself among the trees in front of the lodge. They had to draw Toliver out of doors where they could surround him. From her position, Dana watched Tom duck beneath the back porch which overhung the sloping bank. Lobbing a rock onto the deck, he ducked back under the rotting wooden structure. She could hear rusty hinges squeak as a door swung open, but couldn't see anyone on the porch. After a brief moment the door slammed shut. Had Pete been alerted to their presence? There had to be a better way to draw him out.

From the corner of her eye she watched Walter step from behind the trees to hurl something at the front porch. She waited for the door to open. Instead, she heard the sound of breaking glass and saw a gun barrel protrude through the window. A rapid series of gunshots riddled the trees where Walter had been standing. Breathless, she noticed Walter flatten himself in the brush. More gunshots penetrated the trees and undergrowth.

Had Walter been wounded? Gripping a rock at her side, she hurled it at the window and ducked back into the buck brush. Crawling away from her previous position, she peered at the back porch, where she watched Tom swing onto the rotting deck. With his gun drawn, he kicked at the back door.

Heart threatening to pound from her chest, Dana continued to crawl away from the gunman's line of fire. She could no longer see Tom but heard a burst of gunfire from inside the lodge. Had Tom been killed? Dana bit her lip to prevent herself from shrieking. She glanced back to Walter's last position and was unable to locate him. Was he still alive? She then heard a man's voice yelling from the front of the lodge and crawled back far enough to peer at the porch.

Pete Toliver held his gun to Tom's head and pushed him toward the SUV. Tom's arm was a bright patch of red as he stumbled toward the Honda. She was too far away to get off a clear shot without risking killing Tom.

"Stay back and don't shoot or I'll kill your buddy," Pete yelled as he shoved Tom inside the Honda.

Where was Walter and what was he planning? And what had happened to Charley? He must be dead.

Hesitating, she watched Tom back the SUV down the lane and negotiate a turn that had the Honda facing the dirt road. As they drove out of sight, she heard noises that sounded like breaking glass and tires screeching to a halt. Up and running, she raced after them. When she reached the SUV, she found that Walter had jerked the passenger door open and pulled Toliver from his seat. The windshield was broken and a large rock rested on the seat. Tom had his head on the steering wheel and Dana rushed to help him. He'd lost a lot of blood and needed medical attention.

Pulling the bandana from her head, she used it as a tourniquet to stop the bleeding. She then helped Tom into the back seat. Pulling her cell phone from her back pocket, she was surprised to find two bars of service. Calling 911, she asked the dispatcher to send a flight for life helicopter to meet them at the vacationer's cabin. There wasn't a clear space for a chopper to land anywhere near the lodge.

Walter pulled a pair of handcuffs from his pocket and spread-eagled Toliver on the ground. He told Dana to find rope in the lodge and to hurry back. Afraid of what she might find, she pushed the front door open and searched the lodge for Charley. She found him unconscious in one of the bedrooms, the back of his head a bloody mess. His hands and feet were tied but Pete hadn't taken time to gag him.

She could find nothing resembling a rope so she stripped a bed and tore strips of muslin to braid as a short rope. When she had tied off both ends, Dana ran back to the SUV and told Walter that Charley needed help. As soon as he'd tied Toliver's feet, he picked him up and placed him face down in the back of the SUV. After checking on Tom, Walter backed the Honda to the lodge. There he and Dana bandaged Charley's head with remnants of the torn sheet and carried him to the Honda. If there was a speed limit, Walter exceeded it as he drove back to the vacationers' cabin.

The helicopter was waiting when they arrived. Kerrie and Charley's family stood back, crouching to avoid the worst of the rotor wash. Walter pulled up next to the loading bay and Charley and Tom were loaded aboard following hugs from Amelia and Kerrie.

When the chopper lifted off, Walter unlocked the Honda's back door to check on Pete Toliver. When the killer began to swear, he used his bandana to gag him. The kids didn't need to hear what he had to say.

Charley's family climbed into their sports utility vehicle with Walter at the wheel. Within minutes they were on their way to deliver Pete Toliver to the county jail.

Dana worried where to house everyone. She then remembered that Jeff would no longer be needed and Kerrie would take the first plane back to Denver in the morning to finish her feature story. As soon as Gus was out of the hospital, Marietta would return home. And Walter had no reason to stay. So the Logan Hotel would soon become a taxi service.

There was still the missing partner and the need to retrieve Jeff's car from the Toliver cabin. Gus's cabin needed a major overhaul—as did Marietta's—and his new wolf clinic had to be built. Dana smiled and rested her head against the seat back for the ride home.

Chapter Twenty Four

Next morning Dana asked Kerrie about her future plans as she drove her to the airport. She was puzzled by the wry expression on her daughter's face. Kerrie was noncommittal although she talked about the feature article she was writing for City Magazine.

"What about Roger?"

"He seems to have developed an ailment known as cold feet," Kerrie said.

"So the engagement's off?"

"As far as I'm concerned it is."

Dana hesitated. "What about Tom?"

"As soon as his arm heals he'll drive to Denver to look for a job."

"So you plan to stay on at the magazine?"

Kerrie smiled. "Maybe. We'll see what develops. Who knows? We might come back to Wyoming."

"That would make me happy."

"What about all your guests? You really need a housekeeper, Mom."

"They'll be leaving as soon as Charley's out of the

hospital. Then Sarah and I will help Gus and Marietta get resettled."

Kerrie laughed. "From what I've observed, they'll only need one house from now on, although Marietta's playing hard to get."

"I think they know they need each other."

"What about you and Walter?"

"He's retiring next month and I can't stop him from moving to Wyoming."

"That's not an answer, Mom. Are you going to marry him?"

"To quote my daughter, 'Who knows?'"

"Not to change the subject, but are you serious about selling the mansion?"

Dana hesitated because she hadn't made up her mind. "I love it here in Wyoming, but the mansion seems to be jinxed. First, your Aunt Georgi is murdered, then a terrorist breaks in while we were gone and the drug gang vandalizes the house twice. And it happened again this week. What would you do?"

"I'd consider my bad luck over and make repairs and stay."

"Are you trying to tell me something, dear?"

Kerrie smiled again. "If you move back to California and I move here—"

"Aha, so you *are* considering marrying Tom."

"Could be."

"Has he asked?"

"Not yet but he will."

"Pretty sure of yourself, aren't you?"

Dana's cell phone rang and she recognized Walter's voice. "After you see Kerrie off on her plane, would you mind making another run to the airport?"

"Something important brewing in Modesto?"

"I'm afraid so. I'll have to stay there the three weeks

I have left until I retire."

Only three weeks? Dana's fingers tightened on the wheel.

"By the way, love. I think you should get yourself another dog. I know you're not over Bert yet, but I woke up this morning remembering Frank Toliver's wolf dog and thought you might like to adopt her."

"A great idea if we can locate her. I hope she hasn't starved to death. I wondered about Gus's cat too. Wouldn't he be happy if we were able to locate him?"

She heard the sheriff chuckle on the other end of the line.

"You're an incurable caretaker, Dana. That's one of the things I love about you."

Dana pulled into the airport parking lot and told Walter she would see him soon. Clicking off, she helped Kerrie unload her luggage from the Jeep. They no longer needed camouflaged transportation and she would think about acquiring another SUV.

* * *

After seeing Walter off at the airport, Logan & Cafferty made one more trip to the mountain in search of the missing pets. Dana vowed that it was their last trip and Sarah agreed that she'd had enough of Mother Nature. They decided to look for Frank's dog near the burned out cabin, hoping that Pete hadn't shot the animals and buried them.

"I doubt he buried them," Sarah said. "That's not his modus operandi."

"You're right. He didn't bother to bury all the wolves he killed."

They left the Jeep with a package of sirloin steak for Jenny and a packet of food for Gus's cat. The entire area still reeked of ashes and smoke, which had probably repelled the animals. They unwrapped their purchases and sat on flat rocks to wait.

"I wonder what happened to Gladys and Frank Toliver's truck."

Sarah frowned. "You don't think the animals were left in their respective pickups to die, do you?"

"The last time we were here, there were a couple of signal bars." Dana pulled out her cell phone and punched in the Stanton County sheriff's number. When someone answered she asked if the pickup trucks had been found. After a few moments, a deputy confirmed that the trucks had been spotted in a canyon not far from the vacationer's cabin on the eastern slope, but hadn't been recovered.

Dana clicked off smiling. "Wrap that meat and let's go. Good thing we wore our hiking boots and brought some water." She worried the pets had not survived in the heat without food or water. It had been three days since Gus had been found but they didn't know how long he'd been bound and gagged in the cabin.

They began their search when they were within sight of the vacation cabin. Walking along the dirt road in opposite directions, they peered into the canyon, which wasn't as deep as Dana had feared. A few minutes into their search she heard Sarah whistle and jogged around the bend to see her pointing downward. Frank's pickup truck was lodged in a depression, its bumper caught by a large pine tree. Gladys had suffered a similar fate when it struck another tree. Dana thought it was a miracle the old truck hadn't caught fire.

"I thought I heard a dog bark when I whistled for you, Dana."

"Whistle again. It's probably Jenny calling for help."

They both heard the dog bark after Sarah's second whistle. Dana took a step forward and nearly lost her balance when the earth crumbled beneath her feet.

Sarah asked how they could get down there.

"Slide on our backsides," Dana said.

"How about getting back up?"

"We need to find a rope."

They scanned the area for some sign of a vacationing cabin owner. No one seemed to be around. Dana hated to leave the animals stranded while they found someone to help, but it seemed their only option. Why hadn't they thought to bring along a rope?

"Too bad there isn't another Gus Blake cruising the dirt roads looking for—"

"Speak of the devil, Sarah." Dana pointed to a cloud of dust on the road they had just traveled. She said a quick prayer that the vehicle was headed their way. Sure enough, an old pickup truck came into sight. Not as old or rusty as Gladys, but the man behind the wheel was about Gus's age. Talk about déjà vu.

"Got a rope?" Sarah asked when the old truck pulled alongside.

"I have one in the back," the old man said. "Whatcha need it for, girlie?"

Sarah laughed. "Are you related to Gus Blake by any chance?"

"I'm Ben Blake," he said, extending a questionable hand. "Gus's my first cousin. How'd you know?"

"Your cousin's in the hospital. Maybe you ought to go and see him."

"I heard about that and figured I oughta visit the old geezer."

Sarah laughed. "Old geezer?"

"Yeah, he's a coupla months older'n me."

Dana walked up to the driver's door to explain their need for a rope. She then pointed to the canyon. Ben Blake reluctantly left his truck and sauntered over to the edge. Recognizing Gladys, he asked why they'd bother to pull it out of the canyon.

"That's not our plan." Dana told him they needed to rescue the trapped animals.

"Why didn't you say so sooner." Sauntering back to his truck, he pulled a long greasy coiled rope from the bed of his truck, asking who was going to climb into the canyon. Dana knew Sarah was out of shape so she volunteered. She watched as he drove close to the edge and tied one end of the rope to his bumper hitch. He then attached the other end to her waist.

This is a really fine idea. Holding her breath, Dana plotted her course to the trucks, which were only a few feet apart. Digging in her heels, she used a broken limb she found along the road to aid her balance. Then, as Ben played out a small amount of rope, she climbed and slid her way to Frank Toliver's truck.

The door was locked and Jenny was whimpering with her paws on the glass. The window had been lowered several inches, so Pete Toliver wasn't totally heartless. He had played with the dog since it was a pup so he must have some feelings for the wolf named for his mother.

Dana tried to unlock the door by squeezing her arm between the glass and door frame. When that failed, she picked up a palm-sized rock and made her way to the passenger side. Telling Jenny to sit, she hit the glass three times before it shattered. She then used the limb to punch a hole large enough to run her arm through. When the door unlocked she pulled her arm back and noticed it was bleeding. It didn't matter. The dog was safe.

Jenny still wore a leash so she hooked the end to the bumper hitch and went in search of Gus's cat. Rubbing her bleeding arm on her jeans, she peered inside the old truck. When she tried the door, it creaked open. Gladys was so old that the locks had rusted. The cat was crouched on the back corner of the passenger seat, so Dana walked around the truck and opened the door. By that time the cat had moved to the other side.

She should have pocketed some cat food before she made her descent. Dana didn't know the cat's name but it probably wouldn't have mattered. She climbed onto the passenger seat and tried to close the door but the rope attached to her waist prevented it. Her arm was dripping blood again and all she needed were cat scratches to add to her injuries. Dana was a dog person and had never owned a cat, so how was she going to persuade the feline to accompany her? She thought of Sarah, who was afraid of cats, especially one as large as this one.

Jenny was barking and she knew she couldn't take both animals up the embankment at the same time. She'd take the dog first and get some first aid for her arm. She'd then return with cat food. Climbing out of the truck, she signaled Ben Blake that she was bringing the dog, and hoped he wouldn't try to pull them up too fast. The old man looked a bit frail and would probably need Sarah's help.

It was then she noticed an old gray van further down the canyon and almost hidden in undergrowth. Could it be the one they had seen at Gus's place when the two masked men left with his computer?

Dana didn't think there was enough rope to reach the van so she untied herself and yelled that she was going to investigate. She heard Sarah yell no, but she was already sliding down the embankment, grabbing roots and bushes to keep her from tumbling to the canyon floor.

When she reached the van she found it unlocked. Carefully reaching into the glove compartment on the passenger side, she found the registration and insurance cards. The van was registered to Rhonda Bailey. Shocked, she sat down beside the van and reread the cards.

She decided to conduct a brief inspection of the van

for further evidence and found an envelope under the front seat. Pete Toliver's name was surrounded by a large heart. The envelope wasn't sealed so she opened it. Inside was a note from Rhonda.

Dear Pete,
You must know that I love you but I'm tired of all this wolf killing. I don't know why you think it's necessary to cover up the drug sales and I'm tired of that too. No one else wants any part of your plans and I can't persuade them to take part in any more rallies.
Please leave the mountain and come live with me in Laramie.
Rhonda

Pete must have read the note and decided that Rhonda was a liability, especially after her stay in the hospital. She had to have been his only partner in crime. Stuffing the cards and note in her back pocket, Dana prepared to climb up the canyon wall to the site where she had left the rope.

She was definitely feeling her sixty years although she considered herself in good shape. Hands scratched and bleeding, Dana at last reached the area where she had left the rope and Jenny tied to Toliver's bumper hitch. Retying the rope to her waist, she signaled Sarah and Ben to pull her up to the road.

Jenny seemed happy to climb out of the canyon and Dana looped her leash around her uninjured arm. Some ten minutes later they were both sitting on the edge of the road, the dog licking Dana's face. Sarah poured water into the pan they'd brought along and watched as the dog lapped it up. She then offered Jenny a small steak.

Like his cousin Gus, Ben had a first aid kit in his truck and skillfully applied antiseptic and a bandage to Dana's arm. She looked back into the canyon and dreaded another trip down. But it was Gus's cat and it needed rescuing, whether it wanted her help or not.

Sarah handed her a packet of cat food, which she stuffed in a pocket. When she started back down, she realized that she had forgotten to close Gladys's passenger door. What she feared most had happened. The cat had leaped out and disappeared. There was only one thing to do. She tore open the cat food package and left a trail up the side of the canyon as she climbed out. She knew Sarah would be afraid to grab the cat but maybe Ben wouldn't mind. Dana would probably have to capture the cat herself as she sat on the canyon rim.

Jenny licked her face as Dana petted her. What a lovely wolf dog. If Bert was looking down on them, she was sure he would approve.

Sarah groaned as she sat down beside her. Placing an arm around her shoulder, she said, "I'm sure glad you like dogs and wolves."

"Why?"

"Because you're going to have to build a kennel behind the mansion."

Dana laughed. "Jenny can stay in the house. She doesn't need a kennel."

Sarah pulled the leash so that Dana could view the dog in profile. "Haven't you noticed? We're going to be grandparents?"

* * *

If you enjoyed *Gray Wolf Mountain*, you may also like to sample a chapter from each of the other Logan & Cafferty mysteries.

A Village Shattered
Diary of Murder
Murder on the Interstate

A Village Shattered

Chapter 1

Alice's porch light always served as a beacon on Saturday nights, but her house at the end of Mulberry Lane was as dark as a mausoleum. Dana eased her car along the curb and stopped in front of the house. Her dashboard clock said 7:46, so they were only a minute late.

"Something's wrong, Sarah."

Her companion leaned to have a better look. "You're right. Alice would never miss bingo night, unless..."

Dana retrieved a flashlight from beneath the driver's seat. It was then she noticed that all the houses on Alice's street were dark. "How strange," she said, opening the Audi's door. "There hasn't been a brown-out in the village in years."

"Harold must have driven his pickup into one of the power poles."

Envisioning the village's "Mister Magoo," Dana wondered how Harold Samuels had renewed his driver's license. He was much too vain for glasses, and contacts were more than he could manage. Her attention returned to the house. Momentarily scanning the windows for candlelight, she started up the walk, leaves crunching underfoot. The door should be open by now. Alice was always anxious to get there early.

They hesitated on the edge of the jungle Alice called a garden. A giant willow stood dead center in the overgrown tangle of plants, its weeping limbs restless in the evening breeze. The camellias were tall enough to hide a mountain lion, but it was something considerably smaller that streaked past.

Dana turned to track the animal's path. Her flashlight caught two gold eyes peering from behind Sarah's legs. Sighing, Dana knelt to scoop up Alice's cat.

"It's only Mr. Tiger."

"What's he doing out here?" her friend said as she backed away. "Alice never lets him roam at night."

"Something's definitely wrong." Dana prayed it wasn't another heart attack. She tucked the cat beneath her arm and stepped onto the porch. Ringing the bell, they waited long moments for someone to answer. Rummaging through her purse, she found the key Alice had recently given her. When the door creaked open, an overpowering sweet smell greeted them. Sarah held a tissue to her nose and shrieked, "Alliicceee?" in a voice pitched high enough to crack the entry glass.

Dana flipped a switch along the foyer wall. When a lamp failed to light, she flashed her beam around the living room. The coffee table was overturned, knickknacks scattered and broken. The room resembled a miniature battlefield.

Alice was there among the rubble. Face down on her green Berber rug, she clutched a short, knotted cord in her bloated hand. A shattered lamp lay on the floor, its slivers gleaming in her snowy hair. Slowly kneeling beside her, Dana searched for a pulse she sensed wasn't there. "She's gone, Sarah."

"But who would kill sweet Alice?"

Dana felt her throat constrict and made no attempt to reply.

"Everybody loved her."

"Not quite everyone."

A cold, nauseous lump settled in Dana's rib cage. Get a grip, she told herself. You've got to remember the crime scene. Reading glasses were on the floor with the novel Alice had been reading. They knew she watched the

2

afternoon soaps, so she must have died that morning.

Sarah lifted the phone with a soggy tissue. Using a pen, she punched in 911. Moments later she concluded the line was as dead as Alice.

Despite her bulk, their friend had put up quite a struggle. She apparently tried to escape to the kitchen when struck with the lamp from behind. Dana's stomach tied itself in knots. Struggling to her feet, she signaled Sarah to follow. They skirted what they considered evidence and cautiously left through the foyer. After locking and testing the door, they made their way to the car. They then noticed that lights were on and the neighbors were filing into the recreation hall, Alice's favorite hangout. The killer must have known the body would be found on bingo night, unless a stranger had committed the murder.

A light mist settled over the red-tiled roofs of the Valley Retirement Village. As the night deepened, tule fog would form an opaque mist. Dana vowed every fall to leave the San Joaquin Valley, but she couldn't leave her friends. They had saved her from the black hole she'd fallen into when Earl died. Her mystery novels also helped fill the void left by her husband's death.

Dana glanced down at her chubby friend, who seemed to be hyperventilating. Worried, she said, "First, a quick cup of chai tea. Then we'll call the sheriff."

* * *

Sheriff Walter Grayson stood like a military guard. Well over six feet, his once-impressive chest had lost the war with gravity. Most middle-aged men acquired some social polish, but the newly-elected sheriff had all the charms of film patrolman, Robocop. Even his voice was robotic.

"We're not suspects," Dana sputtered. "Sarah and I play bingo with Alice every Saturday night."

Disbelief registered in his heavy, arched brow.

"Not much happens here on weekends when you live a mile from town. Especially when the fog rolls in." Dana wondered why she was making excuses. They had nothing to hide.

The sheriff lifted a notepad from his crisp uniform pocket, his pen ready for answers. "Your full names, ages, and addresses?" he said.

"What does age have to do with the murder?"

"Routine questions, ma'am."

She hesitated long enough to make the sheriff scowl. "Dana Marie Logan. I'm...fifty-nine and I live here in the village." She waited for him to ask for her social security number. Before long they would be tattooed on everyone's wrists.

"You don't look old enough for a retirement village," he said.

"My husband was sixty-seven when he died two years ago."

"I see." He abruptly turned to Sarah. "And you, ma'am?"

"Sarah Anne Cafferty. I'm the same age as Dana. My husband, Terry, was sixty-four when lightning struck him last fall. He was swinging a five iron on the village course."

"How long'd you know Alice Zimmer?"

"Several years." Dana was acutely aware of the sheriff's impatience. "We're all members of the Sew and So Club."

"So and So?"

"Needlework and gossip." Dana pantomimed sewing.

"I want all the members' names. And her friends while you're at it."

"They're one and the same, Sheriff." Dana listed nine women, including herself and Sarah.

"The two of you break in the Zimmer house together?"

"Alice gave us keys. She was afraid of another heart attack."

4

"Everybody in the club have one?"

"Just Lana, Sarah, and I."

"Three with opportunity." He continued scribbling.

"You can't suspect us." Sarah's voice was shrill. "Alice was our friend."

"Everybody's suspect, Miz Cafferty. Where were you all day?"

"Home," she said indignantly.

"Together?"

"We talked on the phone. I was telling Dana—"

"No alibis," he said, without looking up.

Before they could protest, he asked when they had last talked to the victim.

"Last evening," Dana said, glaring. "Sew and Sos met at her house."

"Any squabbling at the meeting?"

"No, Sheriff, we all get along quite well."

"The Zimmer woman must have had an enemy."

"Alice was well liked in the village. That's what makes her death so baffling."

* * *

Settled among her sofa pillows, Dana watched as Sarah scanned the floor-to-ceiling bookcases.

"You have enough mystery novels to start your own bookstore, Dana. How many do you read a week?"

"Two or three."

"Looks like everything Doyle and Christie ever wrote."

"You'll find contemporary writers as well: Hart, Clark, Grafton, Leonard, Sayers—"

Sarah thoughtfully sipped her tea. "They can help us solve the murder."

"How?"

"We know more about sleuthing than that newbie sheriff ever will."

5

"That doesn't give us the right to snoop."

"All those mystery novels you've read," Sarah said, "and the tons of reports I typed for Terry—"

Dana envisioned the pink marble urn containing Terry's ashes, which *rested* on Sarah's mantle. Terry Cafferty had been an anomaly, an unassuming P.I. with one apparent vice, an occasional pipe bowl of Prince Albert.

"...and between us, we can track down Alice's killer."

"This isn't a 'Murder, She Wrote' board game we're playing, Sarah. Suppose the killer discovers us first?"

"We'll be careful."

She obviously wasn't herself so Dana decided to humor her. "Let's discuss the case with Terry. A private investigator's advice is exactly what we need."

"A séance, you mean?"

"Our resident psychic conducts them on a regular basis."

"Tamara?"

"She even owns a crystal ball."

Sarah shook her head, apparently dismissing that idea. "We don't look like detectives, so no one would suspect us of investigating the murder."

Dana surveyed her friend's double chin and glittering light blue eyes. "You do resemble Shelly Winters more than Angela Lansbury."

Sarah mimicked the actress. "And you, Logan? A mature Geena Davis."

Dana deliberately dimpled her cheeks, although she wasn't up to smiling. "All right, where do we start?"

"Suspects."

"I can't think of anyone who'd want to kill Alice."

"I can."

"Who?"

"Harold Samuels."

"You can't be serious."

"Remember that sweet smell in Alice's house?"

Dana nodded.

"She's allergic to perfume."

"That's right, she was."

"Kind of smelled like Harold."

"That horse liniment he wears?"

"Harold's bursitis gave him away."

"Honestly, Sarah, how many seniors use arthritic rubs?" Dana answered the question herself. "Nearly everyone."

"Harold must've killed her."

Dana recalled an argument between them at a recent garage sale. "Harold argues with everyone, including Pastor Williams."

"Alice slapped him a good one when he wrestled that trowel away from her. I've never seen her so mad."

"That's still no reason to kill."

"It might've been enough for the village grump."

Dana shook her head in exasperation. "How do you plan to prove your theory?"

"Return to the crime scene and take another whiff."

"The strangest thing I saw," Dana said, attempting to distract her, "was that cord in Alice's hand. She could have snatched it from the killer, and he panicked and used the lamp."

"Harold could've dropped something."

"The police have sealed the house by now. We'd be suspects if they caught us snooping."

"Set your alarm for three o'clock, and don't forget your sneakers. They make 'em in size thirteen, don't they?"

"Eleven-and-a-half, you mush melon. They're hard to find in my size."

"Then wear that old pair of Earl's you use for gardening." Sarah's impish grin dissolved into a determined line. "If you're not up by 3:15, I'll go alone."

Worried, Dana agreed. Her friend was stubborn

enough to investigate on her own, and she thought she knew why. Sarah had understudied her husband for years, just waiting to play detective.

* * *

Both women dressed in dark clothing, each pocketing Terry Cafferty's investigative tools. Heavy flashlights would serve as weapons as well as illuminate the crime scene. The dense fog made Dana claustrophobic, but it didn't deter her friend. Sarah was like an eager child equipped with a magnifying glass.

When they reached Alice's house, yellow crime tape blocked their paths. Carefully ducking beneath the barrier, they stopped for a moment to listen. Satisfied they were alone, Dana fumbled in her pocket, wondering why the sheriff had not impounded their keys. She removed her gloves and crouched to find the keyhole.

"Terry will vacate his urn," she whispered, "when he finds out what we're doing."

The night air was cold and damp, but perspiration trickled from beneath Dana's knit cap, a reminder of the felony they were committing. Her hands trembled as she inserted the key in the lock. At last the tumblers fell and the door swung open, but her friend hesitated on the threshold.

"Where's the cat?" Sarah whispered.

"They must have taken him to the animal shelter." Dana sighed as she nudged Sarah inside. Her fear of felines was a long-standing village joke. Once in the foyer, they switched on flashlights, directing their beams at the floor. Dana cringed when she noticed the chalked outline of Alice's body. The procedure was unnecessary if the body had not been moved, but the inexperienced sheriff must carry his own chalk.

"That sweet smell's gone, Logan."

"It probably aired out when the crime team was here."

"I wonder why they didn't clean up all this fingerprint powder." Sarah swung her light along the baseboards. "Let's search for anything missing."

"Alice's silver tea service is still in place. A burglar would have taken it."

"Somebody might have scared him off."

Dana focused her light on a freestanding bookcase. The contents appeared to have survived an earthquake.

"Her scrapbooks were kept there."

"Why would the killer want them?"

"Sheriff probably took them," Sarah said as she led the way to Alice's bedroom.

Although nothing seemed out of place, the closet door was open. Clothing had been pushed aside and shoes were scattered on the floor.

"Alice's silk blouses are falling off the hangers."

"The bureau drawers have also been searched." Furious, Dana imagined the killer rummaging through Alice's queen-sized underwear. Or had it been the sheriff?

* * *

Dana crouched beneath a window, attempting to peer inside. Dense fog pressed in from all sides, squeezing the air from her lungs. Her peripheral vision picked up a vague figure moving toward her in the fog. An upraised lamp glinted faintly in the haloed street light. Before she could scream, a telephone rang on the sill beside her head. Groping for the receiver, she pulled it to her ear.

Sarah's voice, high-pitched and yawning, jarred her fully awake. "Breakfast, Logan? Crepes are ready for the pan."

"Good grief, Cafferty, don't you ever sleep?"

"Bring some blackberry tea, will you?"

Dana berated herself for agreeing to Sarah's crazy

scheme. She would convince her—gently, of course—that tampering with the crime scene could earn them time in jail. Rehearsing her lecture, she slipped on pale green sweats. Her ancient sociology degree had not prepared her for sabotage, but Sarah's obsession with solving the murder could get them both killed. She'd have to persuade her to investigate from a distance.

Sarah was smiling when she answered the door wearing a new fuchsia pantsuit and stained butcher's apron. *Dana's* mood lightened in response. Reasoning with her friend would be easier than she anticipated. She followed her into the small orange and white kitchen. Better to wait until after breakfast, she decided. She would talk to her later about her diet.

Sarah was buttering her third piece of toast when the doorbell rang. Dana waited at the table, finishing her tea. Recognizing the monotone voice, she braced herself for further questioning. She wondered whether the robotic sheriff had been assembled in Silicone Valley. She much preferred Ed McBain's fictional Detective Carella.

Once they were seated in the living room, the sheriff asked how well they knew Betty Wilson.

Sarah said, "She's a Sew and So, Sheriff."

He scrutinized them both. "When's the last time you saw her."

Sarah's hand crumpled the front of her fuchsia blouse. "You don't mean—?"

"Just answer the question."

"When was it, Dana?"

"Yesterday afternoon. Betty was fine."

When Dana pressed, the sheriff admitted that Betty had disappeared. Her husband reported her missing at midnight when she failed to return from bingo.

She sensed Sarah's anxiety and slid an arm around her shoulder.

"I strongly advise you to keep your doors locked until the perpetrator's arrested," he said. "If you have to go out, use the buddy system."

"We're no longer suspects, Sheriff?" Dana noticed he had relaxed his rigid stance.

Ignoring her question, he cautioned them again about security.

Once the door was double-locked behind him, Sarah insisted, "We've got to find Betty."

* * *

Diary of Murder

Chapter 1

"There's nothing worse than a Rocky Mountain blizzard," Dana complained. "Not even our San Joaquin Valley fog."

Her friend whimpered like a frightened puppy when the motorhome swerved on the ice. A massive storm had assaulted them without warning, spattering the windshield with flakes the size of sand dollars. They had already decided that March was *not* the month to travel Colorado.

"We should have listened to the weather report."

"That wouldn't have stopped me, Sarah. I have to know why Georgi died."

"But they said it was suicide." Sarah's grip on the safety handle was turning her fingers blue.

"My sister would never have taken her own life, and I'm going to prove it."

"If we don't get off this highway soon, we're going to kill *ourselves*."

Dana lifted her foot from the accelerator. "If I pull off now, we could wind up in a ditch. Or hit by an eighteen wheeler." Activating emergency lights, she squinted to locate the center line, which had already disappeared under a thickening layer of snow.

Snowfall increased, forcing Dana to adjust the wipers. At their highest speed, they clattered like a band of castanets. The motorhome swayed, causing something to crash to the floor behind them.

"My laptop," Sarah wailed. "I forgot to put it away."

Snow was swamping the wipers. Their only hope was to prevent the coach from leaving the northbound, two-lane highway. Wind had picked up, driving snow in hypnotic swirls. Nauseated, Dana blinked repeatedly, feeling trapped inside a kaleidoscope. Snow was falling so heavily that it seemed they were standing still.

"We'll never get out of this," Sarah shouted over the wiper's clattering noise.

"Sure we will," she shouted back, doubting her own words. "Watch for exit signs and delineator posts."

"I can't see until we're on them, Dana." Her voice bordered on hysteria.

The lonely stretch of interstate between Denver and the Wyoming border had already drifted in, with visibility reduced to less than twenty feet. If they managed to survive, Dana vowed she would never leave an RV Park again, without first checking the weather. A brief glance at the temperature gauge told her it was twelve degrees. So why did she feel that she had just stepped out of the shower?

Hours seemed to pass before visibility increased. Then intermittent lights appeared in the midst of a blinding whiteout.

"Snowplow," Sarah said. "Stay a ways behind him."

"Or her."

"Women don't drive snowplows, Dana. At least not while I lived in Nebraska."

"That was before the snowplow was invented, Sarah."

Their laughter helped to relieve the stress, but Dana's fingers would have to be pried from the wheel when they reached their destination. *If* they reached it.

"Steer into a skid," her friend advised. "At least I remember that much."

"Maybe you'd like to drive."

"No, no, you're doing fine." Peering through the side window, Sarah said, "An off ramp should be coming up soon. I can't wait to wade through all that white stuff in my tennis shoes."

"And I can't wait to reach Wyoming." Dana swallowed a lump in her throat when she thought of her sister Georgi.

Snow had tapered off by the time they reached Cheyenne, where an early lunch at a truck stop revived them. Sarah replaced her shoes with boots while Dana fueled the motorhome. Impatient to resume their trip, she hurriedly removed ice from the wipers and swiped at the windshield. Road grime coated the front of her parka and their new RV appeared to have developed Progeria, rapid aging disease. Dana sighed, feeling a similar fate.

Snowflakes disappeared a few miles north of Wheatland, and she relaxed enough to loosen her grip on the wheel. Checking the map, Sarah said they had less than two hours remaining. Reaching across the console to pat Dana's arm, she said, "Illnesses often cause people to react in strange ways."

"Georgi would have told me if she were sick."

"Tell me again what her husband said."

"Rob was nearly incoherent when he called. He found her in bed when he arrived home at noon. Georgi was still in her nightgown and had a hand to her throat as though she were choking."

"What kind of sickness would cause that?"

"I wish I knew, Sarah. That's something we need to find out. We also need to talk to her doctor and insist on an autopsy."

"What if her husband objects?"

"I assume he'll agree, but I really don't know him that well."

They rode the rest of the way in silence. Before they reached the outskirts of town, Dana called her sister's number. Her brother-in-law answered and gave her directions to a rural subdivision. Before they reached the circular drive, they stopped to stare in awe at the elaborately built house with its towers, wings and gables.

"Dana, this place looks like Queen Elizabeth's castle."

"It's actually a Queen Anne colonial. Breathtaking, isn't it?"

A shiny black sports car, with its engine running, was parked in the three-stall garage.

"Nice car," Sarah said. "Looks like somebody's leaving."

Georgi had mentioned the sports car, a birthday gift from her husband. Why was it running now when Rob was expecting them? Dana climbed down from the motorhome and opened the passenger door. "Take a deep breath." she said, "We've got some investigating to do."

A tall, tanned, well-built man opened the entry door. For a moment she didn't recognize him. He seemed older and more haggard than Dana remembered. Rob Turnsby gasped when he noticed her standing on the expansive wood porch.

"I thought you were expecting us, Rob."

"I'm sorry, I forgot how much you look like Georgi."

"I'm a year older but some thought we looked like twins." We were once as close as twins, she thought as she stepped across the threshold.

She wasn't sure why Rob made her uneasy. Maybe it was his standoffishness, as though he didn't want anyone invading his space. He led them into the living room and motioned them into two matching arm chairs. After introducing Sarah, she glanced about the well-appointed room with its mahogany mantle, large landscape paintings, and Oriental rug. The oak floor gleamed as though recently polished. Rob had done well for himself since marrying her sister.

"Can I get you something to drink?"

"Thank you, Rob. I'll have some herbal tea." She glanced at Sarah, who nodded her agreement.

"I was thinking of something a bit more relaxing, after your long trip," he said.

"Tea's fine, if you have it."

"I'm sure there's some in the cupboard." His eyelids appeared to twitch.

Glancing again at Sarah, she noticed her questioning expression.

Rob started from the room but turned back to say, "If you don't mind, I'll have a drink."

"Of course not. You look as though you need one."

His face seemed to have lost its previous tan. "What are you implying, Dana?"

"Nothing, you just seem on edge."

His sigh was drawn-out and heavy. "It's been a nightmare since Georgi's death."

"Please sit down. The drinks can wait."

"No, I insist." He turned and left the room.

Sarah leaned toward her, whispering, "What's going on?"

"I don't know but we're going to find out." She left her chair and moved to a large, elaborately draped window. From the corner of her eye she noticed a young woman carrying a packing box into the garage. She turned to watch as a shapely redhead slid into the car and backed it from its stall. *Who can that be? Isn't that Georgi's new car?*

Dana resumed her seat. "Keep your eyes and ears open," she whispered.

Patting her short blond curls into place, Sarah nodded and glanced about the room. "What did you say Rob does for a living?"

"He owns a construction company."

"He built this gorgeous house?"

"I believe he did."

"Very expensive house and furnishings. He must be

quite successful."

"I've noticed."

"And young."

"Yes, ten years younger than Georgi."

"Sounds like a novel plot."

Dana shifted uneasily in her chair. "Strange that you should say that. Are you aware that Georgi was a writer?"

"Yes, you mentioned it."

"Did I tell you she's been writing mystery novels?"

"No, is that why you had so many in your library?"

"Partly. Her books piqued my interest in the genre. She was a very gifted writer." Dana quickly wiped the dampness from her eyes. She then nodded in the direction Rob had taken. Raising a finger to her lips, she settled back in her chair, resting her head against the leather back. Within seconds Rob returned with a tray.

"I hope you don't mind that I microwaved your tea," he said. "The kettle takes forever."

Sarah smiled. "As long as you don't microwave dinner."

"My friend's been reading alternative medicine books," she said, reaching to squeeze Sarah's arm. "We need to discuss Georgi's death certificate as well as the funeral arrangements."

"Already taken care of." He set the china tea service on a marble-topped coffee table. "I wasn't sure you would arrive in time, so I took care of the arrangements, myself."

"But Georgi's only been gone two days."

Rob excused himself and made his way to the bar in an alcove adjoining the living room. He returned with a cocktail. "I knew you would be exhausted from your long trip and I didn't want to burden you with it."

"What are the arrangements?"

"Cremation tomorrow morning."

"Cremation? But Georgi wouldn't–"

"She said that's what she wanted, Dana. I'm surprised you didn't know."

"She had a living will?"

"No, but there's an estate will. I thought that would interest you."

"Why?"

"She left you some money as well as her books. You're her only blood relative, other than your daughter, Kerrie, so naturally she would leave you something."

"I see."

"By the way, where is Kerrie?"

"Working as an editorial assistant for a news magazine in California. I haven't called her yet."

Rob seated himself in a burgundy leather recliner. "Georgi didn't leave you much because the majority of our assets are tied up in the construction business."

Dana felt her scalp prickle. "I didn't expect—"

"The housekeeper's packing her books so you can take them with you."

"We'll have to put them in storage for the time being."

"In that case, you're welcome to leave them here until you've finished traveling." He smiled benevolently.

"Thank you, Rob. That's very accommodating. By the way, was that the housekeeper I noticed leaving in Georgi's sports car?" She watched him wipe his shiny upper lip.

"Uh–yes, I'm allowing her use of the car until her pickup is repaired. She's been very helpful about packing Georgi's things."

"What are you planning to do with them?"

"Give them to charities."

"Would you mind if I go through them and keep a few mementos for Kerrie and myself?"

He shrugged. "By all means. I know that sisters have a special bond. I'm sure you'd like some of her things."

"You're most generous." Dana rose and offered Sarah her hand.

"You can do that tomorrow after the memorial service," he said, sitting upright.

"Would you mind if we look through them before the housekeeper finishes packing?"

"Not at all. I'll show you to her room." He glanced at his watch. "I have a business meeting in half an hour. I should be back in time for dinner."

"You're not taking time off to grieve Georgi's death?"

"We all handle grief in our own way," he said. "I have a business to run and I need to stay busy."

Dana shivered as he guided them up the oak stairs to his wife's room, which was filled with packing boxes. He left before she could ask about the official cause of death. Mentally tabling the question for his return, she opened the closet door.

Shocked, she turned to Sarah. "It's empty. My sister has only been gone two days and he's already getting rid of her clothes."

"I wouldn't be surprised if the housekeeper's making off with them, Dana."

"From the looks of her, she's already taken Georgi's place, including Rob and the sports car."

"We need evidence to go to the police."

"I have to stop the cremation so cause of death can be determined."

"How?"

"I'll think of something. Let's go through these packing boxes to see what we can find."

The first carton contained leisure clothing, the second high-heeled shoes. Five additional boxes were filled with formal wear wrapped haphazardly as though dirty laundry. Dana cringed when she noticed the expensive labels. Her sister must have worn them while married to

8

her former husband, a San Francisco lawyer.

While sorting through a box of designer jeans, Sarah said, "Look at this. A locked, black velvet box."

"It must be Georgi's jewelry. I'm surprised it's still here."

"It's heavy, Dana. Do you think we should open it?"

"How? Pry it open? I don't feel right about that."

"The key must be here somewhere." Sarah opened dresser drawers to feel beneath them. Disappointed, she turned to the white Victorian desk that matched the four-poster bed. Opening the drawer, she extracted a carved wooden pill bottle, which rattled when she shook it. Removing the lid, she discovered a key.

"This has to be the one."

Dana was surprised when the box opened. Carefully lifting the lid, she discovered a matching book, its black velvet cover etched in gold with the name Georgiana Turnsby. Hands trembling, she opened the cover and discovered a diary. The beginning entry was dated June 21st, which she quietly read aloud:

I had serious misgivings about moving to Wyoming, but it's beautiful here. I miss San Francisco Bay, but the air is so clear that you can see the mountains forever. I'm glad I allowed Rob to talk me into moving to his home state.

"Sounds like she was happy, Dana."

She scanned the next few pages and stopped. "Listen to this:"

I can't tell anyone that I've made a terrible mistake. I should have listened to my friend, Angela. Now, I'm too embarrassed and ashamed to tell anyone. How could I have been so blind that I allowed myself to be fooled and rushed into this. What am I going to do?

"Oh, my." Sarah dropped a black sequined dress back into a packing box. "What do you think she's referring to?"

"If my instincts are right, she's referring to her marriage, but the entry was written nearly two years ago. Why didn't she confide in me?"

"She said she was embarrassed, Dana."

Turning the page, she noticed the next entry was dated four days later.

I've decided to make the best of it. I've secretly transferred half my divorce settlement to an offshore account. The rest has been loaned to my husband for the business. He promised to build me the most beautiful house in the state, and seems so eager to please me. How can I turn him down?

"Sounds as though she changed her mind." Sarah picked up another box and set it on the bed.

"Georgi was a generous person. I'm sure she was willing to help Rob establish himself in business."

"Then why would he kill the proverbial goose?"

"The housekeeper, maybe. Georgi may have discovered they were having an affair and threatened to divorce him."

"Wasn't there a prenuptial agreement?"

"I would hope she was smart enough to have one, but Rob's a former salesman and a very charming guy. He could have talked her into nearly anything." Dana had turned another page when she heard a door slam somewhere in the house. Thrusting the diary into its box, she hid them under a pile of clothing.

* * *

Murder on the Interstate

Chapter 1

Lulled by a lack of traffic and the steady beat of rain, Dana was in danger of nodding off when a convertible roared past, followed by a late model pickup. The heavy downpour obscured her view, but they appeared to be coupled like boxcars. Why they were driving that dangerously close, and why so fast in the rain?

An I-40 highway sign signaled an approaching curve so she clicked off the cruise control and slowed to forty-five. Their taillights had vanished and she glanced in both side mirrors. The earlier truck traffic had also disappeared and no headlights were visible in either direction. Darkness was closing in on her.

Sarah groaned from the passenger seat, apparently still asleep. *Must be the anchovies.* Her friend had insisted on stopping for a pizza at a Kingman roadside cafe. Dana groped for the Tums. As she rounded the curve, she noticed two sets of brake lights not far ahead.

The motorhome swayed as she stepped into her own brakes and skidded on the pavement. Road signs had warned of animal crossings. The convertible appeared to have swerved to avoid hitting a deer and had gone off the mountain road. Dana pulled onto the shoulder as the pickup following the convertible screeched back onto the pavement. Why didn't the pickup driver stop to help?

Bolting upright in the passenger seat, Sarah said, "What happened?" Her words were thick with sleep.

"We're about to find out."

Headlights angled upward from somewhere off the road, illuminating a huge digger pine. Was it the convertible?

Dana opened her door and climbed down. The steps were slick with rain and she nearly lost her balance. She heard the passenger door slam as she started down the embankment. Chilled and miserably wet, she slipped and landed in a bed of pine needles. Why hadn't she grabbed the flashlight?

Dana glanced up at her friend, who stood shivering on the shoulder. "Sarah," she yelled, "Call 911 and hurry."

The smell of gasoline was strong, despite the heavy rain. The convertible had missed several pine trees but a boulder had stopped its forward motion. Both doors were locked. Peering through the driver's window, she could see nothing more than shattered glass, a dime-sized hole centering the web design. She then heard several backfires and a ping of metal as though the convertible had been struck with a rock. Realizing it was a gunshot, she dropped to her knees in the mud.

Sarah!

Slipping and clawing her way up the slope, she crawled onto the shoulder. A pickup was parked behind the RV. The driver had a nervous foot. A moment later another set of headlights emerged from the curve down the road. Tires squealed as the pickup roared off. As it passed, the RV's headlights caught a dark red truck, which appeared to be a newer model.

When Dana glanced in the passenger window, Sarah was crouched between the seats, the cell phone clutched in her hand. She took her time unlocking the passenger door.

"Are you all right?"

"I'm not sure." Sarah patted her chest, breathing heavily.

"What happened?"

"He shot up the motorhome."

"Did he shoot at you?"

"I don't think he saw me. He only seemed interested

2

in wounding Matilda."

Dana hated the name Sarah had christened the RV, but that was the least of her worries. Grabbing a flashlight, she climbed back down the steps. A quick inspection revealed inside tires still inflated but the outer ones in the back were flat. She heard an engine shift down and was caught in the glare of headlights. Signaling with her flashlight, she was relieved when the big truck slowed and pulled in behind the motorhome. The driver seemed to be endlessly checking the gauges before leaving the cab. Once on the ground, a warm, plump hand gripped hers in greeting.

"The name's McCurdy," a husky voice said. "Everybody calls me Big Ruby."

At nearly six feet, she was Dana's height although almost twice her girth.

"I'm Dana Logan. There's a Mercedes convertible down the embankment. Gasoline is leaking and both the doors are locked."

"Lead the way."

Rain had slackened and the area still reeked of gasoline. She signaled Sarah to stay in the coach.

"Ruptured gas tank," Ruby said. "That low slung buggy must of hit a rock." She tried both doors before resorting to her knife that she pulled from a sheath on her belt. Slicing the canvas top, she reached inside the car to unlock the door. Her flashlight illuminated the interior where a young woman was slumped across the steering wheel. Her long blond hair was stained with blood and she didn't appear to be breathing. The vintage car had no airbags.

Ruby felt for a pulse. Lifting the woman as though she were a child, she pulled her from the car and carried her some distance before settling her gently on the ground. The flashlight spotted a wound on the left side of the woman's head. Her wide blue eyes then disappeared under Ruby's windbreaker.

"I'm afraid we're too late."

"She's so young," Dana's pizza threatened to return from her stomach. "And so small."

"We'd better find some I.D."

Dana hurried back to retrieve the woman's purse. Shivering in wet clothing and the cool mountain air, she returned to Ruby and the body.

"The pickup driver had to have killed her," Dana said. "He then came back to disable the motorhome. My friend and I are lucky to be alive."

"Tell me about the pickup." Ruby started back up the slope.

"Dark red or burgundy. A Dodge Ram, fairly new."

"You get the license number?"

"I'm afraid not."

"We'll catch the bastard. I'll call the sheriff on the way."

"There's no cell service here."

"No trucker's without a CB."

* * *

Dana took the passenger seat after Sarah crawled into the sleeper. As rain drummed the windshield, she wondered aloud whether animals would find the body before the police arrived.

"Not likely," Ruby said, "The smell of gasoline should keep the critters away." She picked up her microphone to determine whether anyone was in the area. It was several minutes before someone answered her call.

"What's your twenty, lady?"

"West of Flag. How 'bout you?"

"East of Albuquerque. You've got one helluva power booster," a male voice said, "or we're talkin' some damn good skip." The volume rose and fell as though the other driver were out to sea.

Ruby swore beneath her breath. "Friggin' weather acts like a damn snow blower. Sucks up radio signals and spews 'em across the country." She glanced at her passengers and apologized for her language.

"No problem," Dana said. "I've heard worse on TV."

"You meet a lotta nice drivers out here on the road, but some of 'em are always talkin' trash. It gets lonely on long hauls. If you're out here long enough, you start to sound the same."

Just a matter of fitting in, Dana thought as she squinted through the windshield. There was no sign of the pickup.

Ruby tried her cell phone and reported only static. She returned to the CB. Keying the mike, she said, "Breaker, one nine. This is Big Ruby askin' for some help. Anybody out there got your ears on?" She adjusted the squelch when no one answered.

Dana sighed. "Maybe we should have stayed with the body."

"And let that so-and-so get clean away?"

"Yes, you're right." *I couldn't leave Sarah there alone.*

"Tell me again about the pickup. Did you get a good look at the driver?"

"No, but Sarah might have." She turned to determine whether Sarah was listening from the sleeper.

"A dark red Dodge Ram." Sarah said. "I remember the name on the tailgate. It looked like a young man's truck."

"Was it jacked up?" Ruby asked.

"Don't think so."

"Notice any dings or rust spots?"

"It looked shiny new."

"Rain shines up most trucks." Ruby patted the dash. "Even Old Bertha."

Bertha was barreling down the highway much too

fast for prevailing road conditions. Dana hoped Ruby was a competent driver.

"What about bumper stickers?"

Dana closed her eyes and tried to remember what she'd seen.

"One said something about a Las Vegas casino," Sarah said, "but I don't remember which one."

"Nevada license plate?"

"I didn't notice."

Dana cringed. Some sleuths they were. She consoled herself with the fact that they'd been taken by surprise. If the murder hadn't happened, she might have fallen asleep at the wheel. The motorhome would have run off the road like the Mercedes.

She knew that convertibles have a low center of gravity, but the high profile RV probably would have overturned and killed them both. She shuddered, remembering the young woman with a bullet in her head. No one deserved to die that way.

Ruby said, "It'll come back to you. It's surprising how much we remember the next day."

Truckers were like bartenders, roadside psychologists who seemed to know more about human nature than their high-priced counterparts.

"I wonder if the killer went back."

"I doubt it." Big Ruby picked up her phone. They had reached the top of the grade where cell service might be available. "A lotta people coulda stopped there by now."

While the trucker punched in some numbers, Dana held her breath, hoping the call had gone through. She listened intently as Ruby reported the murder to a 911 dispatcher.

"No, I can't return to the crime scene. I gotta load of produce that'll spoil. In case you didn't know, drivers foot the bill if the lettuce wilts before it gets to market."

Closing the phone she said, "I'll drop you off in Flag. Somebody there can take tires back to your rig."

"What about the killer?"

"Soon as the rain lets up, I'll warn the other drivers to keep a lookout."

"But how will they know it's him? Or if it's a man, for that matter?"

"You're right. Plenty of women drive pickup trucks in Northern Arizona. Quite a few of 'em Hopis and Navajos. There's more than a few dark red pickup trucks."

Sarah startled her by gripping her seat back. "I forgot to tell you, Dana, I got a look at the driver when he grabbed his gun from his glove compartment."

"Why didn't you say something sooner?"

"I was too busy thanking my lucky stars he didn't shoot me too."

"What's he look like?"

"Dark hair with a thin beard that runs along his jaw line. Connects with his hair."

"Long or short hair?"

"It was slicked back but I didn't see a pony tail."

Dashboard lights illuminated Ruby's grin. In profile she resembled a queen-sized Sarah, although her hair was darker. "Most people wouldn't remember anything but the gun."

"We're amateur sleuths," Sarah said.

Dana groaned inwardly. She'd hoped Sarah wouldn't tell anyone about the murders they'd solved, but nodded confirmation when Ruby glanced at her. The driver shook her head in disbelief.

"Dana captured a killer single-handed."

Ruby laughed. "Are you two traveling Jane Marples?"

"I'm only sixty," Sarah said. "Dana does facial exercises so she looks much younger. But we're the same age."

Sarah's main spring had snapped. If she didn't calm down, she'd be hyperventilating.

"Tell me about the cases you solved." Ruby reached to adjust the wipers.

By the time Dana filled her in on all the murders, the rain had stopped and they were taking a Flagstaff exit. The road curved down to a large truck stop and they pulled into the nearest fuel lane.

"All out for Flag." Ruby grinned as she descended from her truck. Her bright red hair was dazzling in the overhead lights.

"She's no spring chicken either," Sarah muttered as they prepared to leave Old Bertha.

Dana reached for the handle, reversed directions and swung down to the step, comparing the dismount to that of the motorhome. She could drive this rig as well, with a few instructions from Ruby.

Sarah's short legs flailed in mid-air when she groped for the lower step. Dana reached to help her down. Groaning and stretching on solid ground, they offered to buy their benefactor a cup of coffee. Ruby agreed, but before she could hook Bertha up to a diesel pump, Sarah stopped mid-stride and gasped.

"It's him."

"Who?"

"The man with the gun."

* * *

About the Author

Gray Wolf Mountain is the author's 18th book and fourth in the Logan & Cafferty mystery/suspense series.

Jean Henry Mead is also an award-winning photojournalist and children's author as well as a western historical novelist. She writes the Hamilton Kids' mystery series and nonfiction interview and history books. She began her career as a California news reporter and editor and later served as editor of In Wyoming Magazine and Mystery Mountain Press. Her magazine articles have been published domestically as well as abroad.

www.ingramcontent.com/pod-product-compliance
Lightning Source LLC
Chambersburg PA
CBHW072207170626
46813CB00003B/827